Fairy
Dreams

5

As seen on
nickelodeon.

Winx Club
Volume 5

Winx Club ©2003-2012 Rainbow S.r.l. All Rights Reserved. Series
created by Iginio Straffi www.winxclub.com

Designer • Fawn Lau
Letterer • John Hunt
Editor • Amy Yu

Printed in China

Published by VIZ Media, LLC
P.O. Box 77010
San Francisco, CA 94107

10 9 8 7 6 5 4 3 2 1
First printing, January 2013

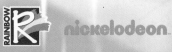

Winx Club™

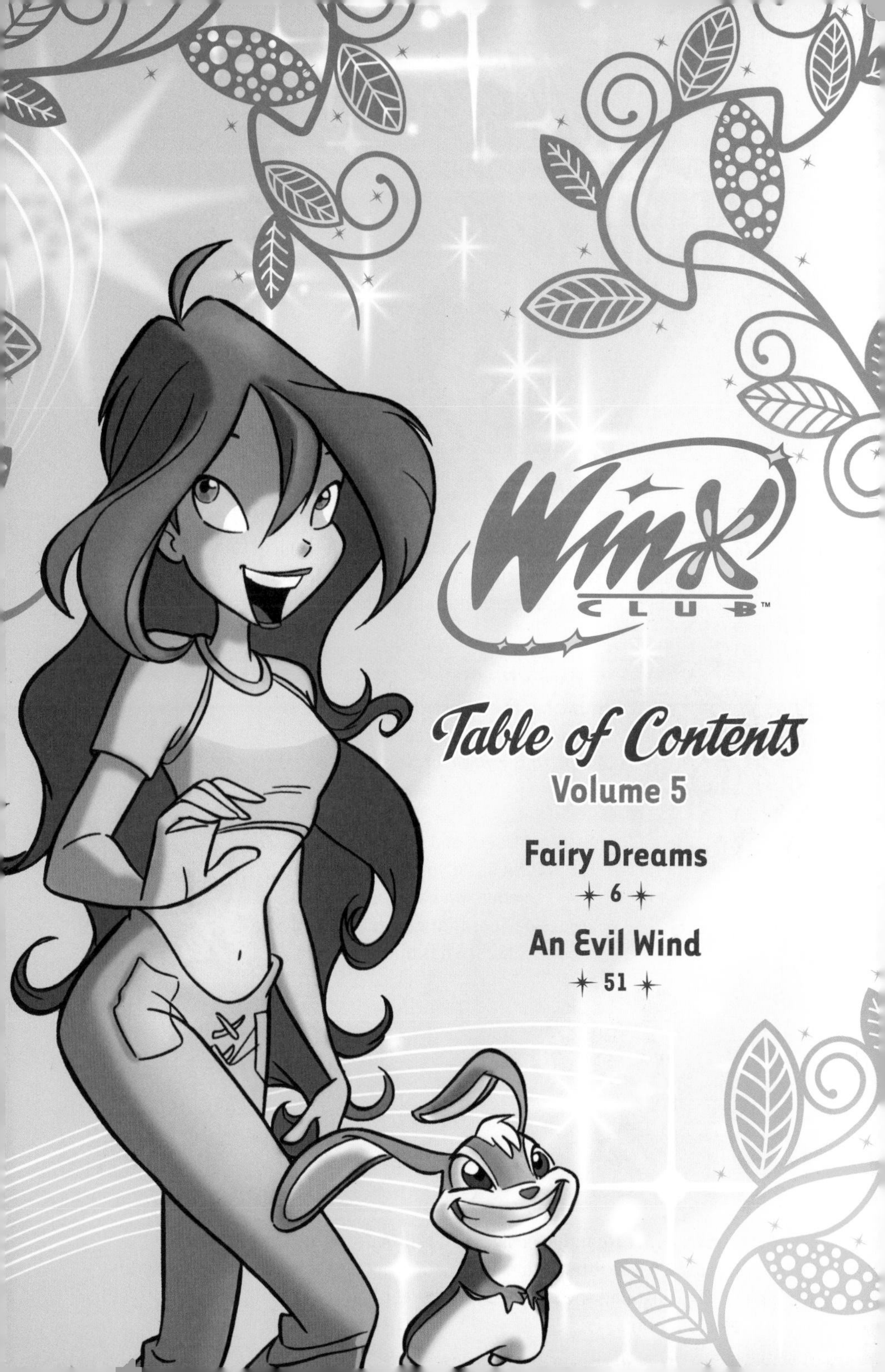

Table of Contents

Volume 5

Meet the Winx Club

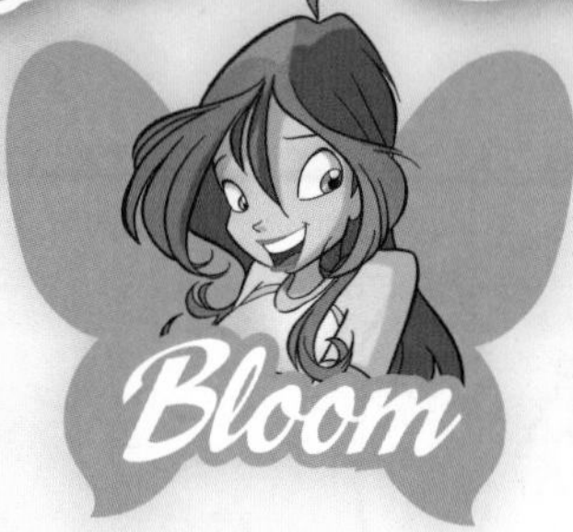
Bloom

Raised on Earth, **BLOOM** had no idea she had magical fairy powers until a chance encounter with Stella. Intelligent and loyal, she is the heart and soul of the Winx Club.

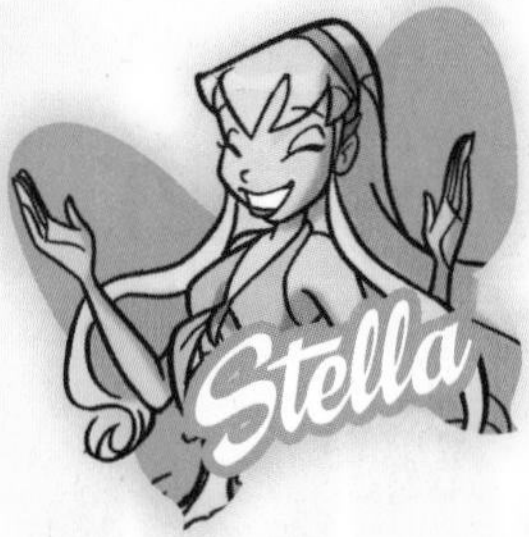
Stella

A princess from Solaria, **STELLA** draws her fairy power from sunlight. Optimistic and carefree, she introduces Bloom to the world of Magix.

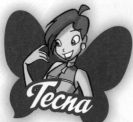

Self-confident and a perfectionist, **TECNA** has a vast knowledge of science, which enables her to create devices that can get her and her friends out of trouble.

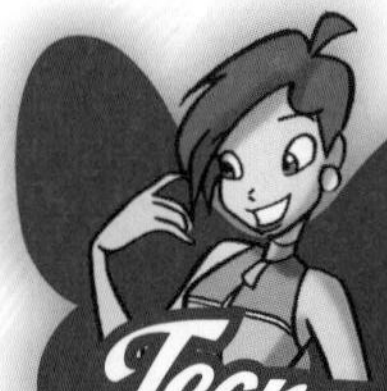
Tecna

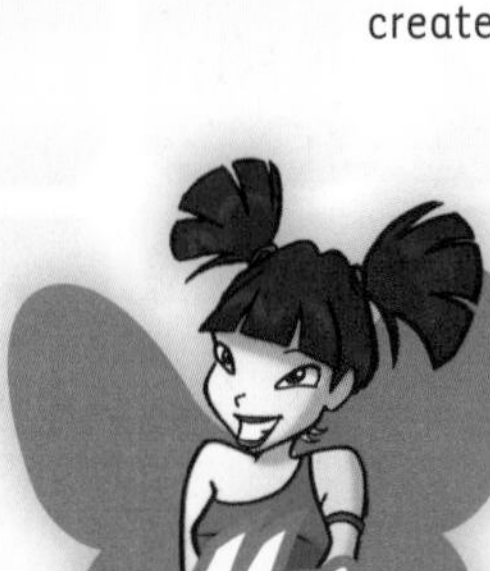
Musa

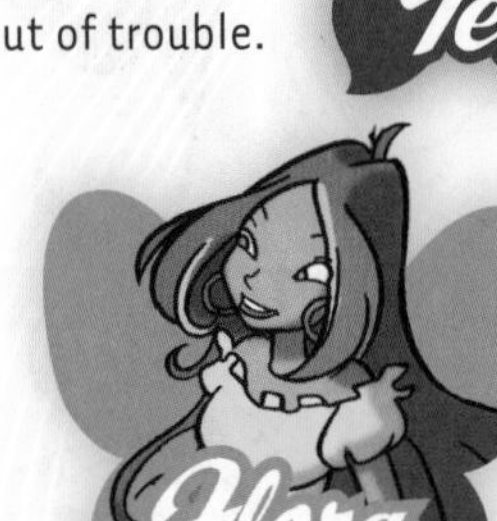
Flora

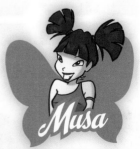

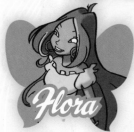

MUSA draws power from the music she plays. She has a natural talent for investigating, and she's got a keen eye for details.

FLORA draws her fairy powers from flowers, plants and nature in general. Sweet and thoughtful, she tends to be the peacemaker in the group.

Their Friends

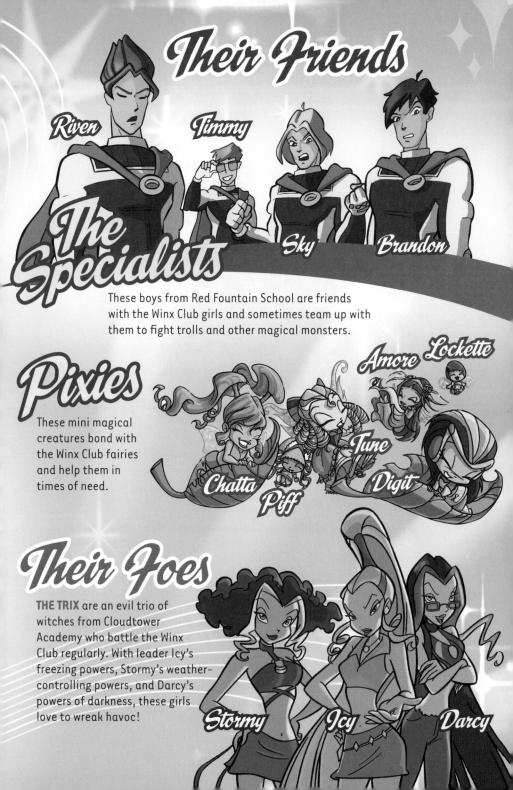

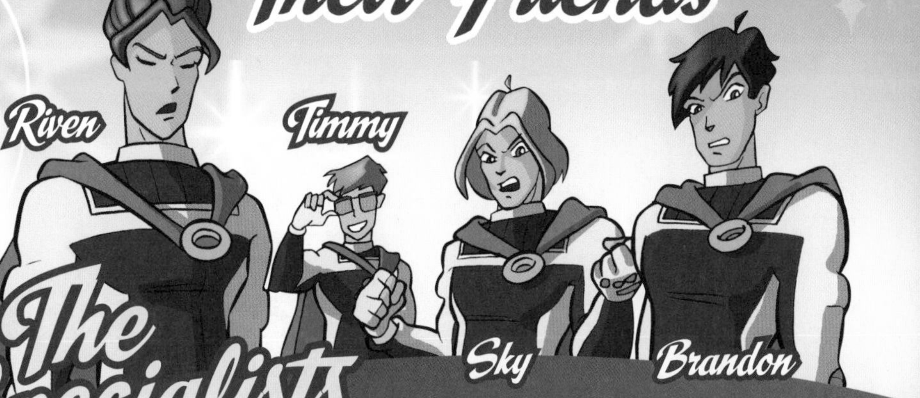
Riven
Timmy
Sky
Brandon

The Specialists

These boys from Red Fountain School are friends with the Winx Club girls and sometimes team up with them to fight trolls and other magical monsters.

Pixies

These mini magical creatures bond with the Winx Club fairies and help them in times of need.

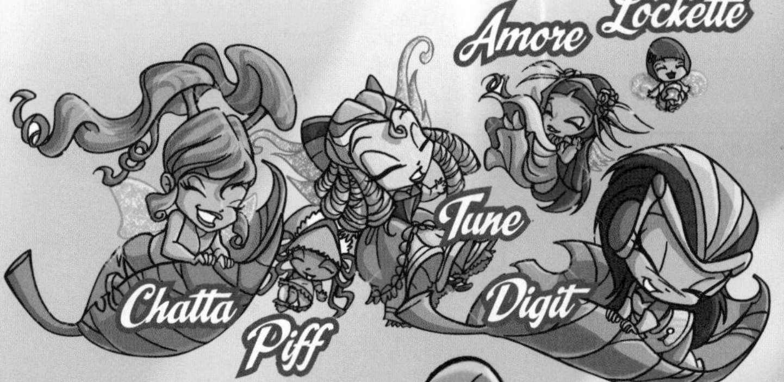
Amore
Lockette
Tune
Chatta
Digit
Piff

Their Foes

THE TRIX are an evil trio of witches from Cloudtower Academy who battle the Winx Club regularly. With leader Icy's freezing powers, Stormy's weather-controlling powers, and Darcy's powers of darkness, these girls love to wreak havoc!

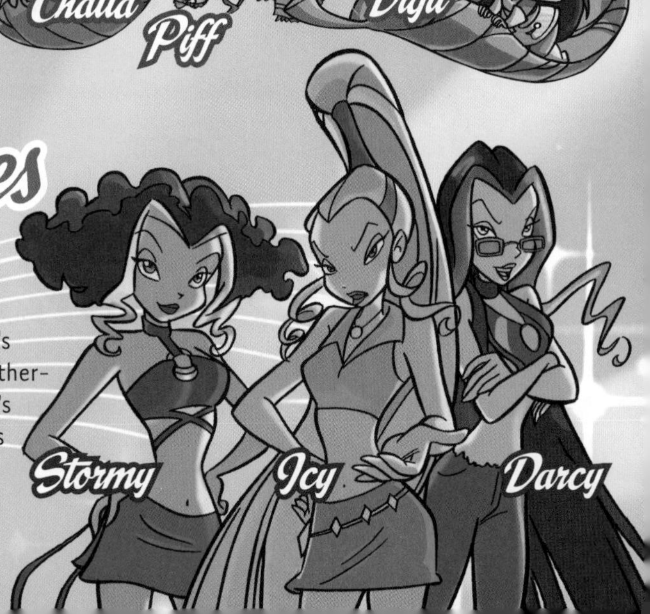
Stormy
Icy
Darcy

Winx Club™

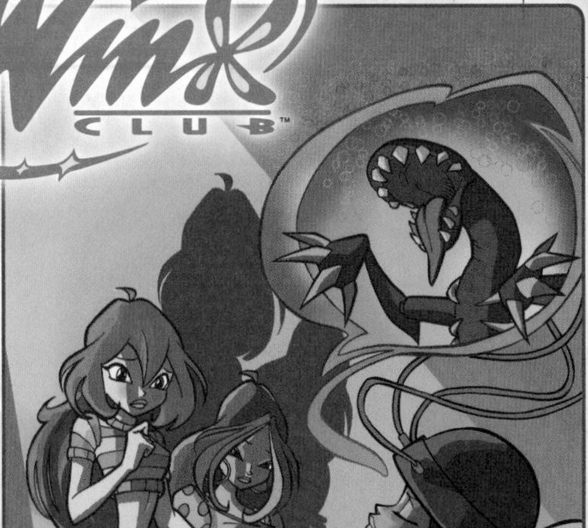

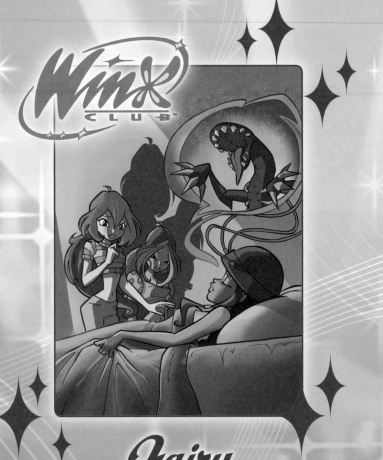

Fairy Dreams

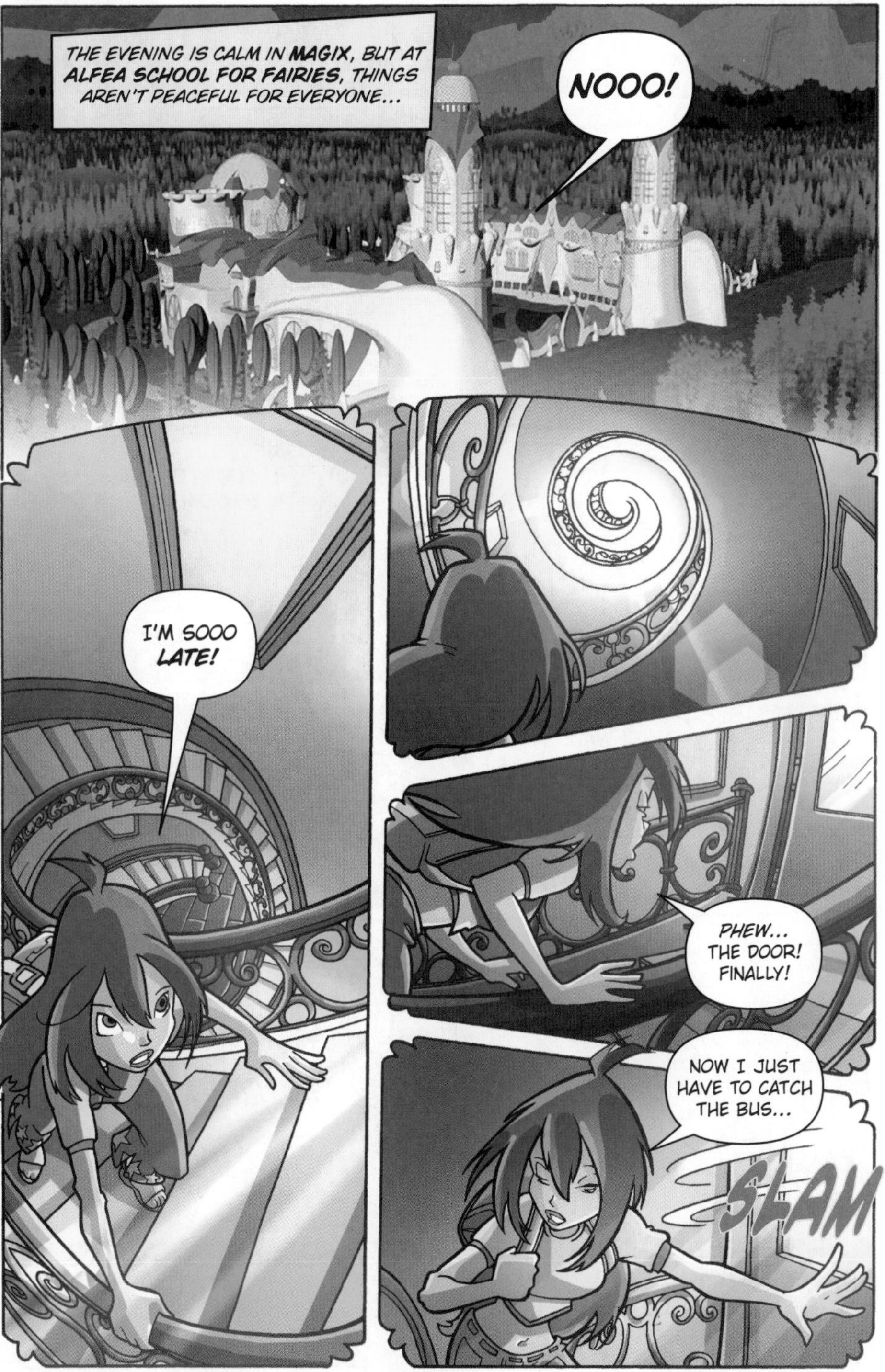
THE EVENING IS CALM IN MAGIX, BUT AT ALFEA SCHOOL FOR FAIRIES, THINGS AREN'T PEACEFUL FOR EVERYONE...
NOOO!
I'M SOOO LATE!
PHEW... THE DOOR! FINALLY!
NOW I JUST HAVE TO CATCH THE BUS...
SLAM

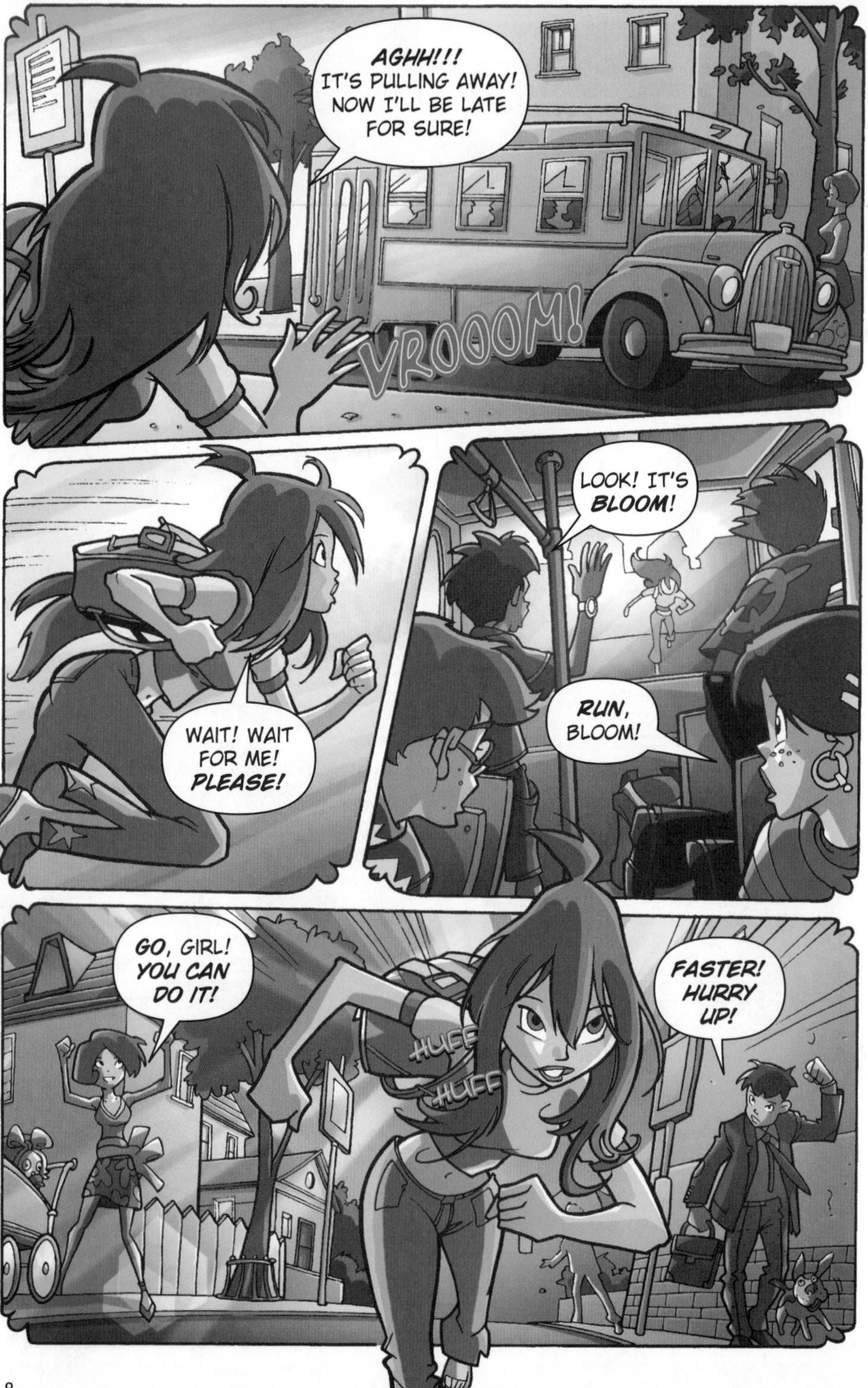
AGHH!!! IT'S PULLING AWAY! NOW I'LL BE LATE FOR SURE!
VROOOM!
WAIT! WAIT FOR ME! PLEASE!
LOOK! IT'S BLOOM!
RUN, BLOOM!
GO, GIRL! YOU CAN DO IT!
HUFF HUFF
FASTER! HURRY UP!

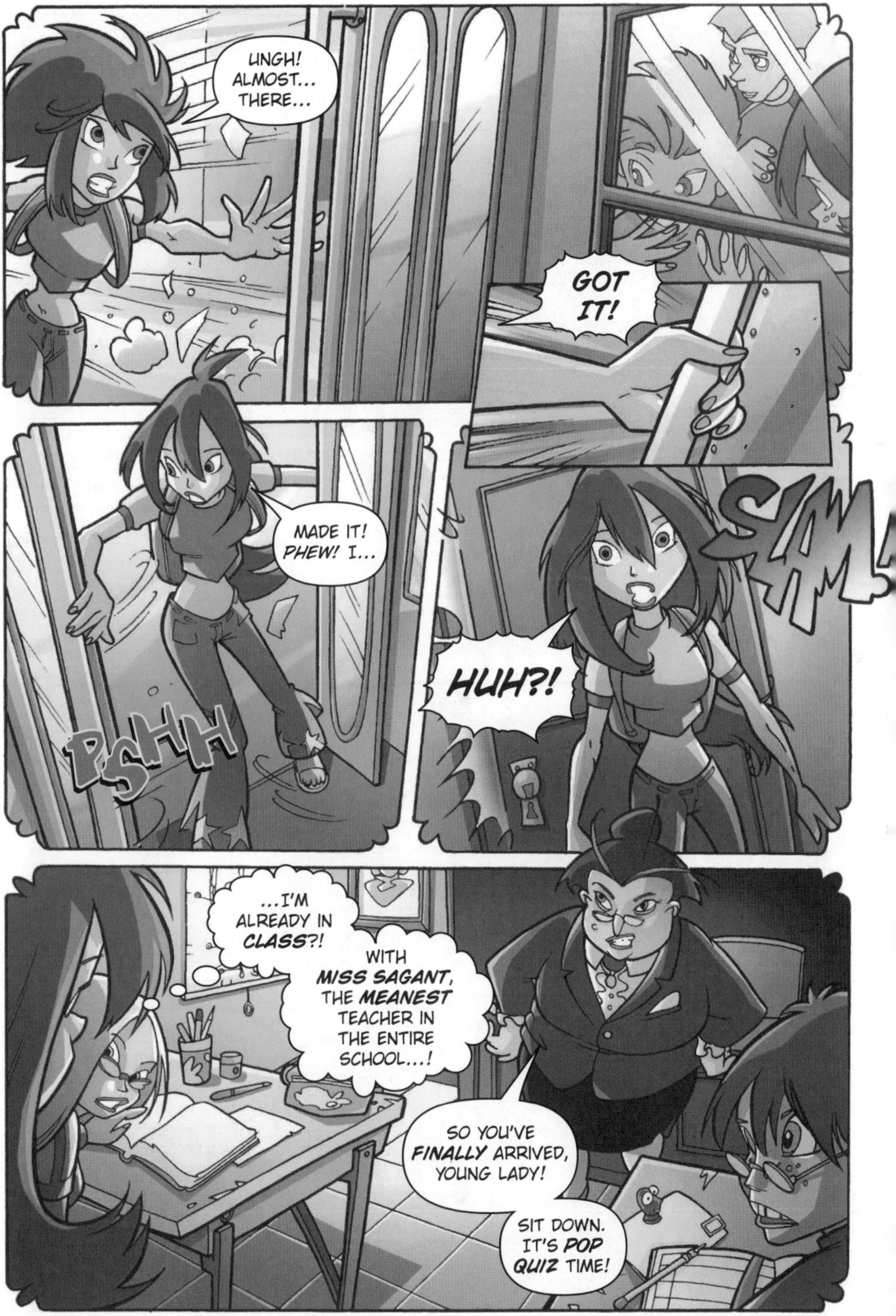
UNGH! ALMOST... THERE...
GOT IT!
MADE IT! PHEW! I...
PSHH
SLAM
HUH?!
...I'M ALREADY IN CLASS?!
WITH MISS SAGANT, THE MEANEST TEACHER IN THE ENTIRE SCHOOL...!
SO YOU'VE FINALLY ARRIVED, YOUNG LADY!
SIT DOWN. IT'S POP QUIZ TIME!

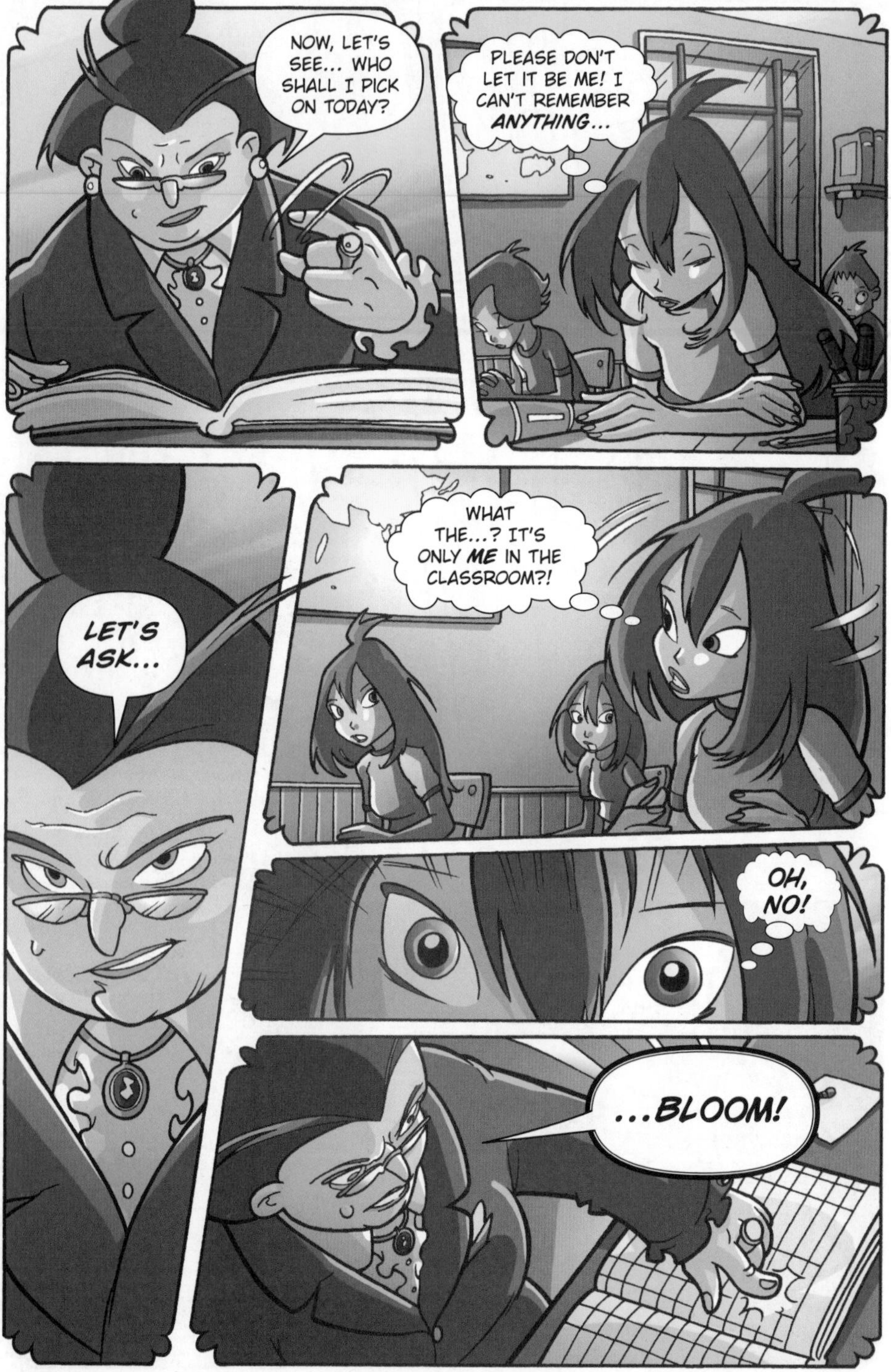
NOW, LET'S SEE... WHO SHALL I PICK ON TODAY?
PLEASE DON'T LET IT BE ME! I CAN'T REMEMBER *ANYTHING*...
LET'S ASK...
WHAT THE...? IT'S ONLY *ME* IN THE CLASSROOM?!
OH, NO!
...BLOOM!

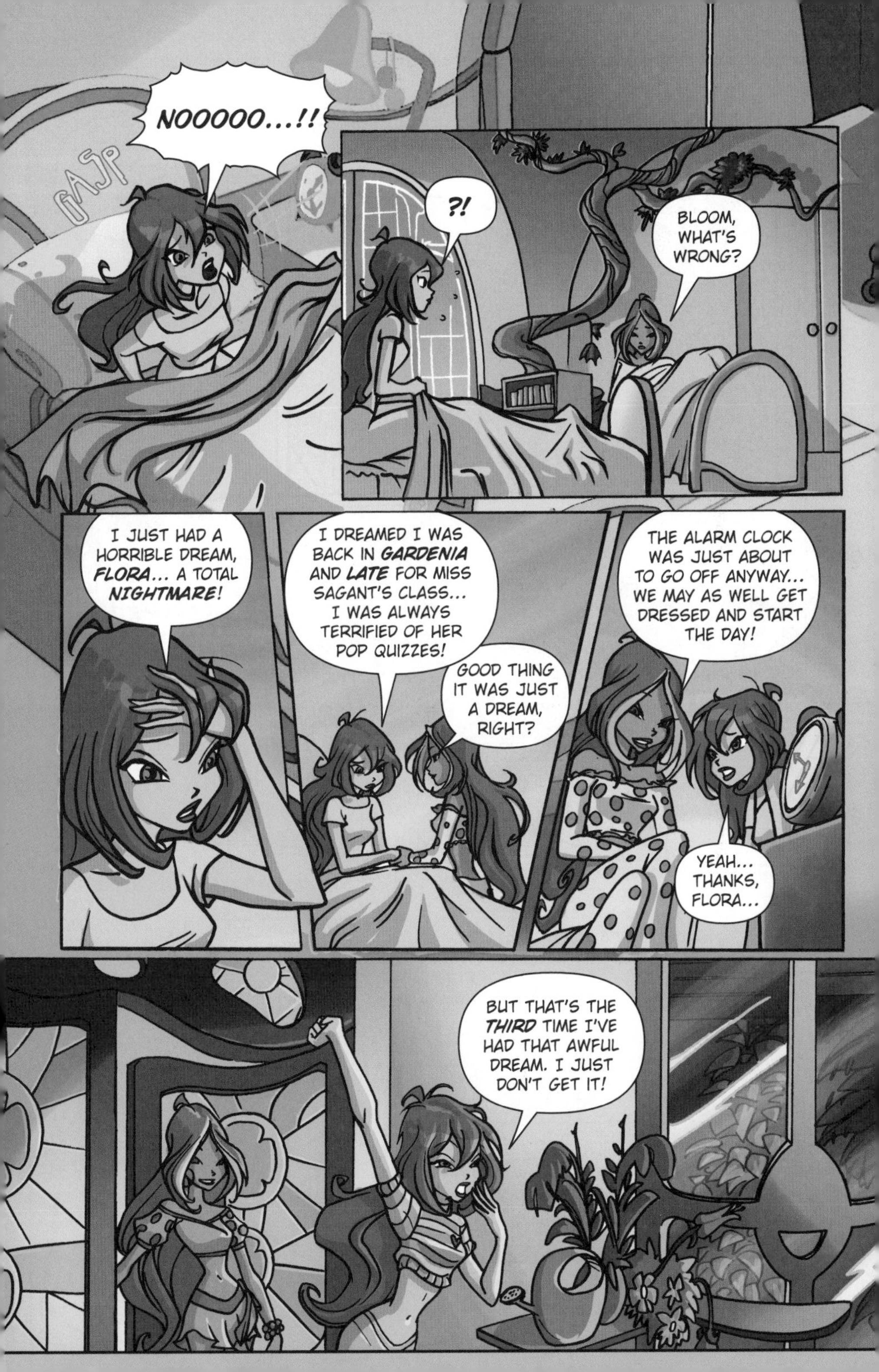
NOOOOO...!!
GASP
?!
BLOOM, WHAT'S WRONG?
I JUST HAD A HORRIBLE DREAM, FLORA... A TOTAL NIGHTMARE!
I DREAMED I WAS BACK IN GARDENIA AND LATE FOR MISS SAGANT'S CLASS... I WAS ALWAYS TERRIFIED OF HER POP QUIZZES!
GOOD THING IT WAS JUST A DREAM, RIGHT?
THE ALARM CLOCK WAS JUST ABOUT TO GO OFF ANYWAY... WE MAY AS WELL GET DRESSED AND START THE DAY!
YEAH... THANKS, FLORA...
BUT THAT'S THE THIRD TIME I'VE HAD THAT AWFUL DREAM. I JUST DON'T GET IT!

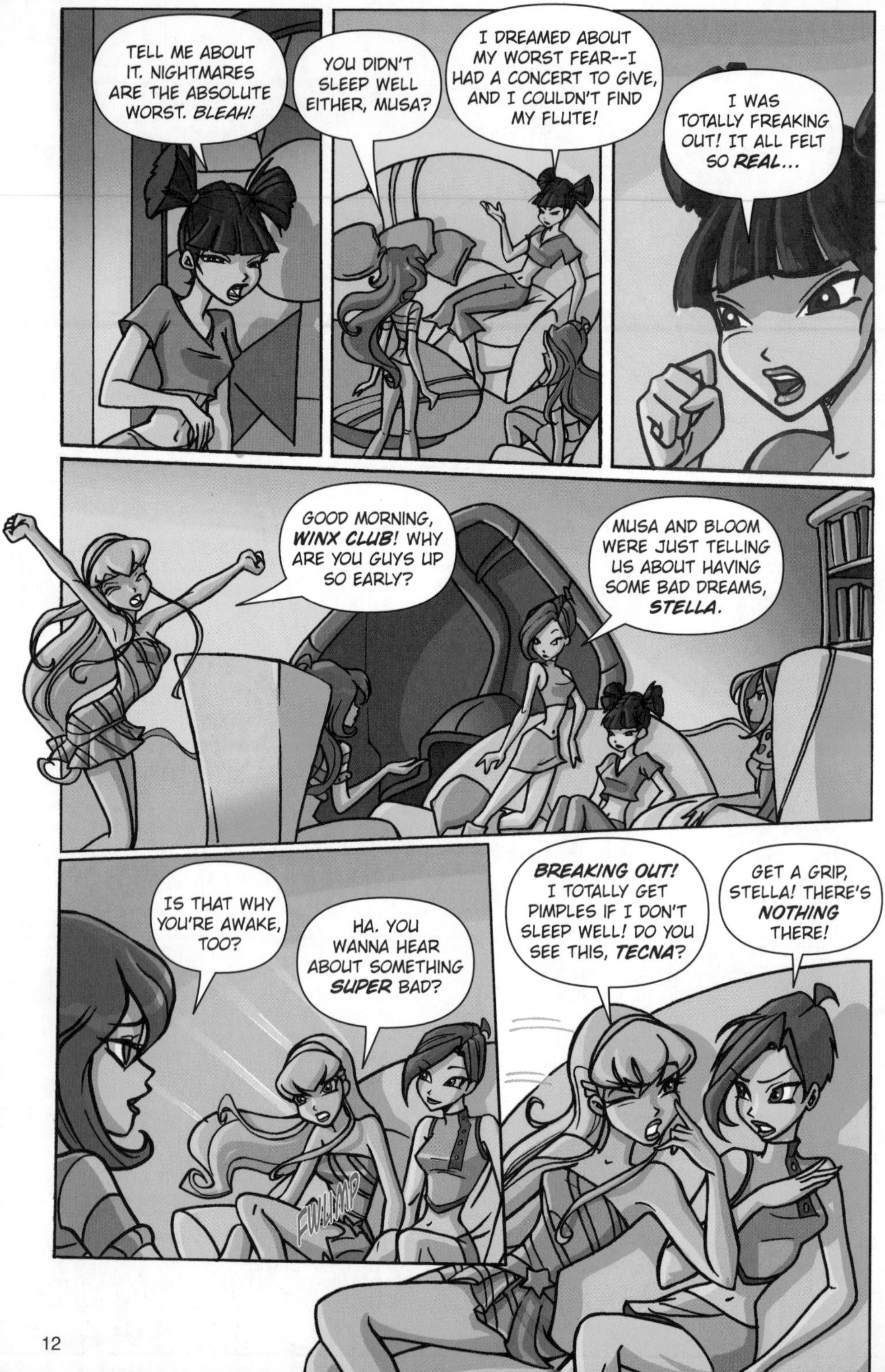
TELL ME ABOUT IT. NIGHTMARES ARE THE ABSOLUTE WORST. *BLEAH!*
YOU DIDN'T SLEEP WELL EITHER, MUSA?
I DREAMED ABOUT MY WORST FEAR--I HAD A CONCERT TO GIVE, AND I COULDN'T FIND MY FLUTE!
I WAS TOTALLY FREAKING OUT! IT ALL FELT SO ***REAL...***
GOOD MORNING, ***WINX CLUB!*** WHY ARE YOU GUYS UP SO EARLY?
MUSA AND BLOOM WERE JUST TELLING US ABOUT HAVING SOME BAD DREAMS, **STELLA.**
IS THAT WHY YOU'RE AWAKE, TOO?
HA. YOU WANNA HEAR ABOUT SOMETHING ***SUPER*** BAD?
FWUMP
BREAKING OUT! I TOTALLY GET PIMPLES IF I DON'T SLEEP WELL! DO YOU SEE THIS, ***TECNA***?
GET A GRIP, STELLA! THERE'S ***NOTHING*** THERE!

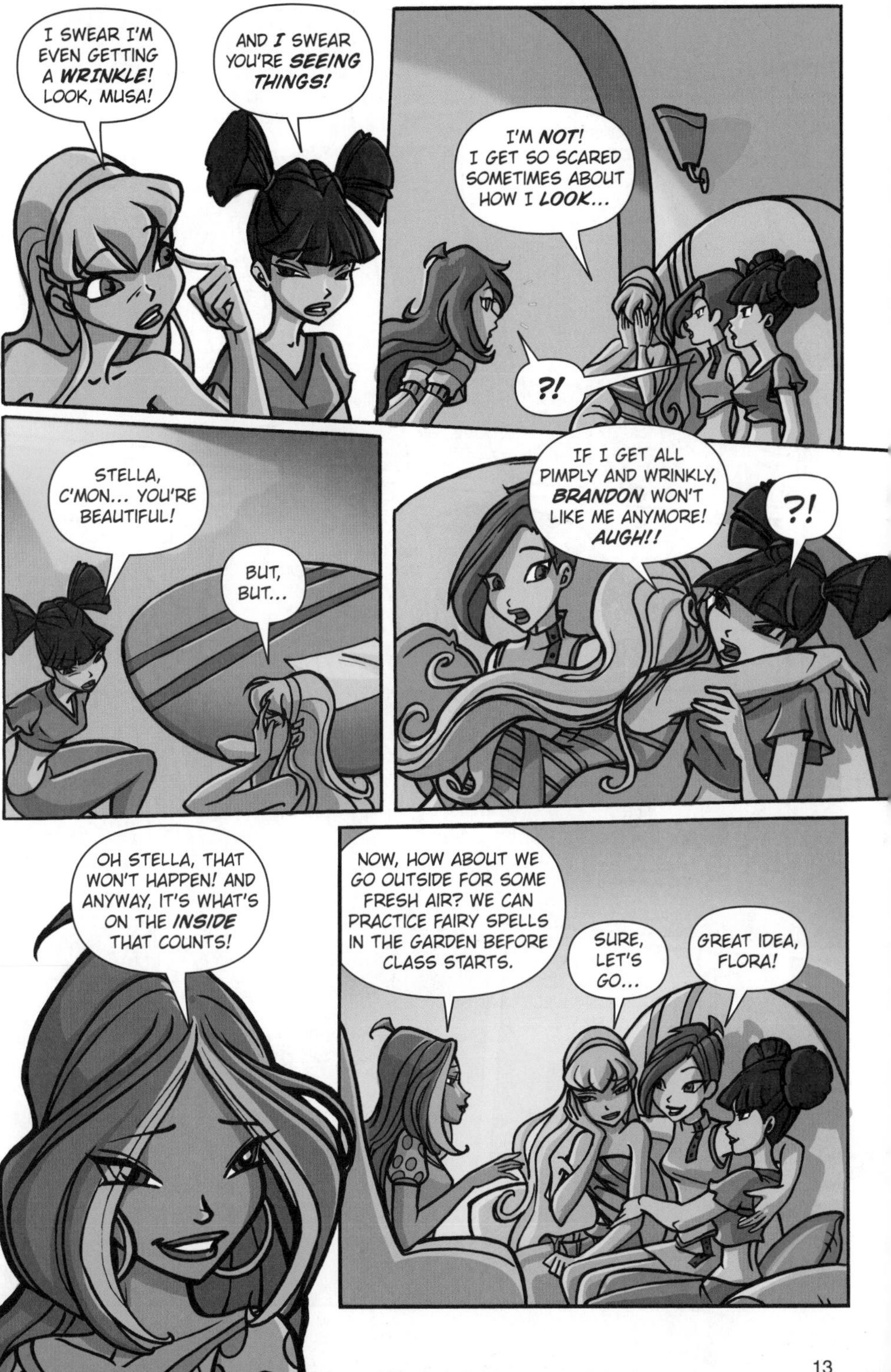
I SWEAR I'M EVEN GETTING A **WRINKLE**! LOOK, MUSA!
AND *I* SWEAR YOU'RE **SEEING THINGS!**
I'M **NOT**! I GET SO SCARED SOMETIMES ABOUT HOW I **LOOK**...
?!
STELLA, C'MON... YOU'RE BEAUTIFUL!
BUT, BUT...
IF I GET ALL PIMPLY AND WRINKLY, **BRANDON** WON'T LIKE ME ANYMORE! **AUGH!!**
?!
OH STELLA, THAT WON'T HAPPEN! AND ANYWAY, IT'S WHAT'S ON THE *INSIDE* THAT COUNTS!
NOW, HOW ABOUT WE GO OUTSIDE FOR SOME FRESH AIR? WE CAN PRACTICE FAIRY SPELLS IN THE GARDEN BEFORE CLASS STARTS.
SURE, LET'S GO...
GREAT IDEA, FLORA!

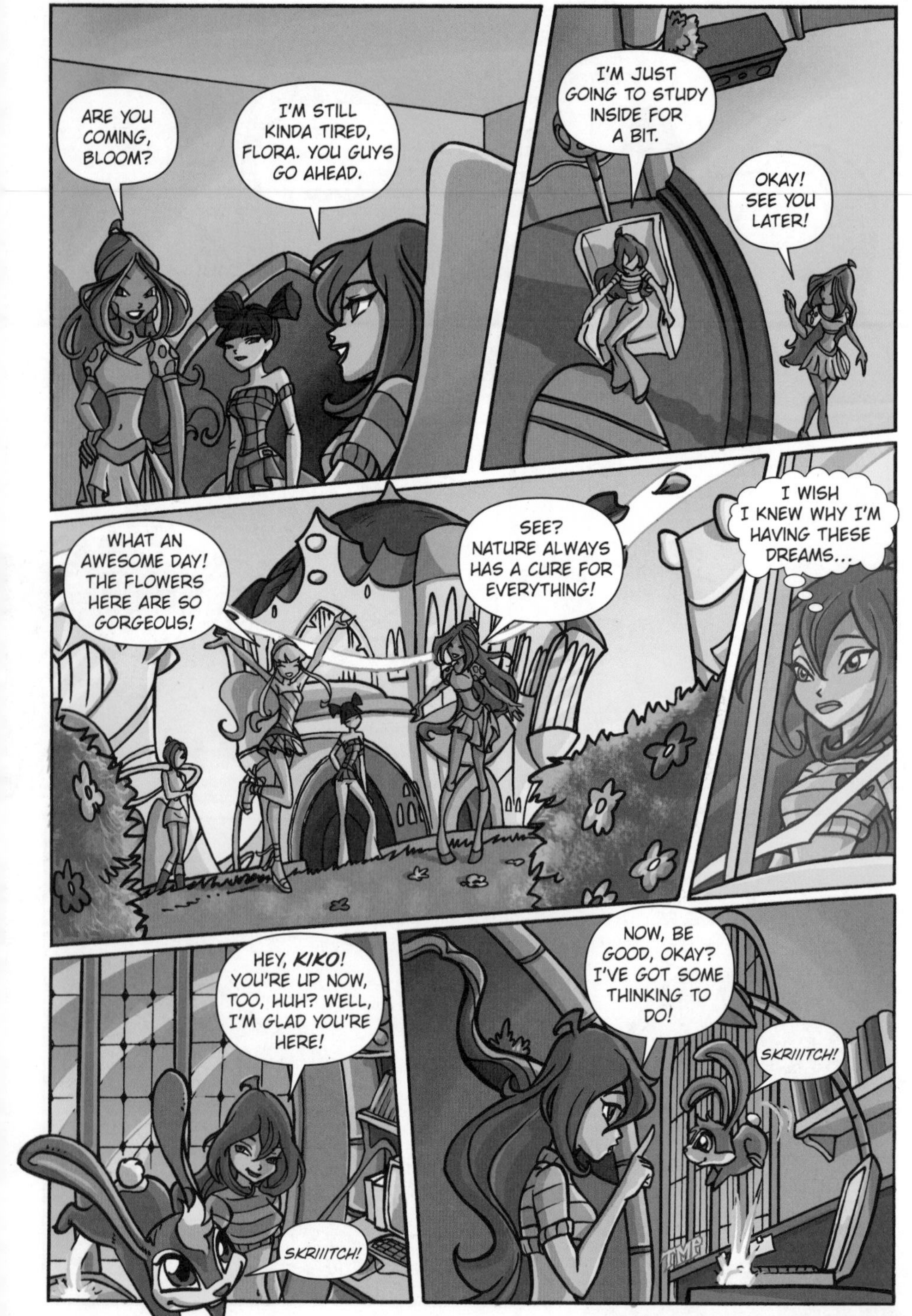
ARE YOU COMING, BLOOM?
I'M STILL KINDA TIRED, FLORA. YOU GUYS GO AHEAD.
I'M JUST GOING TO STUDY INSIDE FOR A BIT.
OKAY! SEE YOU LATER!
WHAT AN AWESOME DAY! THE FLOWERS HERE ARE SO GORGEOUS!
SEE? NATURE ALWAYS HAS A CURE FOR EVERYTHING!
I WISH I KNEW WHY I'M HAVING THESE DREAMS...
HEY, KIKO! YOU'RE UP NOW, TOO, HUH? WELL, I'M GLAD YOU'RE HERE!
SKRIIITCH!
NOW, BE GOOD, OKAY? I'VE GOT SOME THINKING TO DO!
SKRIIITCH!
TMP

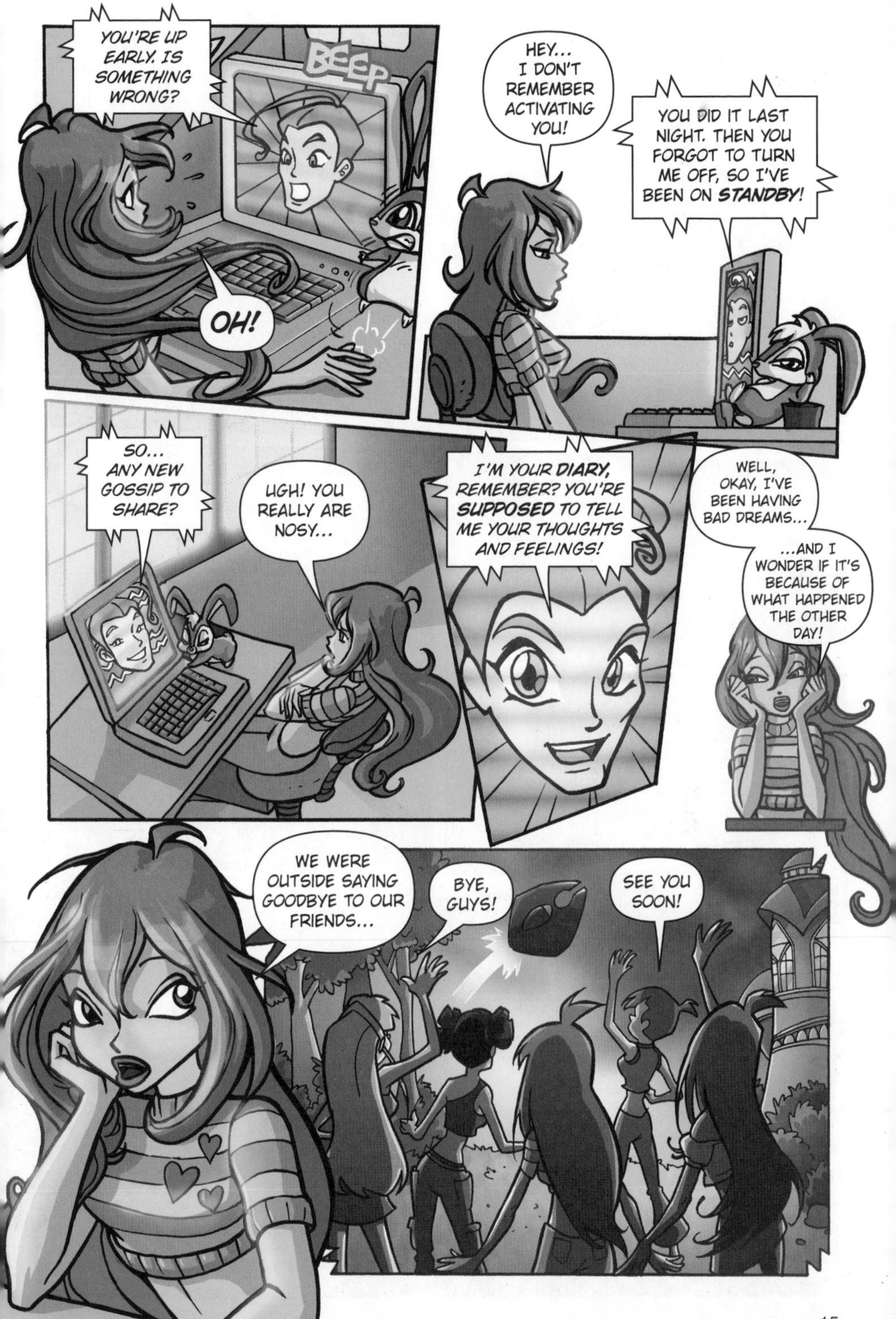

YOU'RE UP EARLY. IS SOMETHING WRONG?
BEEP
OH!
HEY... I DON'T REMEMBER ACTIVATING YOU!
YOU DID IT LAST NIGHT. THEN YOU FORGOT TO TURN ME OFF, SO I'VE BEEN ON STANDBY!
SO... ANY NEW GOSSIP TO SHARE?
UGH! YOU REALLY ARE NOSY...
I'M YOUR DIARY, REMEMBER? YOU'RE SUPPOSED TO TELL ME YOUR THOUGHTS AND FEELINGS!
WELL, OKAY, I'VE BEEN HAVING BAD DREAMS...
...AND I WONDER IF IT'S BECAUSE OF WHAT HAPPENED THE OTHER DAY!
WE WERE OUTSIDE SAYING GOODBYE TO OUR FRIENDS...
BYE, GUYS!
SEE YOU SOON!

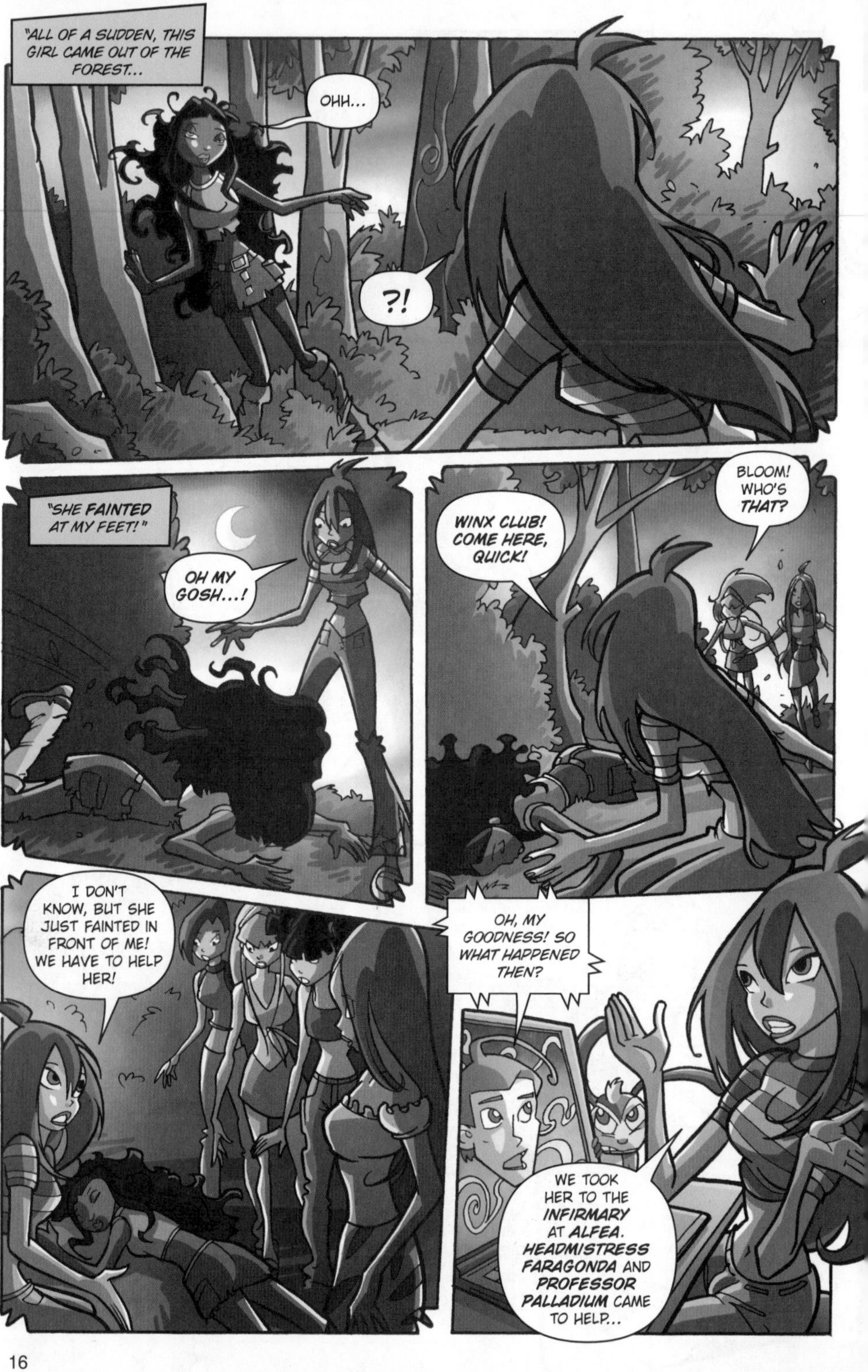
"ALL OF A SUDDEN, THIS GIRL CAME OUT OF THE FOREST...
OHH...
?!
"SHE FAINTED AT MY FEET!"
OH MY GOSH...!
WINX CLUB! COME HERE, QUICK!
BLOOM! WHO'S THAT?
I DON'T KNOW, BUT SHE JUST FAINTED IN FRONT OF ME! WE HAVE TO HELP HER!
OH, MY GOODNESS! SO WHAT HAPPENED THEN?
WE TOOK HER TO THE INFIRMARY AT ALFEA. HEADMISTRESS FARAGONDA AND PROFESSOR PALLADIUM CAME TO HELP...

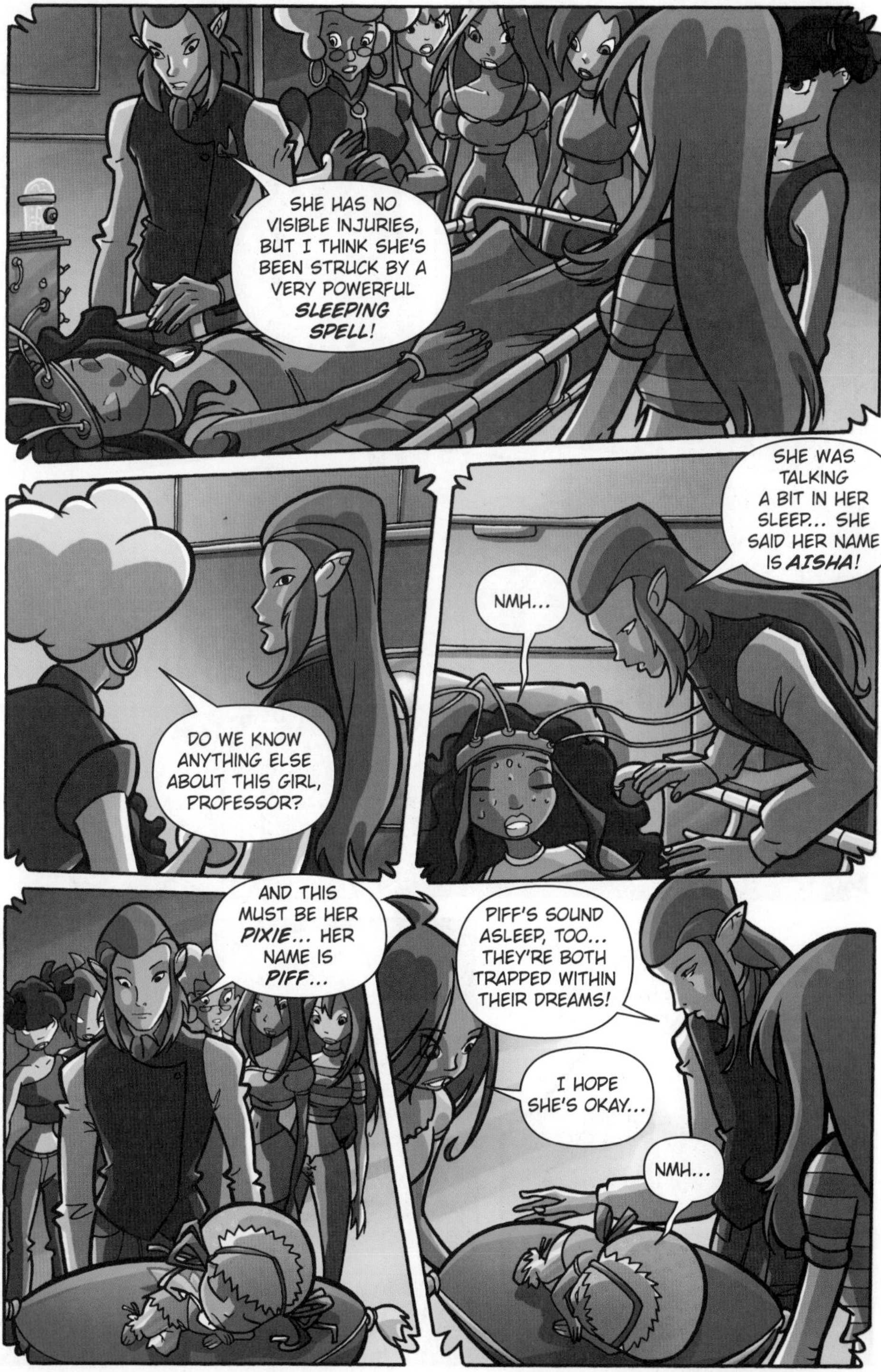

SHE HAS NO VISIBLE INJURIES, BUT I THINK SHE'S BEEN STRUCK BY A VERY POWERFUL SLEEPING SPELL!
DO WE KNOW ANYTHING ELSE ABOUT THIS GIRL, PROFESSOR?
SHE WAS TALKING A BIT IN HER SLEEP... SHE SAID HER NAME IS AISHA!
NMH...
AND THIS MUST BE HER PIXIE... HER NAME IS PIFF...
PIFF'S SOUND ASLEEP, TOO... THEY'RE BOTH TRAPPED WITHIN THEIR DREAMS!
I HOPE SHE'S OKAY...
NMH...

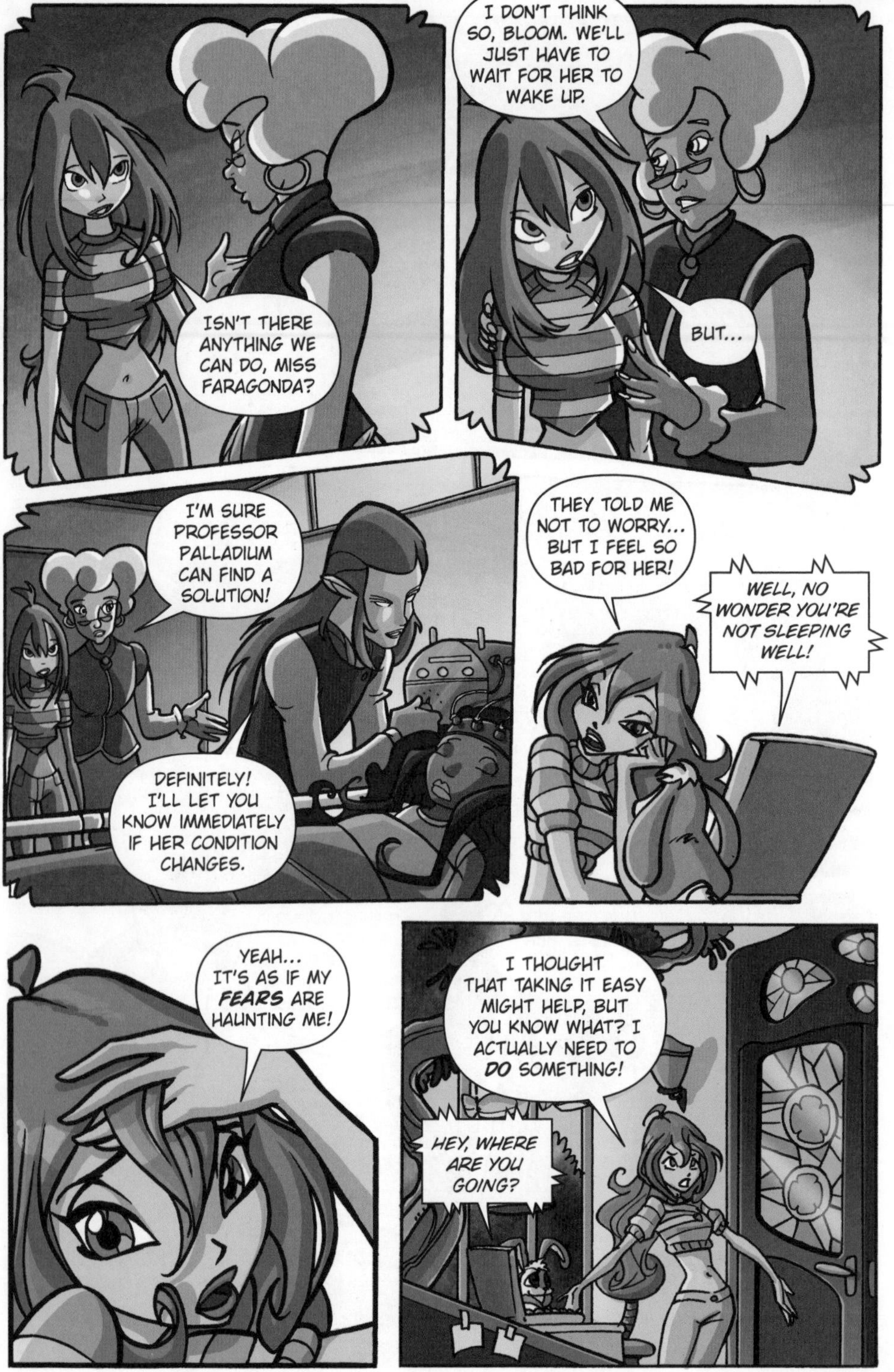
ISN'T THERE ANYTHING WE CAN DO, MISS FARAGONDA?
I DON'T THINK SO, BLOOM. WE'LL JUST HAVE TO WAIT FOR HER TO WAKE UP.
BUT...
I'M SURE PROFESSOR PALLADIUM CAN FIND A SOLUTION!
DEFINITELY! I'LL LET YOU KNOW IMMEDIATELY IF HER CONDITION CHANGES.
THEY TOLD ME NOT TO WORRY... BUT I FEEL SO BAD FOR HER!
WELL, NO WONDER YOU'RE NOT SLEEPING WELL!
YEAH... IT'S AS IF MY FEARS ARE HAUNTING ME!
I THOUGHT THAT TAKING IT EASY MIGHT HELP, BUT YOU KNOW WHAT? I ACTUALLY NEED TO DO SOMETHING!
HEY, WHERE ARE YOU GOING?

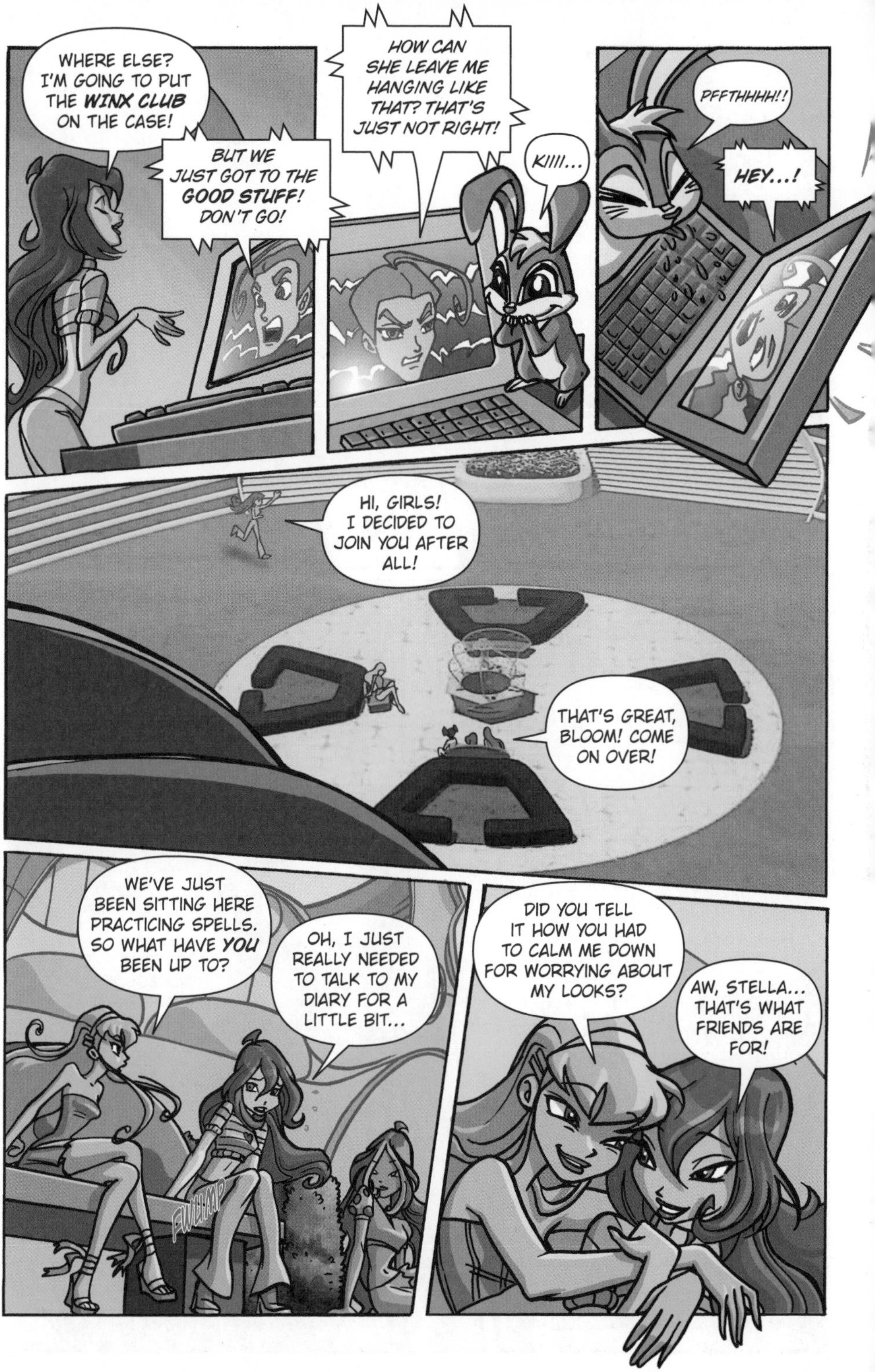
WHERE ELSE? I'M GOING TO PUT THE WINX CLUB ON THE CASE!
BUT WE JUST GOT TO THE GOOD STUFF! DON'T GO!
HOW CAN SHE LEAVE ME HANGING LIKE THAT? THAT'S JUST NOT RIGHT!
KIIII...
PFFTHHHH!!
HEY...!
HI, GIRLS! I DECIDED TO JOIN YOU AFTER ALL!
THAT'S GREAT, BLOOM! COME ON OVER!
WE'VE JUST BEEN SITTING HERE PRACTICING SPELLS. SO WHAT HAVE YOU BEEN UP TO?
OH, I JUST REALLY NEEDED TO TALK TO MY DIARY FOR A LITTLE BIT...
FWUMP
DID YOU TELL IT HOW YOU HAD TO CALM ME DOWN FOR WORRYING ABOUT MY LOOKS?
AW, STELLA... THAT'S WHAT FRIENDS ARE FOR!

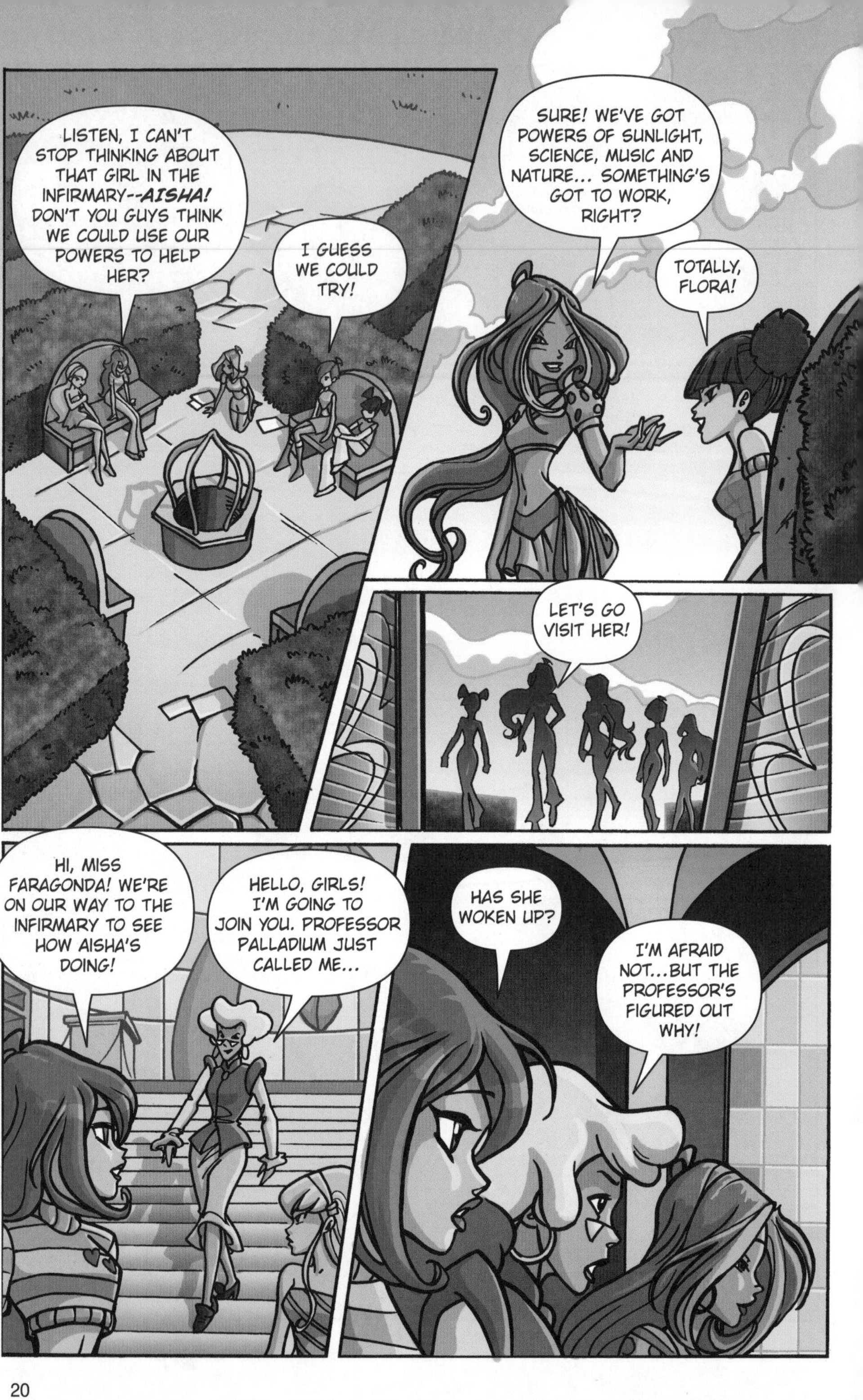
LISTEN, I CAN'T STOP THINKING ABOUT THAT GIRL IN THE INFIRMARY--AISHA! DON'T YOU GUYS THINK WE COULD USE OUR POWERS TO HELP HER?
I GUESS WE COULD TRY!
SURE! WE'VE GOT POWERS OF SUNLIGHT, SCIENCE, MUSIC AND NATURE... SOMETHING'S GOT TO WORK, RIGHT?
TOTALLY, FLORA!
LET'S GO VISIT HER!
HI, MISS FARAGONDA! WE'RE ON OUR WAY TO THE INFIRMARY TO SEE HOW AISHA'S DOING!
HELLO, GIRLS! I'M GOING TO JOIN YOU. PROFESSOR PALLADIUM JUST CALLED ME...
HAS SHE WOKEN UP?
I'M AFRAID NOT...BUT THE PROFESSOR'S FIGURED OUT WHY!

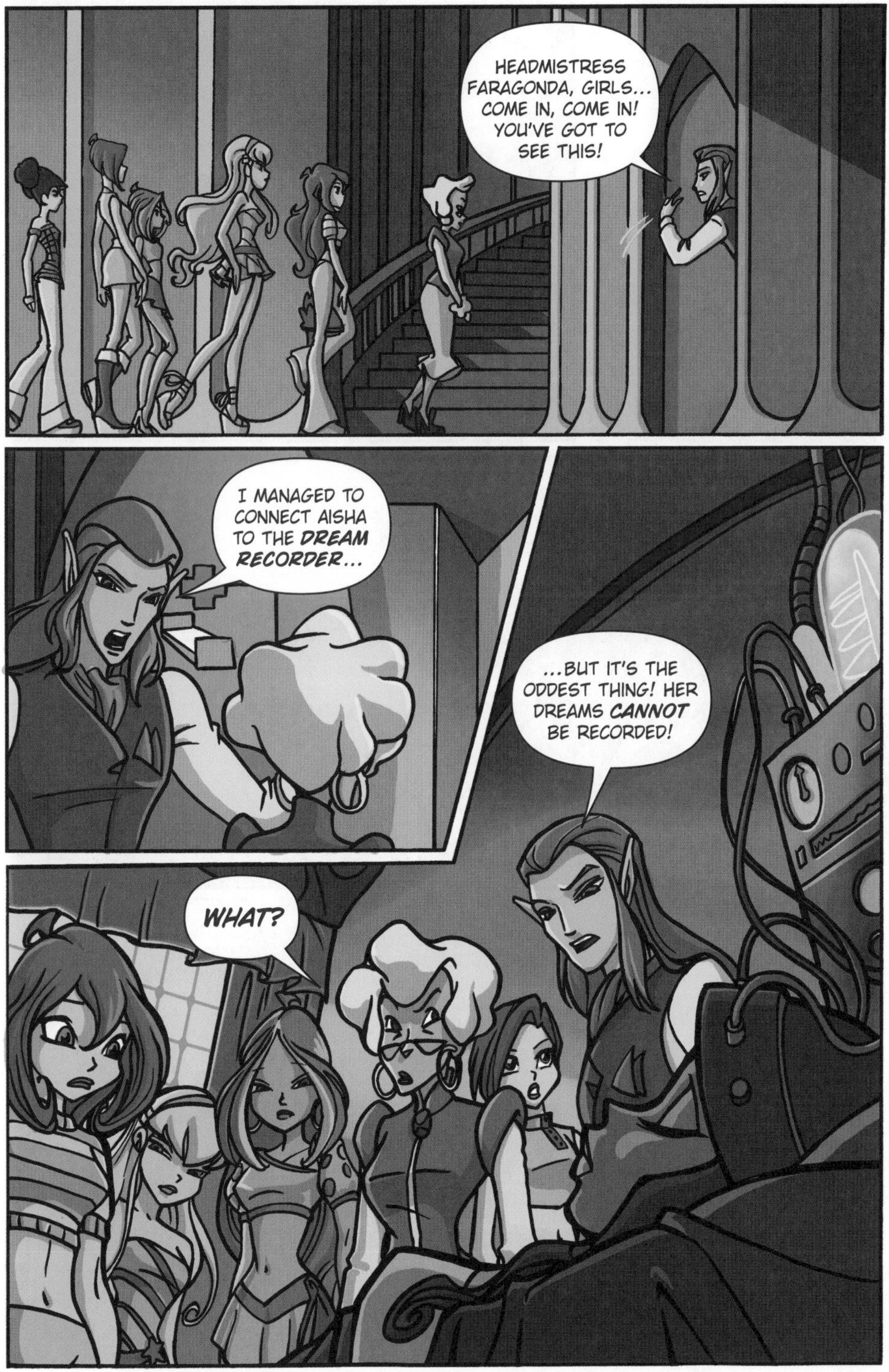
HEADMISTRESS FARAGONDA, GIRLS... COME IN, COME IN! YOU'VE GOT TO SEE THIS!
I MANAGED TO CONNECT AISHA TO THE *DREAM RECORDER*...
...BUT IT'S THE ODDEST THING! HER DREAMS *CANNOT* BE RECORDED!
WHAT?

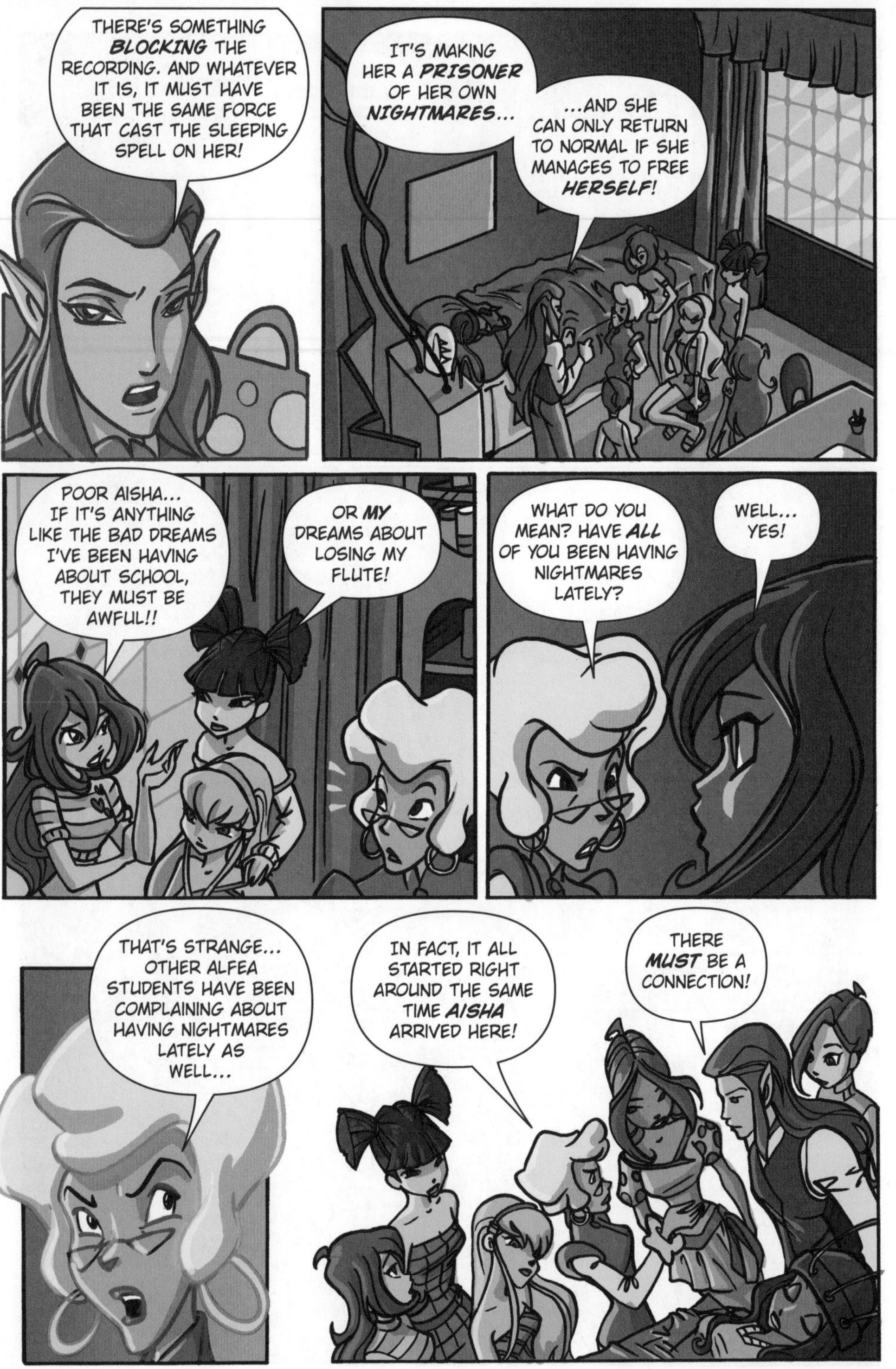
THERE'S SOMETHING BLOCKING THE RECORDING. AND WHATEVER IT IS, IT MUST HAVE BEEN THE SAME FORCE THAT CAST THE SLEEPING SPELL ON HER!
IT'S MAKING HER A PRISONER OF HER OWN NIGHTMARES...
...AND SHE CAN ONLY RETURN TO NORMAL IF SHE MANAGES TO FREE HERSELF!
POOR AISHA... IF IT'S ANYTHING LIKE THE BAD DREAMS I'VE BEEN HAVING ABOUT SCHOOL, THEY MUST BE AWFUL!!
OR MY DREAMS ABOUT LOSING MY FLUTE!
WHAT DO YOU MEAN? HAVE ALL OF YOU BEEN HAVING NIGHTMARES LATELY?
WELL... YES!
THAT'S STRANGE... OTHER ALFEA STUDENTS HAVE BEEN COMPLAINING ABOUT HAVING NIGHTMARES LATELY AS WELL...
IN FACT, IT ALL STARTED RIGHT AROUND THE SAME TIME AISHA ARRIVED HERE!
THERE MUST BE A CONNECTION!

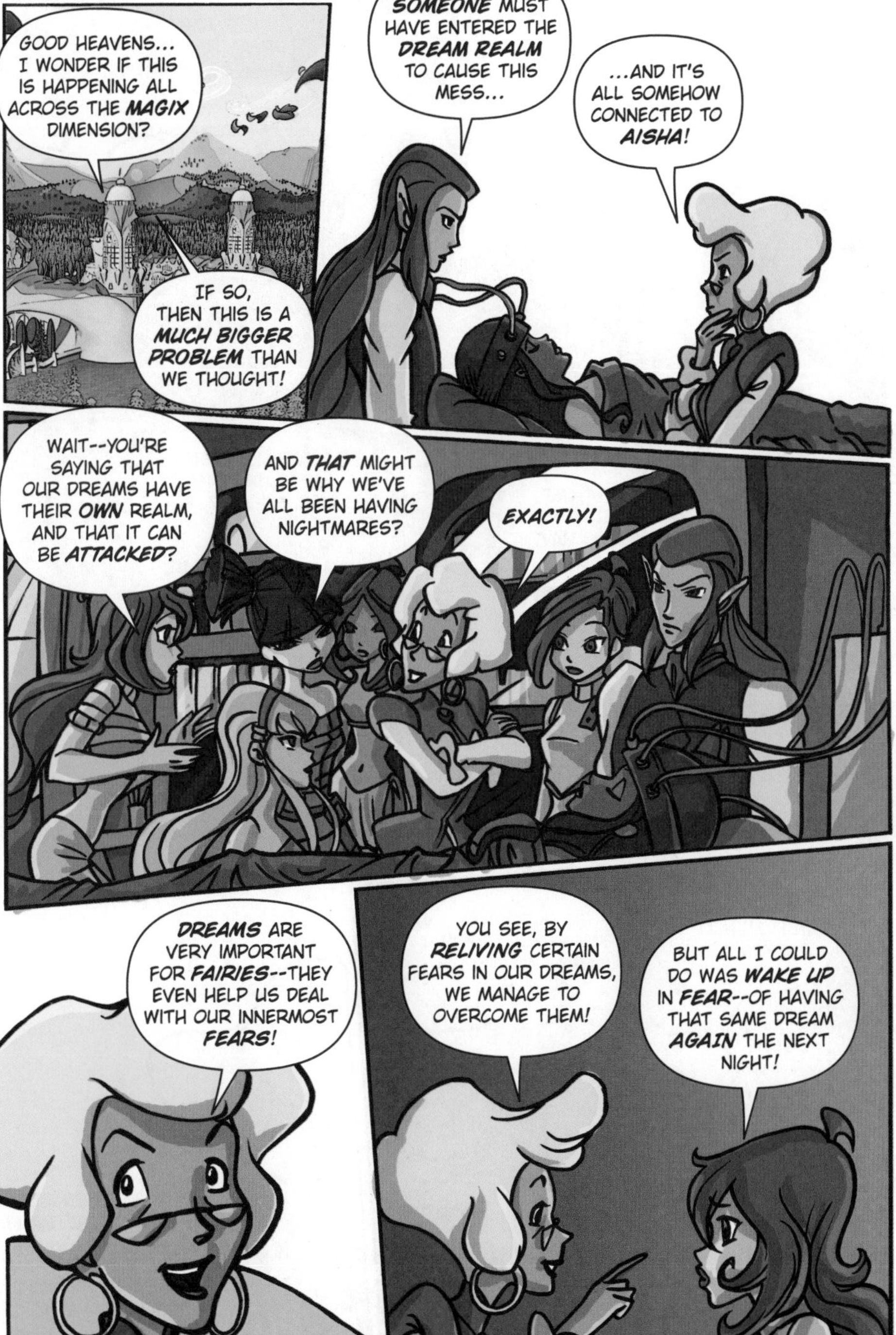
GOOD HEAVENS... I WONDER IF THIS IS HAPPENING ALL ACROSS THE MAGIX DIMENSION?
IF SO, THEN THIS IS A MUCH BIGGER PROBLEM THAN WE THOUGHT!
SOMEONE MUST HAVE ENTERED THE DREAM REALM TO CAUSE THIS MESS...
...AND IT'S ALL SOMEHOW CONNECTED TO AISHA!
WAIT--YOU'RE SAYING THAT OUR DREAMS HAVE THEIR OWN REALM, AND THAT IT CAN BE ATTACKED?
AND THAT MIGHT BE WHY WE'VE ALL BEEN HAVING NIGHTMARES?
EXACTLY!
DREAMS ARE VERY IMPORTANT FOR FAIRIES--THEY EVEN HELP US DEAL WITH OUR INNERMOST FEARS!
YOU SEE, BY RELIVING CERTAIN FEARS IN OUR DREAMS, WE MANAGE TO OVERCOME THEM!
BUT ALL I COULD DO WAS WAKE UP IN FEAR--OF HAVING THAT SAME DREAM AGAIN THE NEXT NIGHT!

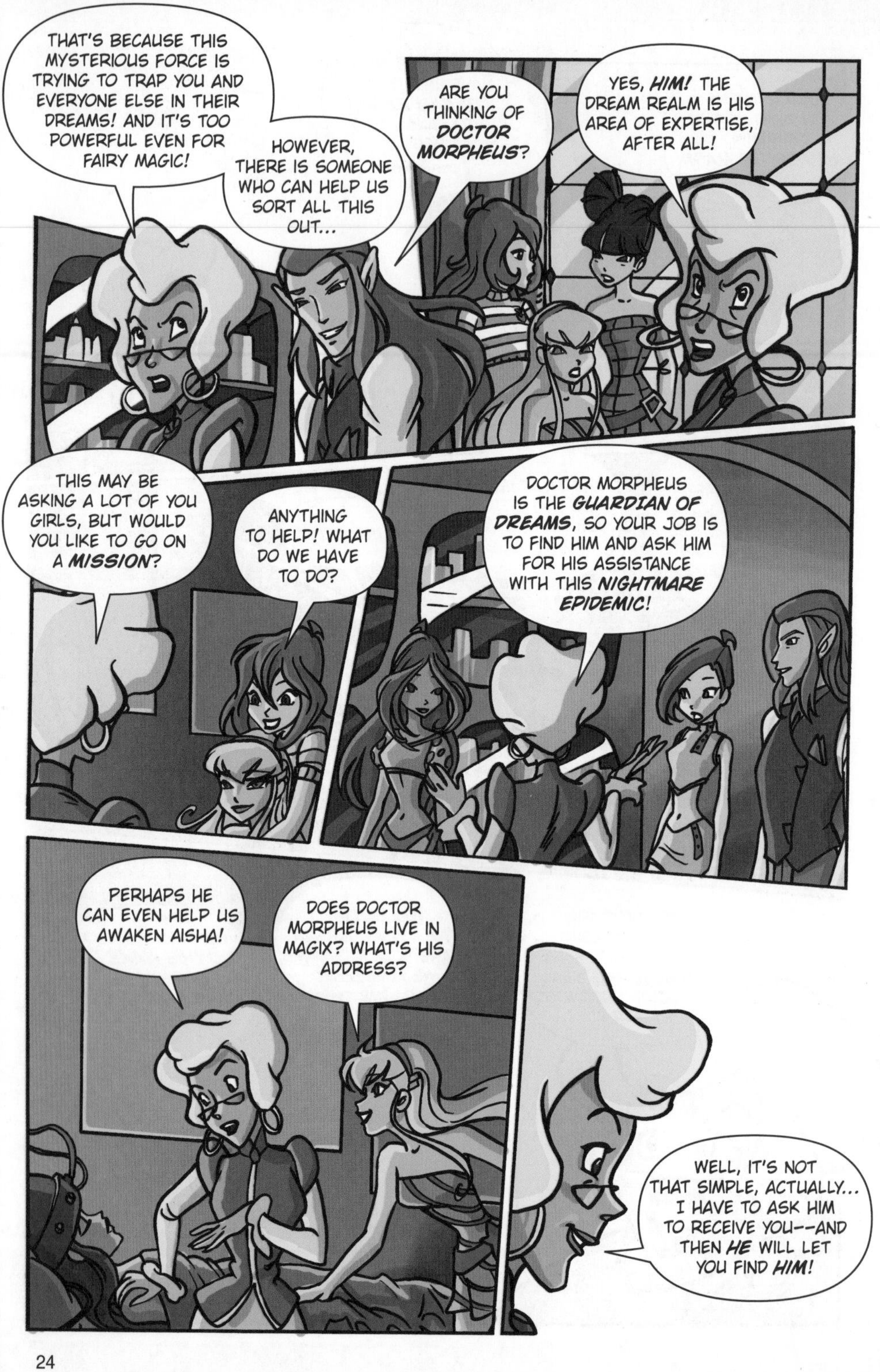
THAT'S BECAUSE THIS MYSTERIOUS FORCE IS TRYING TO TRAP YOU AND EVERYONE ELSE IN THEIR DREAMS! AND IT'S TOO POWERFUL EVEN FOR FAIRY MAGIC!
HOWEVER, THERE IS SOMEONE WHO CAN HELP US SORT ALL THIS OUT...
ARE YOU THINKING OF DOCTOR MORPHEUS?
YES, HIM! THE DREAM REALM IS HIS AREA OF EXPERTISE, AFTER ALL!
THIS MAY BE ASKING A LOT OF YOU GIRLS, BUT WOULD YOU LIKE TO GO ON A MISSION?
ANYTHING TO HELP! WHAT DO WE HAVE TO DO?
DOCTOR MORPHEUS IS THE GUARDIAN OF DREAMS, SO YOUR JOB IS TO FIND HIM AND ASK HIM FOR HIS ASSISTANCE WITH THIS NIGHTMARE EPIDEMIC!
PERHAPS HE CAN EVEN HELP US AWAKEN AISHA!
DOES DOCTOR MORPHEUS LIVE IN MAGIX? WHAT'S HIS ADDRESS?
WELL, IT'S NOT THAT SIMPLE, ACTUALLY... I HAVE TO ASK HIM TO RECEIVE YOU--AND THEN HE WILL LET YOU FIND HIM!

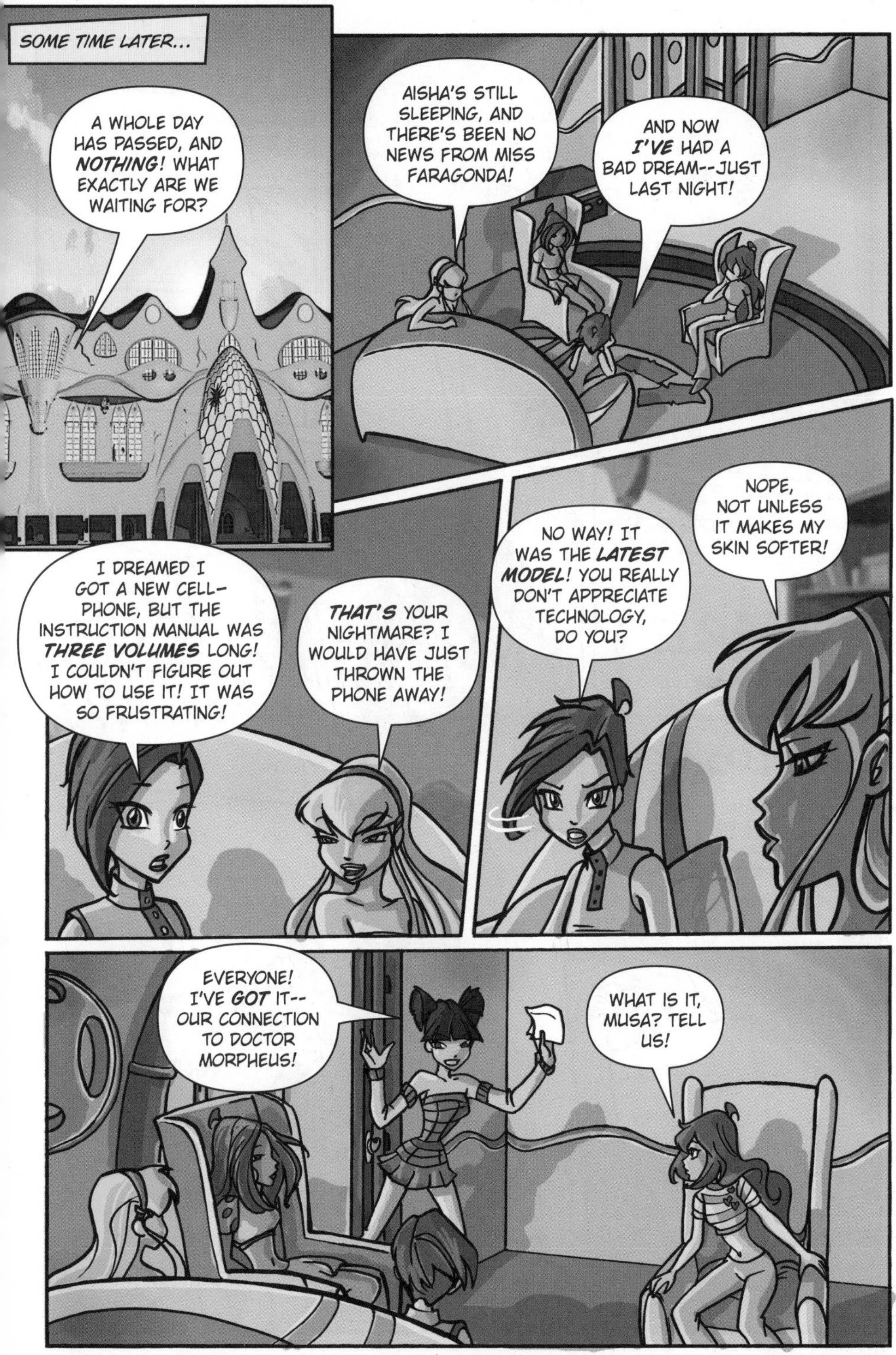
SOME TIME LATER...
A WHOLE DAY HAS PASSED, AND NOTHING! WHAT EXACTLY ARE WE WAITING FOR?
AISHA'S STILL SLEEPING, AND THERE'S BEEN NO NEWS FROM MISS FARAGONDA!
AND NOW I'VE HAD A BAD DREAM--JUST LAST NIGHT!
I DREAMED I GOT A NEW CELL-PHONE, BUT THE INSTRUCTION MANUAL WAS THREE VOLUMES LONG! I COULDN'T FIGURE OUT HOW TO USE IT! IT WAS SO FRUSTRATING!
THAT'S YOUR NIGHTMARE? I WOULD HAVE JUST THROWN THE PHONE AWAY!
NO WAY! IT WAS THE LATEST MODEL! YOU REALLY DON'T APPRECIATE TECHNOLOGY, DO YOU?
NOPE, NOT UNLESS IT MAKES MY SKIN SOFTER!
EVERYONE! I'VE GOT IT--OUR CONNECTION TO DOCTOR MORPHEUS!
WHAT IS IT, MUSA? TELL US!

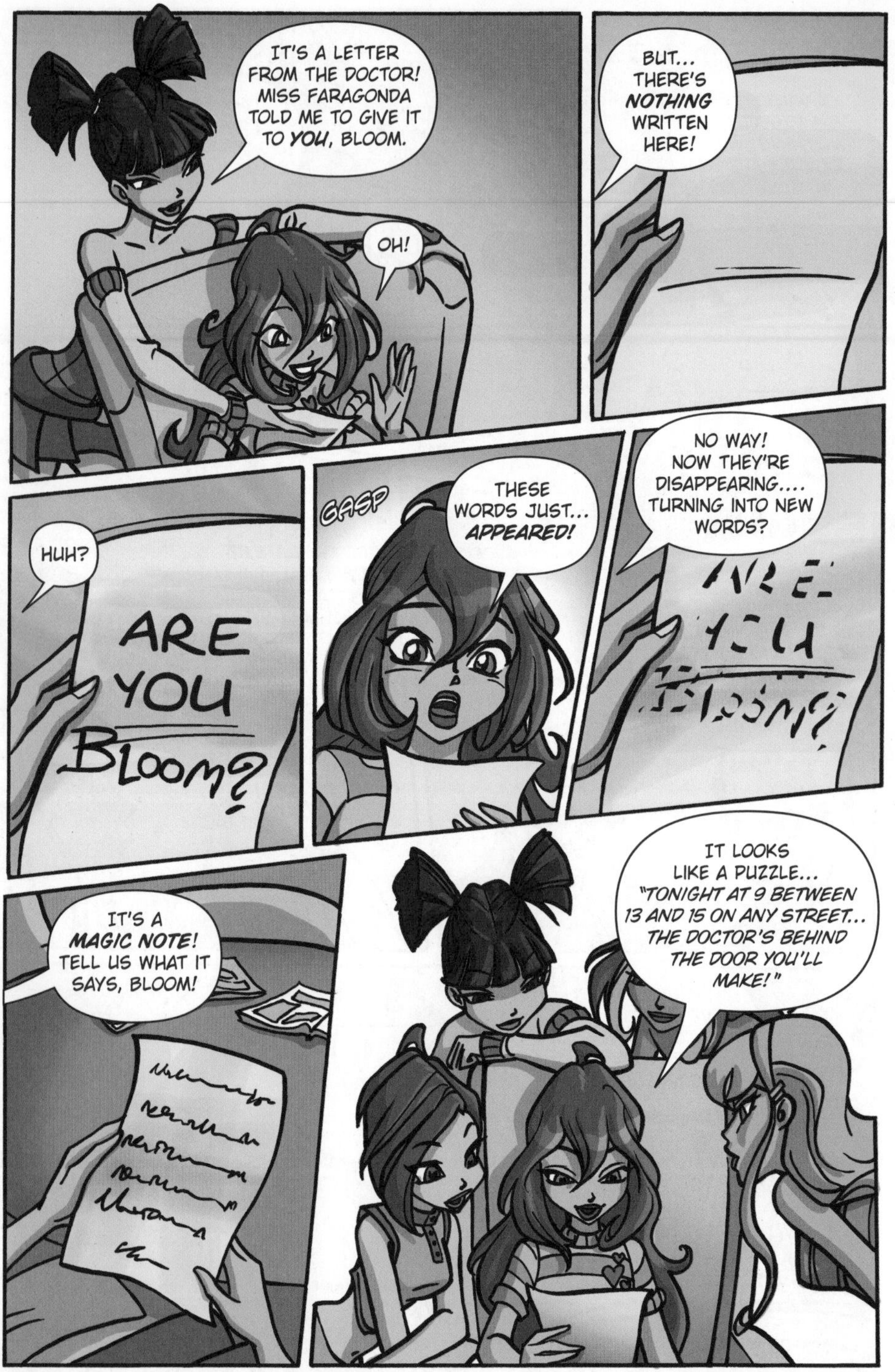
IT'S A LETTER FROM THE DOCTOR! MISS FARAGONDA TOLD ME TO GIVE IT TO YOU, BLOOM.
OH!
BUT... THERE'S NOTHING WRITTEN HERE!
HUH?
ARE YOU BLOOM?
GASP
THESE WORDS JUST... APPEARED!
NO WAY! NOW THEY'RE DISAPPEARING.... TURNING INTO NEW WORDS?
IT'S A MAGIC NOTE! TELL US WHAT IT SAYS, BLOOM!
IT LOOKS LIKE A PUZZLE... "TONIGHT AT 9 BETWEEN 13 AND 15 ON ANY STREET... THE DOCTOR'S BEHIND THE DOOR YOU'LL MAKE!"

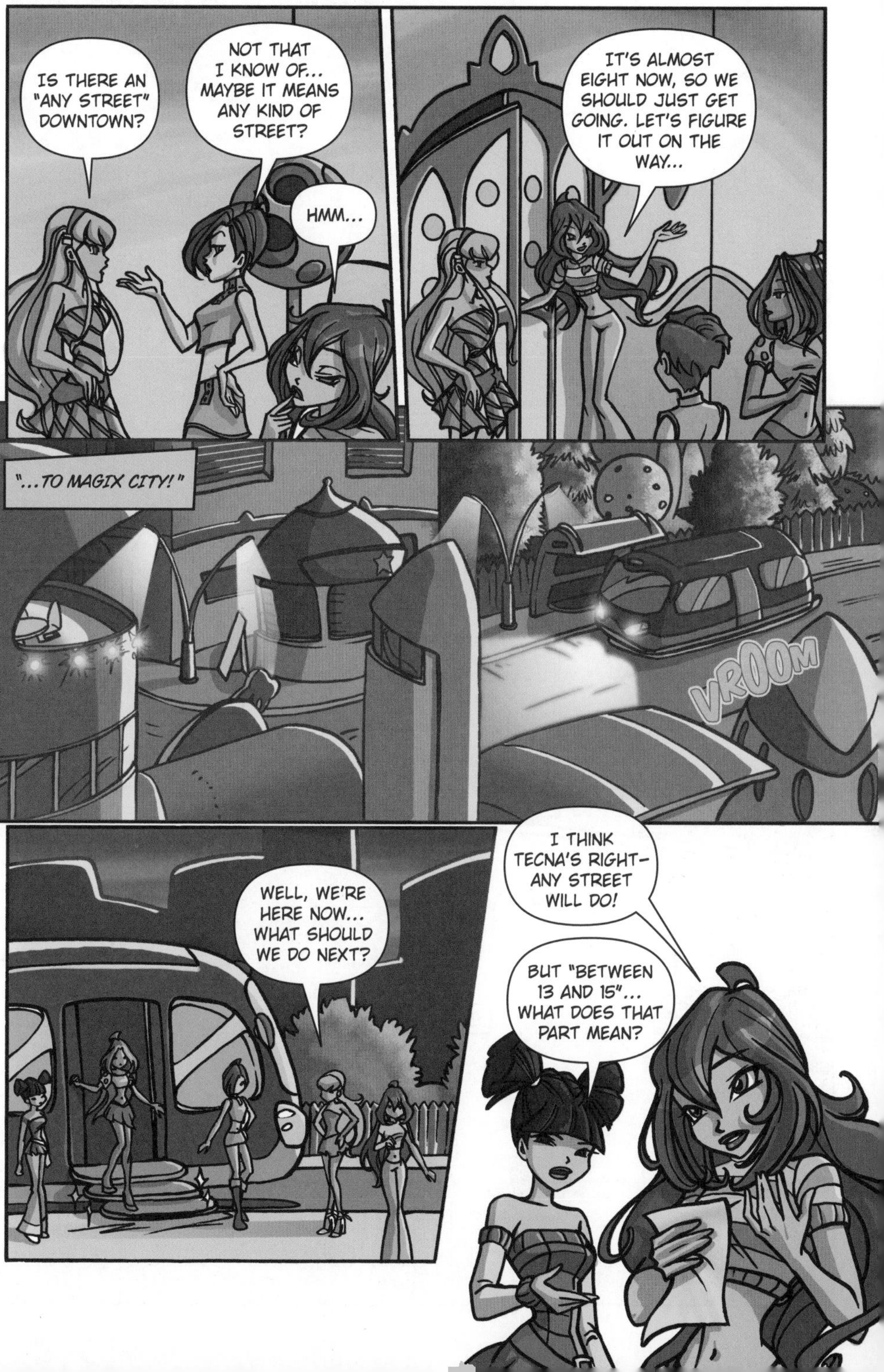
IS THERE AN "ANY STREET" DOWNTOWN?
NOT THAT I KNOW OF... MAYBE IT MEANS ANY KIND OF STREET?
HMM...
IT'S ALMOST EIGHT NOW, SO WE SHOULD JUST GET GOING. LET'S FIGURE IT OUT ON THE WAY...
"...TO MAGIX CITY!"
VROOM
WELL, WE'RE HERE NOW... WHAT SHOULD WE DO NEXT?
I THINK TECNA'S RIGHT-ANY STREET WILL DO!
BUT "BETWEEN 13 AND 15"... WHAT DOES THAT PART MEAN?

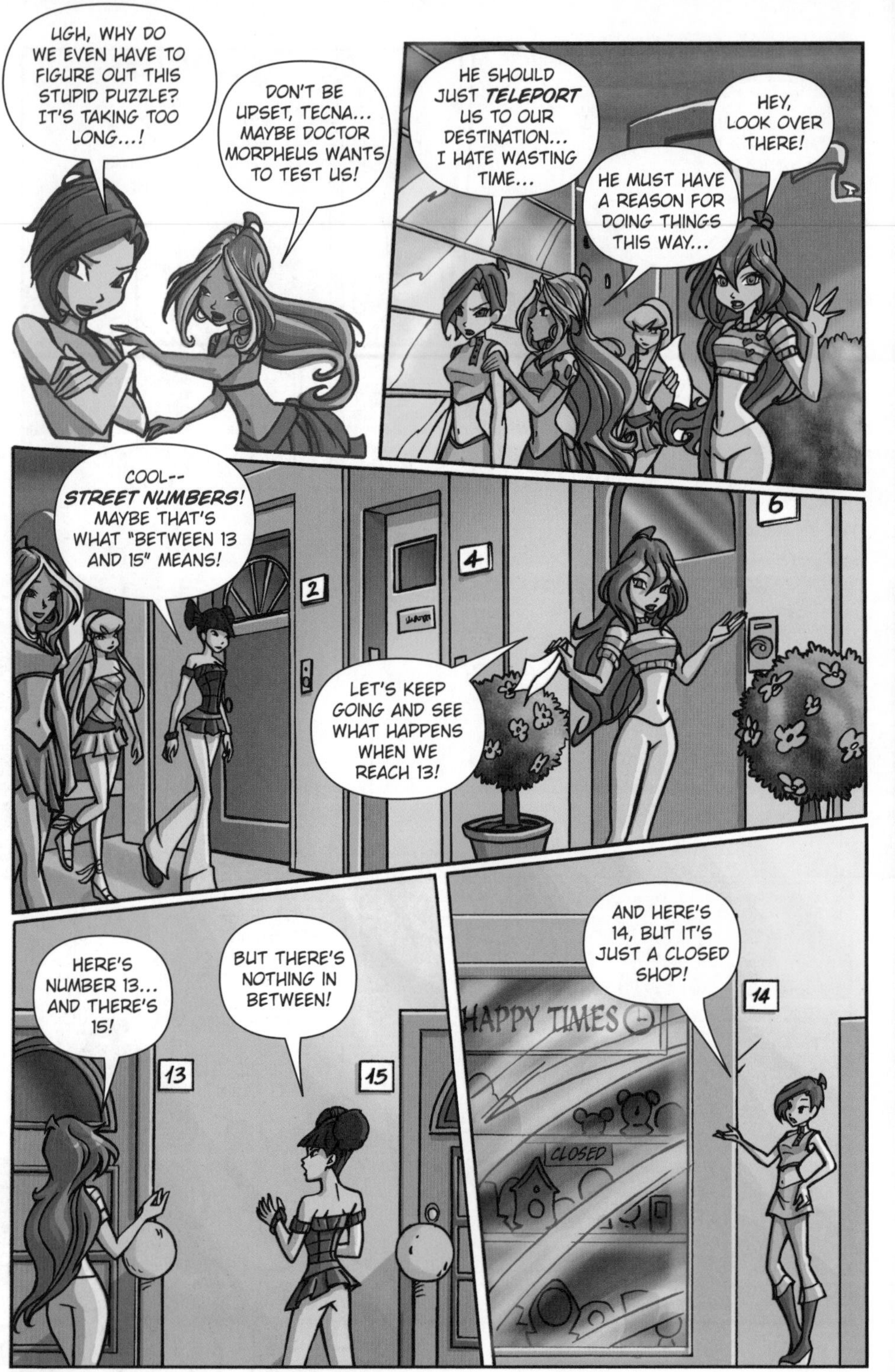
UGH, WHY DO WE EVEN HAVE TO FIGURE OUT THIS STUPID PUZZLE? IT'S TAKING TOO LONG...!
DON'T BE UPSET, TECNA... MAYBE DOCTOR MORPHEUS WANTS TO TEST US!
HE SHOULD JUST TELEPORT US TO OUR DESTINATION... I HATE WASTING TIME...
HE MUST HAVE A REASON FOR DOING THINGS THIS WAY...
HEY, LOOK OVER THERE!
COOL-- STREET NUMBERS! MAYBE THAT'S WHAT "BETWEEN 13 AND 15" MEANS!
2
4
6
LET'S KEEP GOING AND SEE WHAT HAPPENS WHEN WE REACH 13!
HERE'S NUMBER 13... AND THERE'S 15!
BUT THERE'S NOTHING IN BETWEEN!
13
15
AND HERE'S 14, BUT IT'S JUST A CLOSED SHOP!
14
HAPPY TIMES
CLOSED

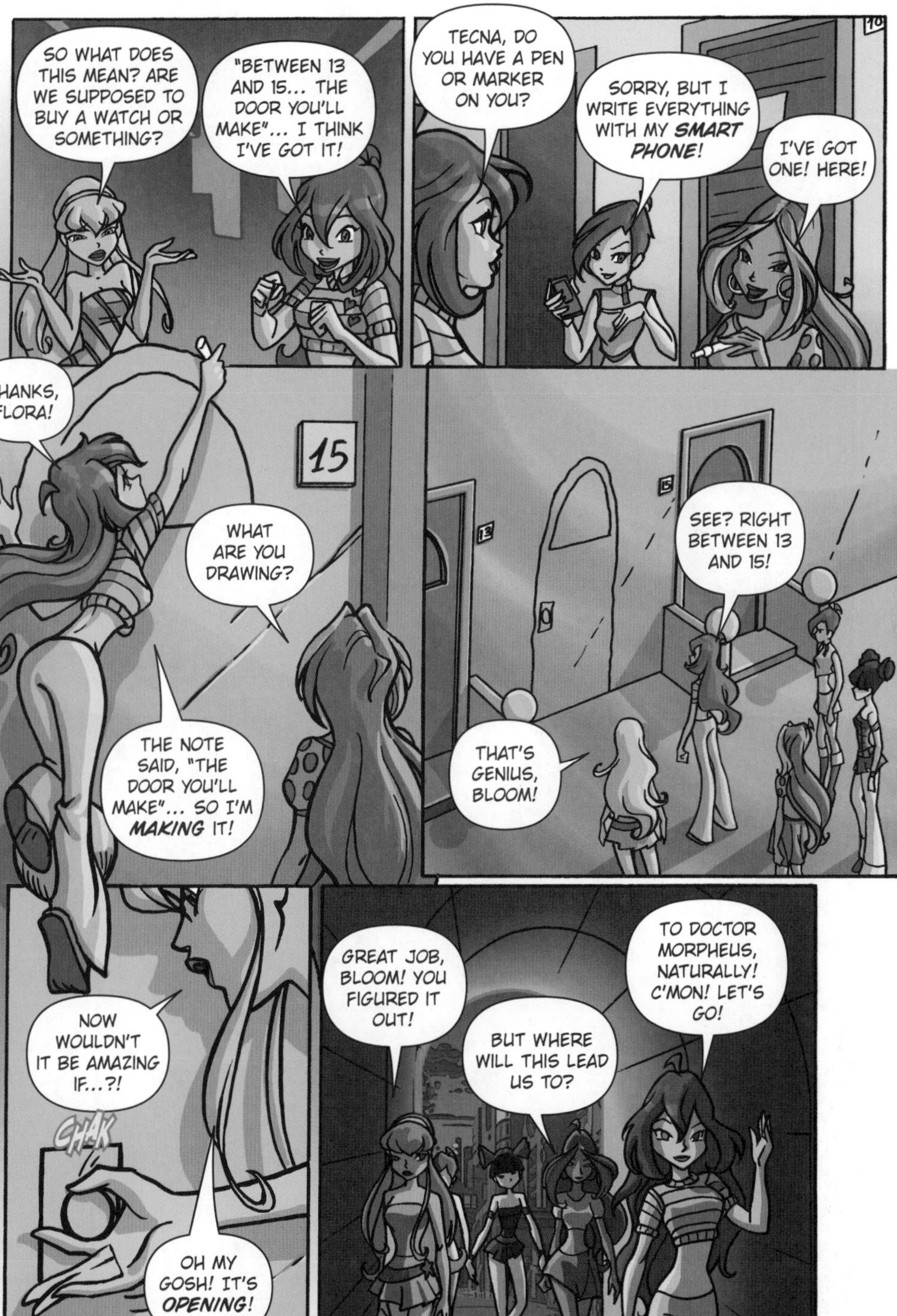
SO WHAT DOES THIS MEAN? ARE WE SUPPOSED TO BUY A WATCH OR SOMETHING?
"BETWEEN 13 AND 15… THE DOOR YOU'LL MAKE"… I THINK I'VE GOT IT!
TECNA, DO YOU HAVE A PEN OR MARKER ON YOU?
SORRY, BUT I WRITE EVERYTHING WITH MY SMART PHONE!
I'VE GOT ONE! HERE!
10
THANKS, FLORA!
15
WHAT ARE YOU DRAWING?
THE NOTE SAID, "THE DOOR YOU'LL MAKE"… SO I'M MAKING IT!
13
15
SEE? RIGHT BETWEEN 13 AND 15!
THAT'S GENIUS, BLOOM!
NOW WOULDN'T IT BE AMAZING IF…?!
CHAK
OH MY GOSH! IT'S OPENING!
GREAT JOB, BLOOM! YOU FIGURED IT OUT!
BUT WHERE WILL THIS LEAD US TO?
TO DOCTOR MORPHEUS, NATURALLY! C'MON! LET'S GO!

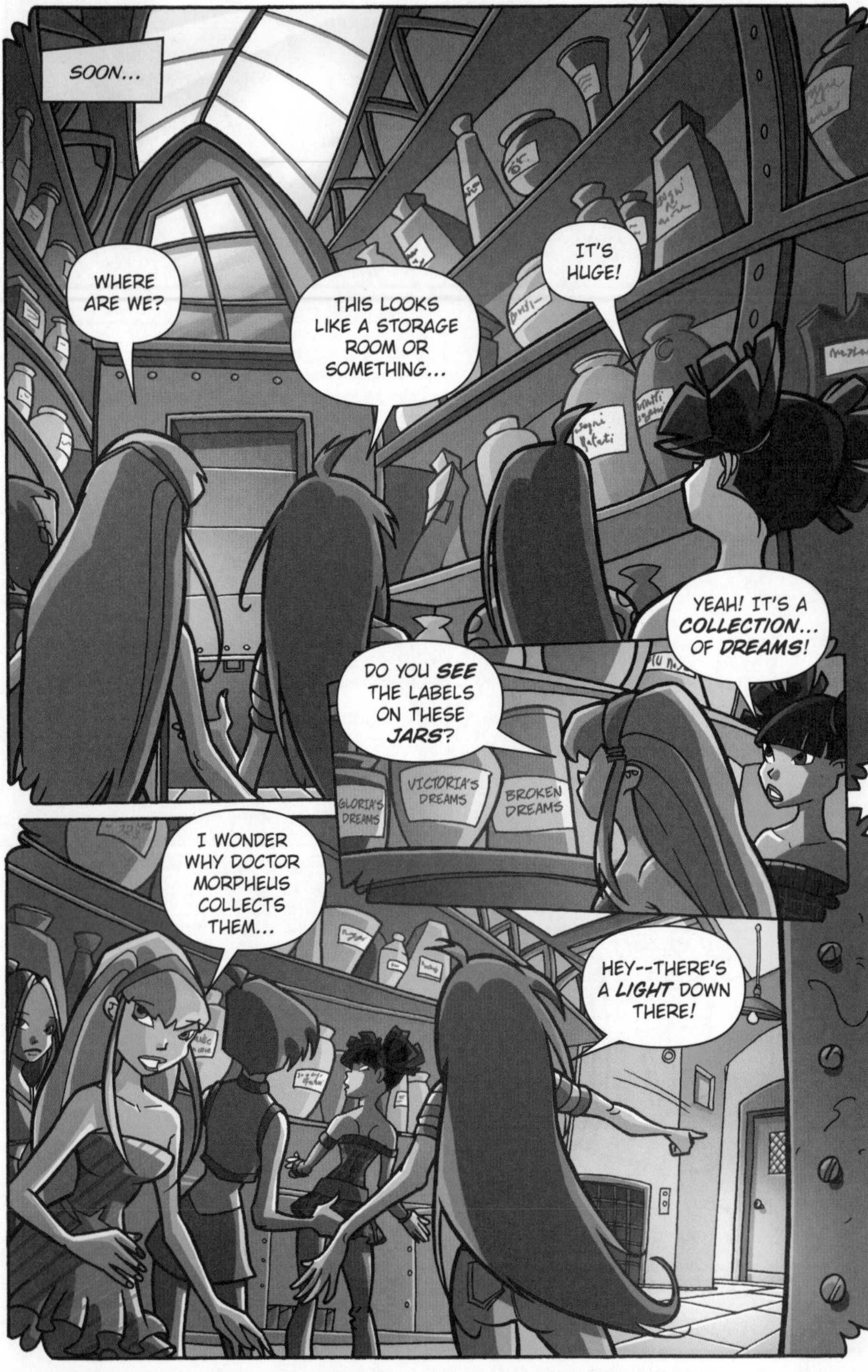
SOON...
WHERE ARE WE?
THIS LOOKS LIKE A STORAGE ROOM OR SOMETHING...
IT'S HUGE!
YEAH! IT'S A COLLECTION... OF DREAMS!
DO YOU SEE THE LABELS ON THESE JARS?
GLORIA'S DREAMS
VICTORIA'S DREAMS
BROKEN DREAMS
I WONDER WHY DOCTOR MORPHEUS COLLECTS THEM...
HEY--THERE'S A LIGHT DOWN THERE!

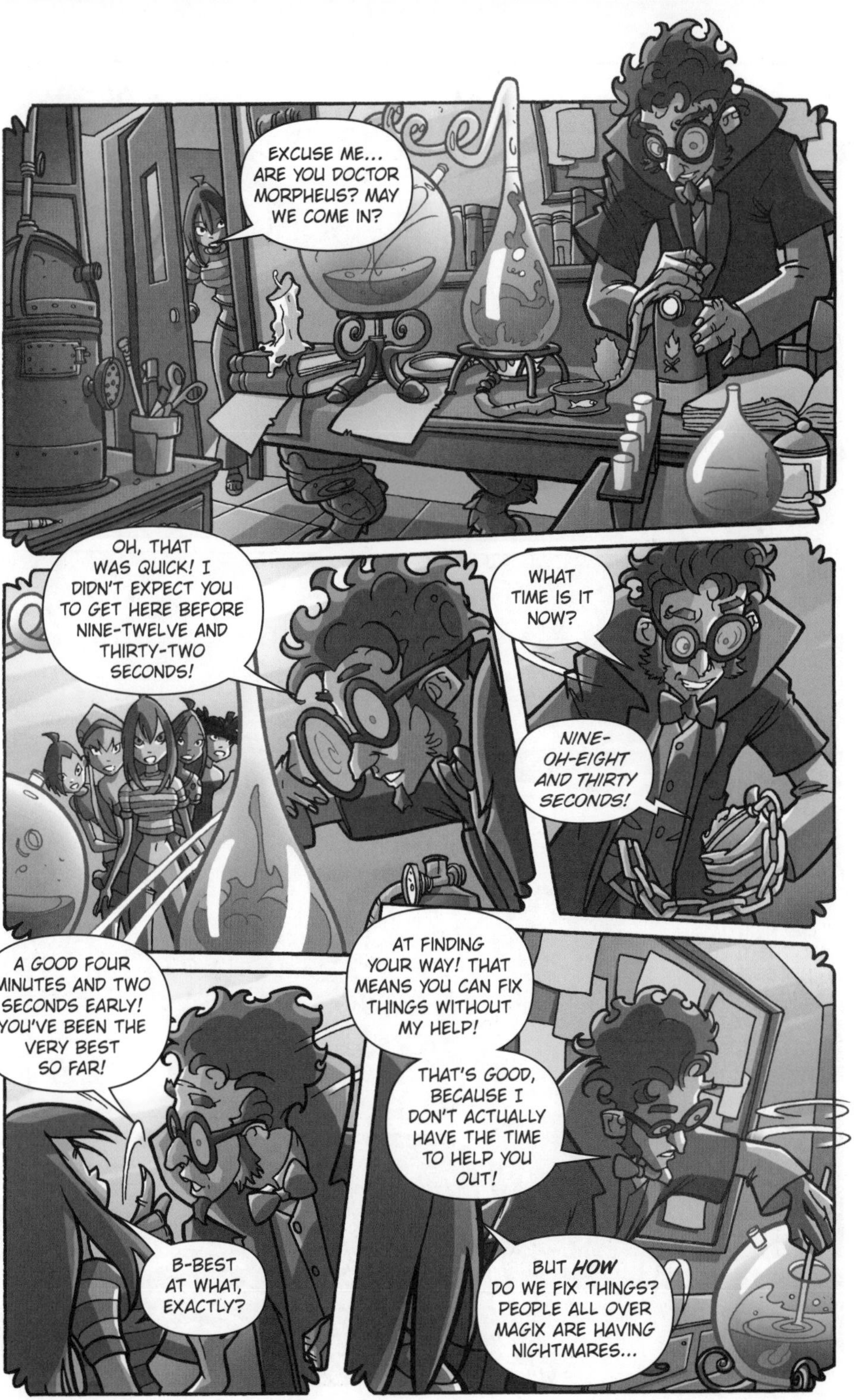
EXCUSE ME... ARE YOU DOCTOR MORPHEUS? MAY WE COME IN?
OH, THAT WAS QUICK! I DIDN'T EXPECT YOU TO GET HERE BEFORE NINE-TWELVE AND THIRTY-TWO SECONDS!
WHAT TIME IS IT NOW?
NINE-OH-EIGHT AND THIRTY SECONDS!
A GOOD FOUR MINUTES AND TWO SECONDS EARLY! YOU'VE BEEN THE VERY BEST SO FAR!
B-BEST AT WHAT, EXACTLY?
AT FINDING YOUR WAY! THAT MEANS YOU CAN FIX THINGS WITHOUT MY HELP!
THAT'S GOOD, BECAUSE I DON'T ACTUALLY HAVE THE TIME TO HELP YOU OUT!
BUT **HOW** DO WE FIX THINGS? PEOPLE ALL OVER MAGIX ARE HAVING NIGHTMARES...

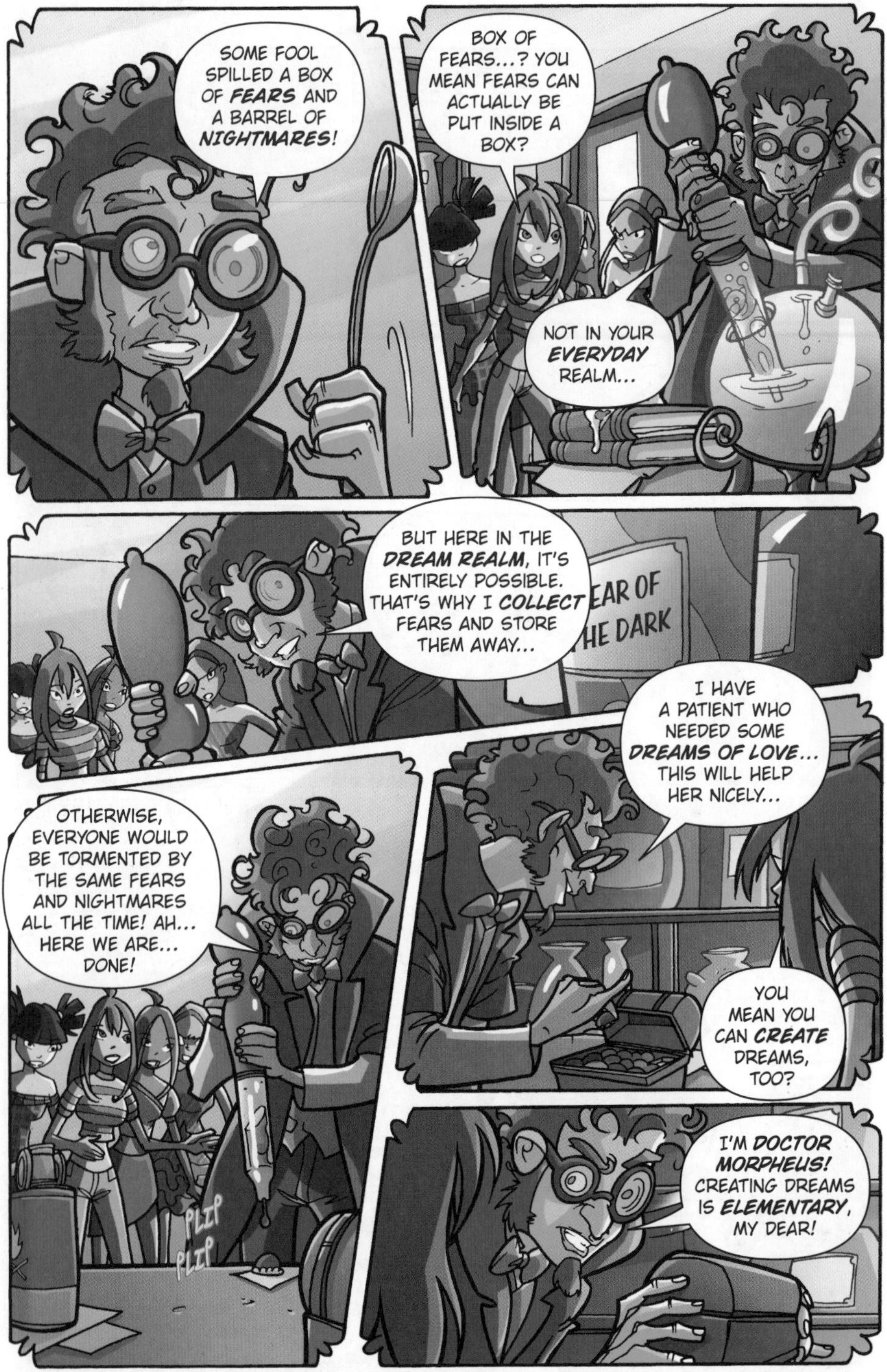
SOME FOOL SPILLED A BOX OF FEARS AND A BARREL OF NIGHTMARES!
BOX OF FEARS...? YOU MEAN FEARS CAN ACTUALLY BE PUT INSIDE A BOX?
NOT IN YOUR EVERYDAY REALM...
BUT HERE IN THE DREAM REALM, IT'S ENTIRELY POSSIBLE. THAT'S WHY I COLLECT FEARS AND STORE THEM AWAY...
EAR OF
HE DARK
OTHERWISE, EVERYONE WOULD BE TORMENTED BY THE SAME FEARS AND NIGHTMARES ALL THE TIME! AH... HERE WE ARE... DONE!
PLIP
PLIP
I HAVE A PATIENT WHO NEEDED SOME DREAMS OF LOVE... THIS WILL HELP HER NICELY...
YOU MEAN YOU CAN CREATE DREAMS, TOO?
I'M DOCTOR MORPHEUS! CREATING DREAMS IS ELEMENTARY, MY DEAR!

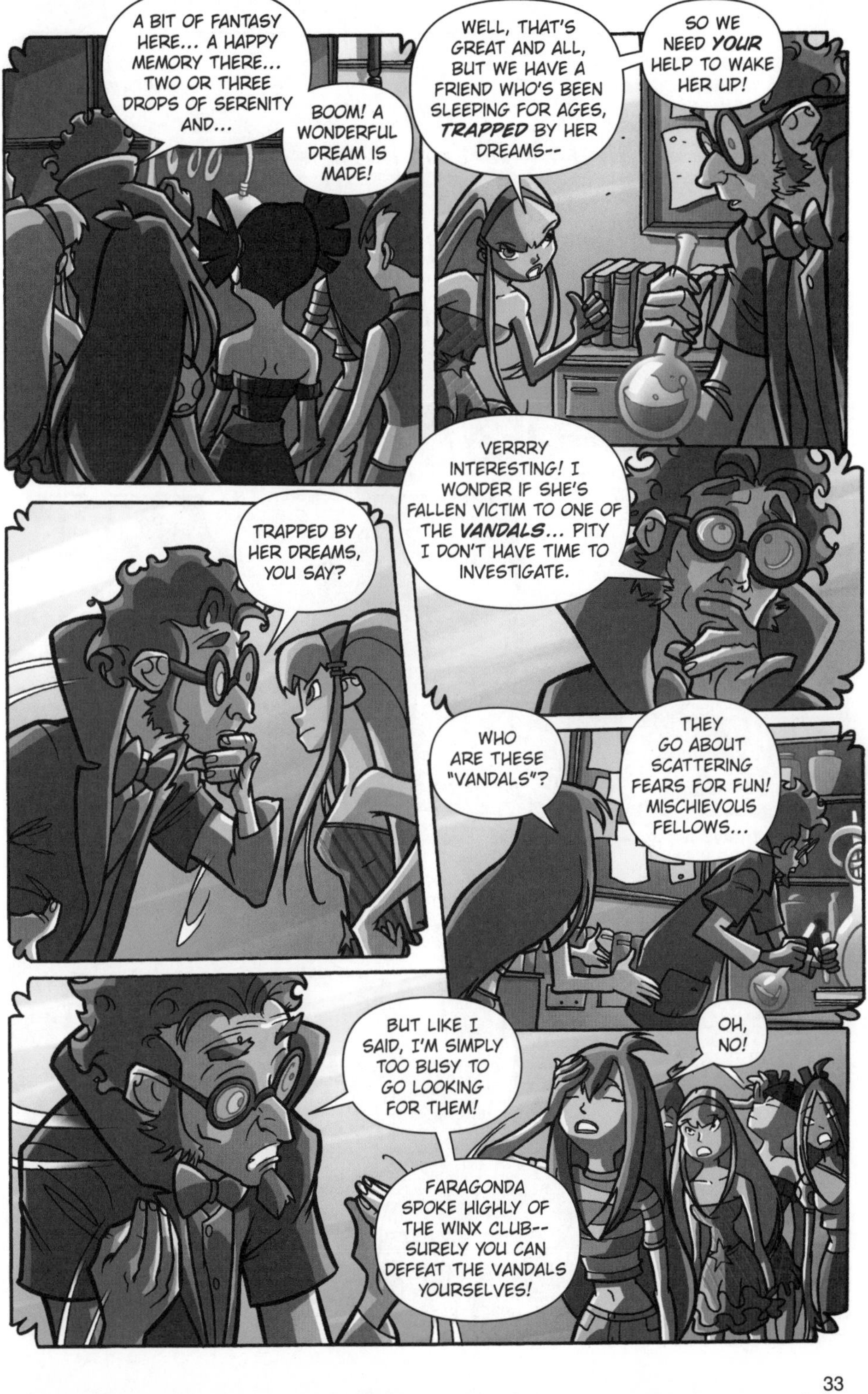
A BIT OF FANTASY HERE... A HAPPY MEMORY THERE... TWO OR THREE DROPS OF SERENITY AND...
BOOM! A WONDERFUL DREAM IS MADE!
WELL, THAT'S GREAT AND ALL, BUT WE HAVE A FRIEND WHO'S BEEN SLEEPING FOR AGES, TRAPPED BY HER DREAMS--
SO WE NEED YOUR HELP TO WAKE HER UP!
TRAPPED BY HER DREAMS, YOU SAY?
VERRRY INTERESTING! I WONDER IF SHE'S FALLEN VICTIM TO ONE OF THE VANDALS... PITY I DON'T HAVE TIME TO INVESTIGATE.
WHO ARE THESE "VANDALS"?
THEY GO ABOUT SCATTERING FEARS FOR FUN! MISCHIEVOUS FELLOWS...
BUT LIKE I SAID, I'M SIMPLY TOO BUSY TO GO LOOKING FOR THEM!
FARAGONDA SPOKE HIGHLY OF THE WINX CLUB-- SURELY YOU CAN DEFEAT THE VANDALS YOURSELVES!
OH, NO!

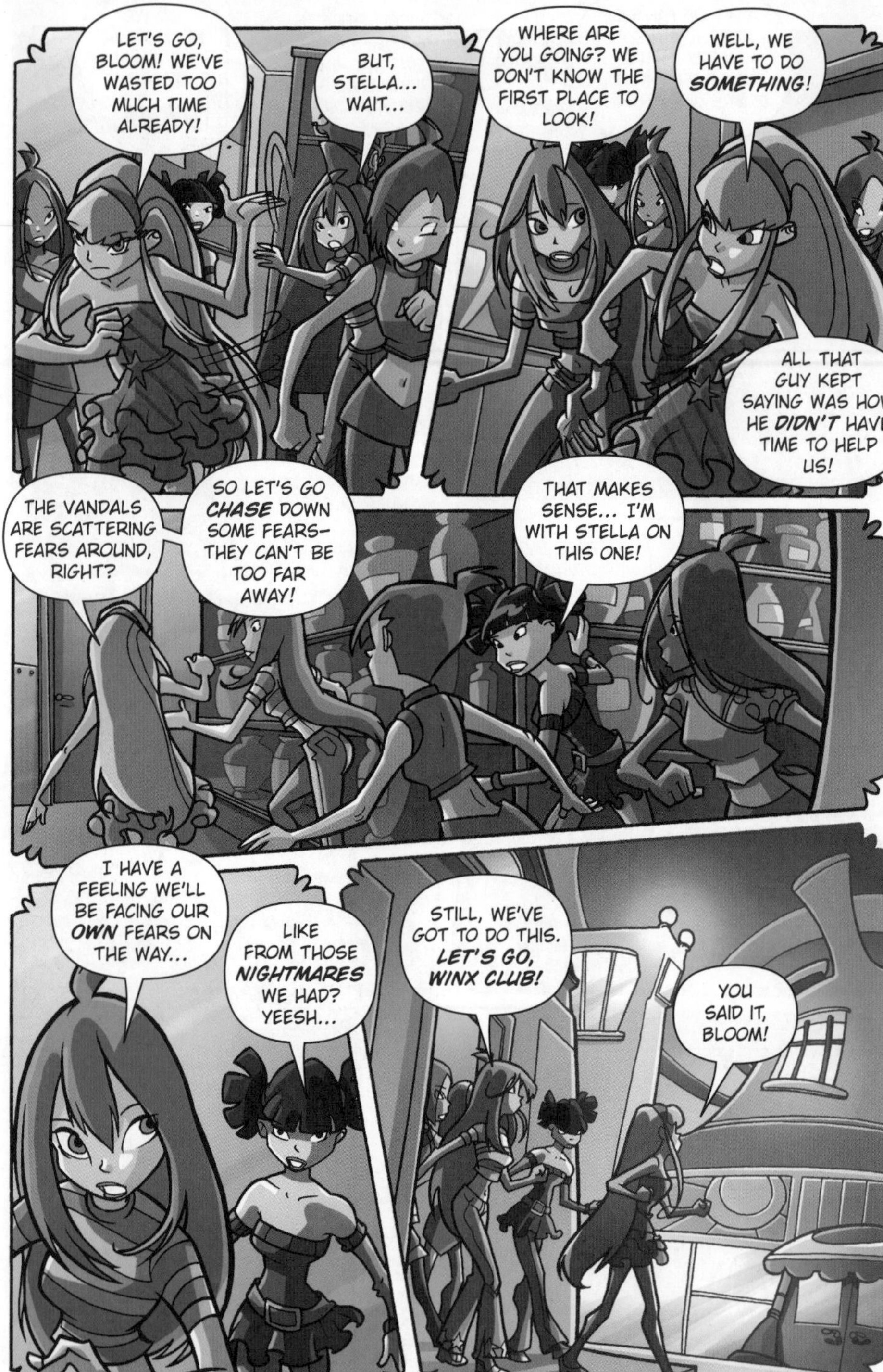
LET'S GO, BLOOM! WE'VE WASTED TOO MUCH TIME ALREADY!
BUT, STELLA... WAIT...
WHERE ARE YOU GOING? WE DON'T KNOW THE FIRST PLACE TO LOOK!
WELL, WE HAVE TO DO SOMETHING!
ALL THAT GUY KEPT SAYING WAS HOW HE DIDN'T HAVE TIME TO HELP US!
THE VANDALS ARE SCATTERING FEARS AROUND, RIGHT?
SO LET'S GO CHASE DOWN SOME FEARS– THEY CAN'T BE TOO FAR AWAY!
THAT MAKES SENSE... I'M WITH STELLA ON THIS ONE!
I HAVE A FEELING WE'LL BE FACING OUR OWN FEARS ON THE WAY...
LIKE FROM THOSE NIGHTMARES WE HAD? YEESH...
STILL, WE'VE GOT TO DO THIS. LET'S GO, WINX CLUB!
YOU SAID IT, BLOOM!

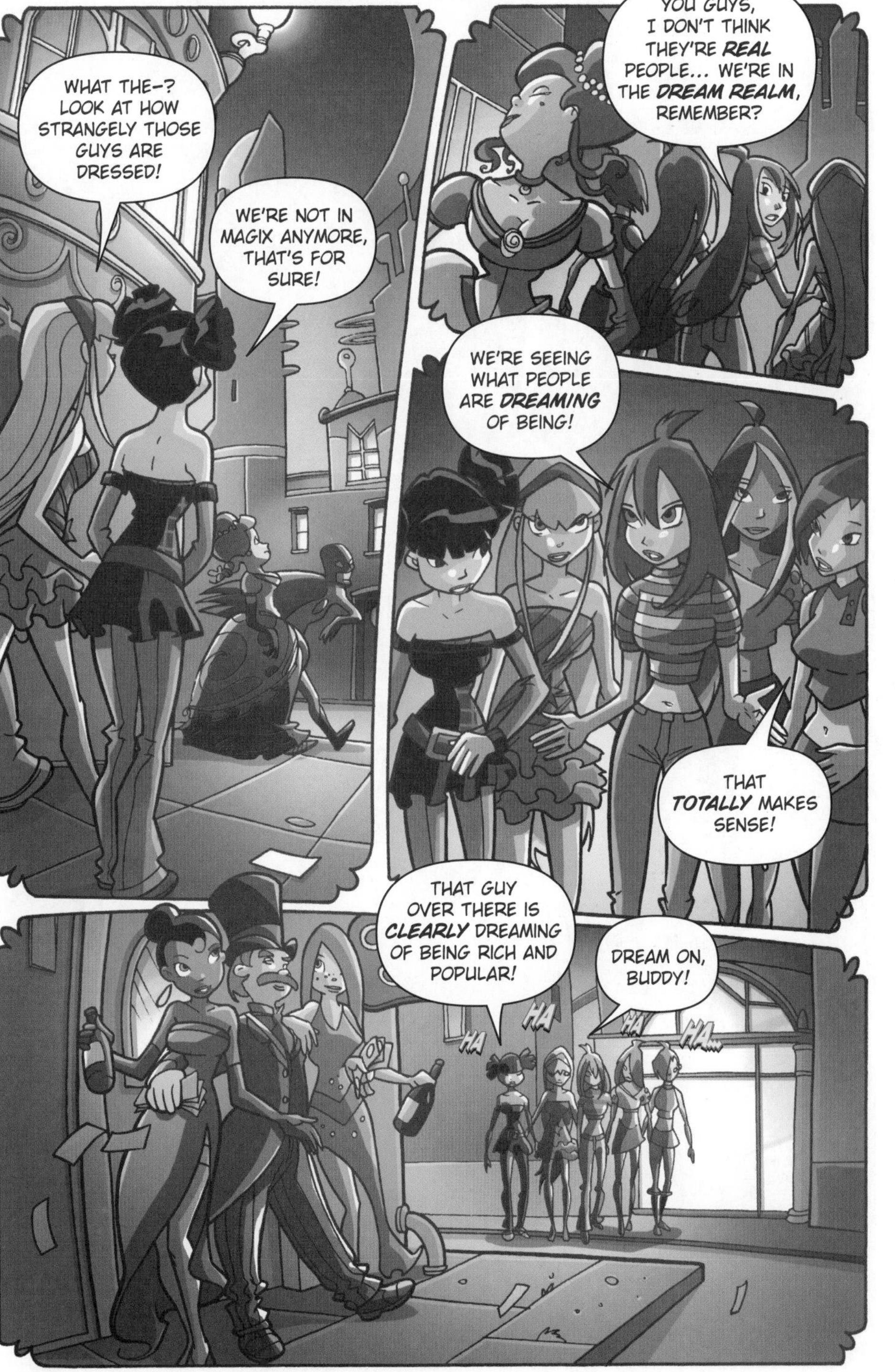
WHAT THE-? LOOK AT HOW STRANGELY THOSE GUYS ARE DRESSED!
WE'RE NOT IN MAGIX ANYMORE, THAT'S FOR SURE!
YOU GUYS, I DON'T THINK THEY'RE REAL PEOPLE... WE'RE IN THE DREAM REALM, REMEMBER?
WE'RE SEEING WHAT PEOPLE ARE DREAMING OF BEING!
THAT TOTALLY MAKES SENSE!
THAT GUY OVER THERE IS CLEARLY DREAMING OF BEING RICH AND POPULAR!
DREAM ON, BUDDY!
HA
HA
HA
HA...

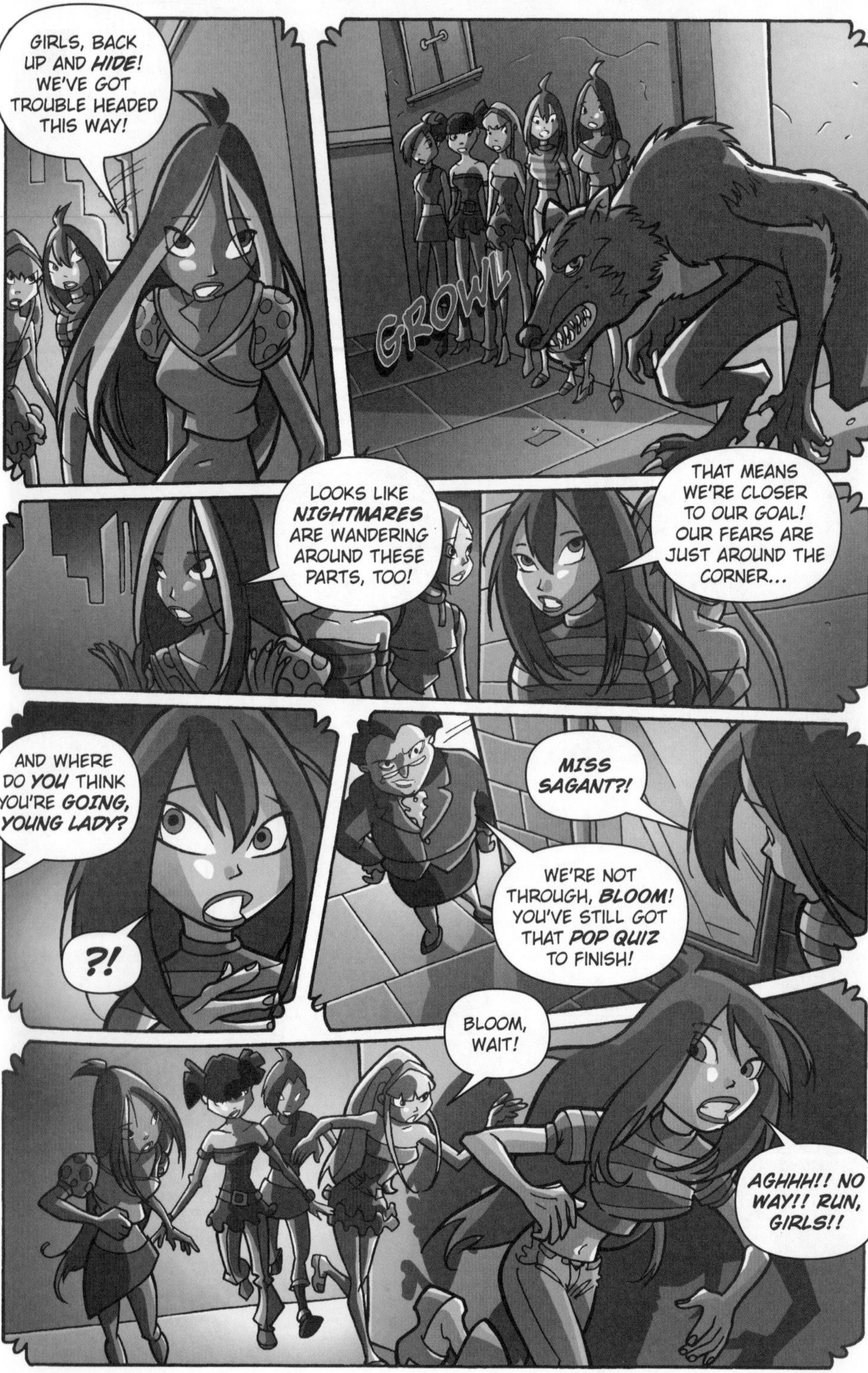
GIRLS, BACK UP AND HIDE! WE'VE GOT TROUBLE HEADED THIS WAY!
GROWL
LOOKS LIKE NIGHTMARES ARE WANDERING AROUND THESE PARTS, TOO!
THAT MEANS WE'RE CLOSER TO OUR GOAL! OUR FEARS ARE JUST AROUND THE CORNER...
AND WHERE DO YOU THINK YOU'RE GOING, YOUNG LADY?
?!
MISS SAGANT?!
WE'RE NOT THROUGH, BLOOM! YOU'VE STILL GOT THAT POP QUIZ TO FINISH!
BLOOM, WAIT!
AGHHH!! NO WAY!! RUN, GIRLS!!

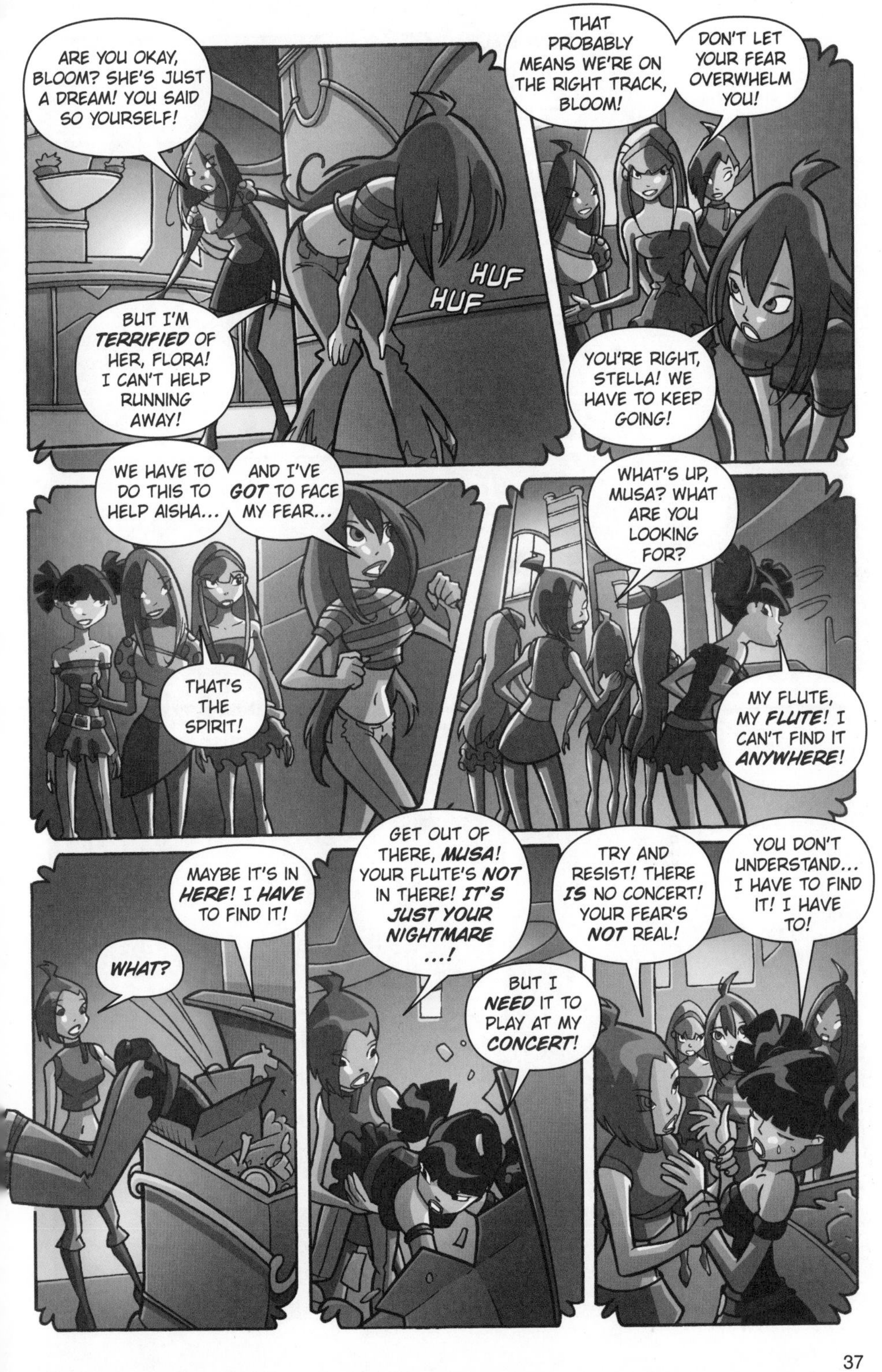
ARE YOU OKAY, BLOOM? SHE'S JUST A DREAM! YOU SAID SO YOURSELF!
BUT I'M ***TERRIFIED*** OF HER, FLORA! I CAN'T HELP RUNNING AWAY!
HUF
HUF
THAT PROBABLY MEANS WE'RE ON THE RIGHT TRACK, BLOOM!
DON'T LET YOUR FEAR OVERWHELM YOU!
YOU'RE RIGHT, STELLA! WE HAVE TO KEEP GOING!
WE HAVE TO DO THIS TO HELP AISHA...
AND I'VE ***GOT*** TO FACE MY FEAR...
THAT'S THE SPIRIT!
WHAT'S UP, MUSA? WHAT ARE YOU LOOKING FOR?
MY FLUTE, MY ***FLUTE***! I CAN'T FIND IT ***ANYWHERE***!
MAYBE IT'S IN ***HERE***! I ***HAVE*** TO FIND IT!
WHAT?
GET OUT OF THERE, ***MUSA***! YOUR FLUTE'S ***NOT*** IN THERE! ***IT'S JUST YOUR NIGHTMARE...!***
BUT I ***NEED*** IT TO PLAY AT MY ***CONCERT***!
TRY AND RESIST! THERE ***IS*** NO CONCERT! YOUR FEAR'S ***NOT*** REAL!
YOU DON'T UNDERSTAND... I HAVE TO FIND IT! I HAVE TO!

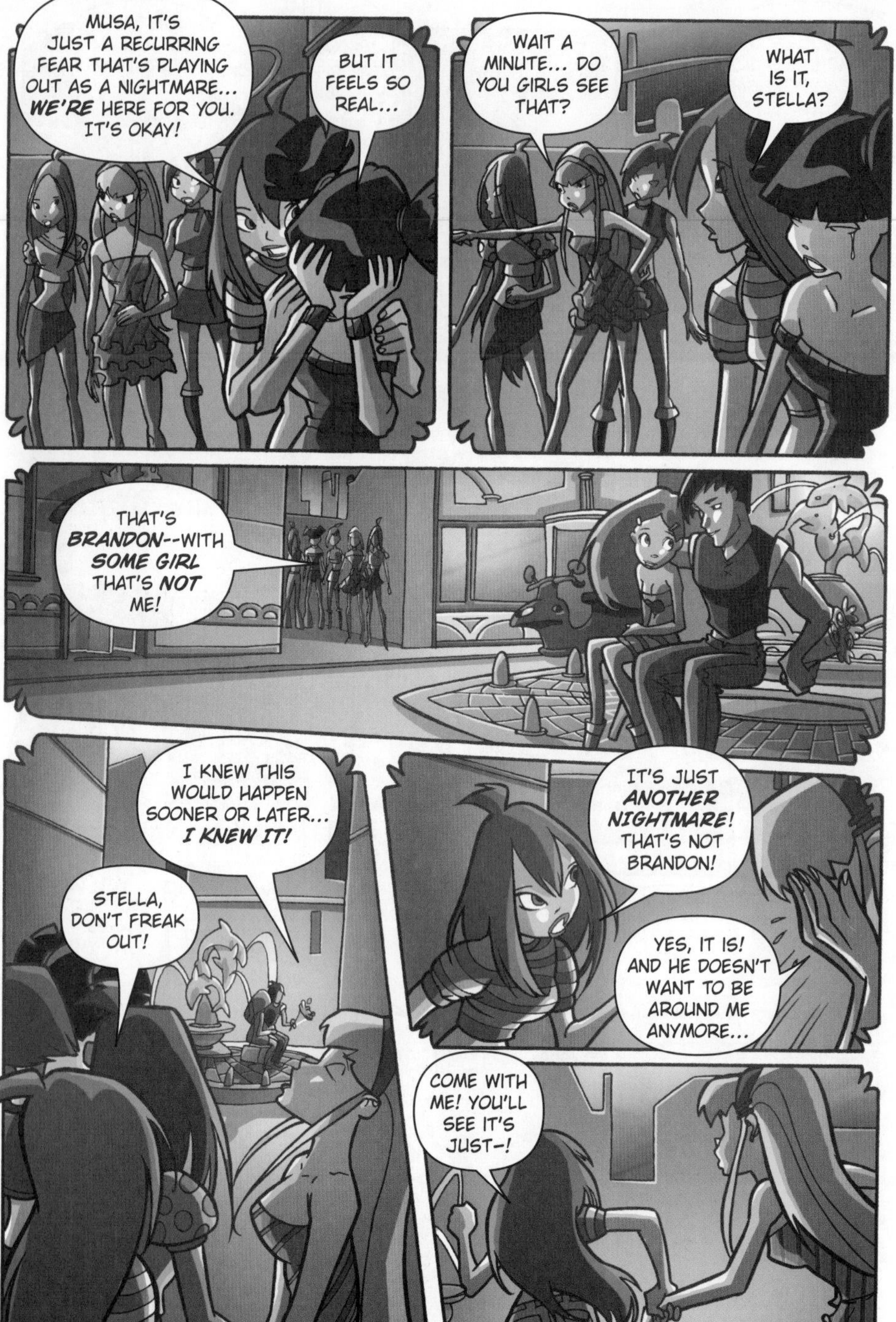
MUSA, IT'S JUST A RECURRING FEAR THAT'S PLAYING OUT AS A NIGHTMARE... WE'RE HERE FOR YOU. IT'S OKAY!
BUT IT FEELS SO REAL...
WAIT A MINUTE... DO YOU GIRLS SEE THAT?
WHAT IS IT, STELLA?
THAT'S BRANDON--WITH SOME GIRL THAT'S NOT ME!
I KNEW THIS WOULD HAPPEN SOONER OR LATER... I KNEW IT!
STELLA, DON'T FREAK OUT!
IT'S JUST ANOTHER NIGHTMARE! THAT'S NOT BRANDON!
YES, IT IS! AND HE DOESN'T WANT TO BE AROUND ME ANYMORE...
COME WITH ME! YOU'LL SEE IT'S JUST-!

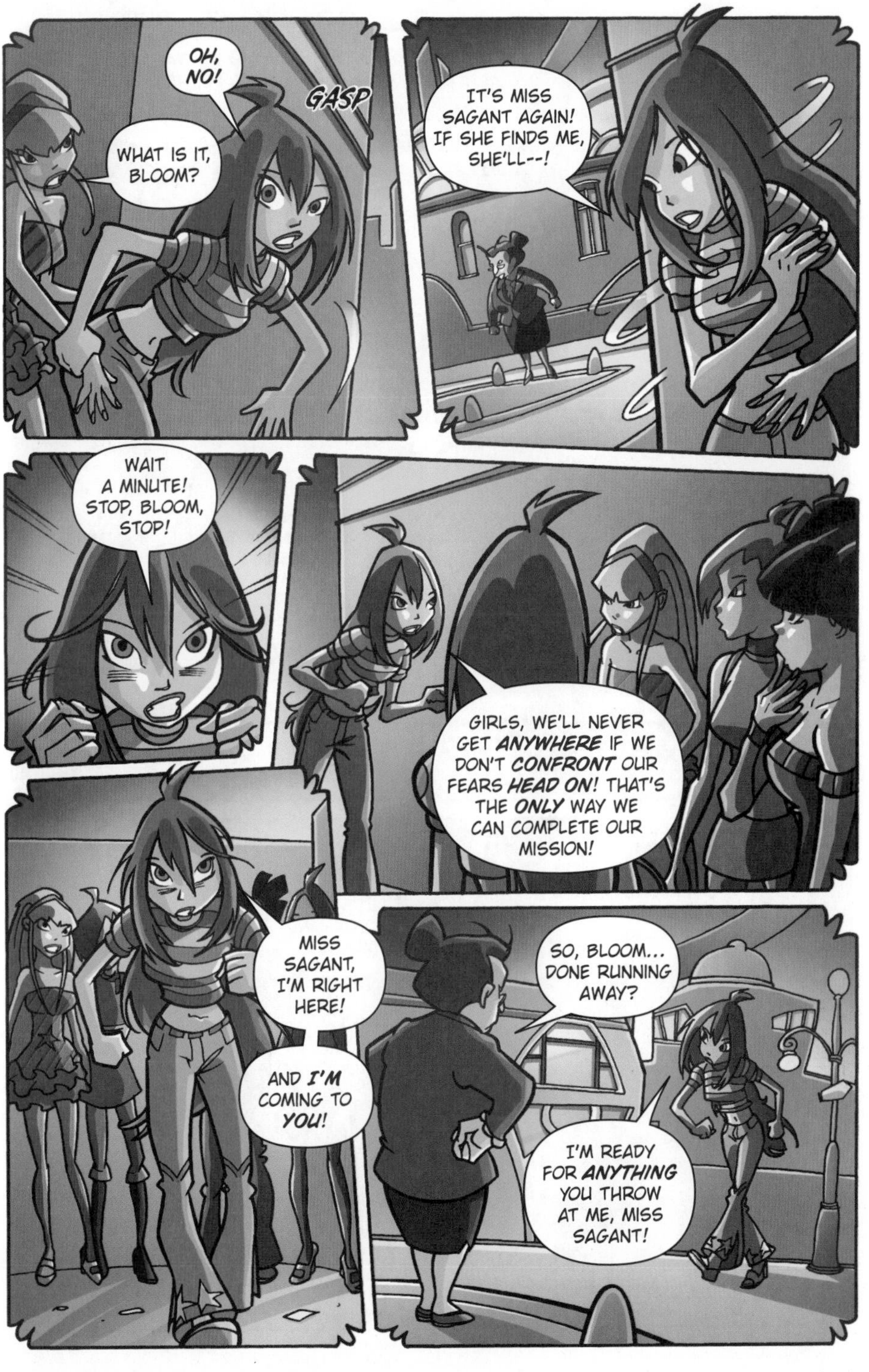
OH, NO!
WHAT IS IT, BLOOM?
GASP
IT'S MISS SAGANT AGAIN! IF SHE FINDS ME, SHE'LL--!
WAIT A MINUTE! STOP, BLOOM, STOP!
GIRLS, WE'LL NEVER GET ANYWHERE IF WE DON'T CONFRONT OUR FEARS HEAD ON! THAT'S THE ONLY WAY WE CAN COMPLETE OUR MISSION!
MISS SAGANT, I'M RIGHT HERE!
AND I'M COMING TO YOU!
SO, BLOOM... DONE RUNNING AWAY?
I'M READY FOR ANYTHING YOU THROW AT ME, MISS SAGANT!

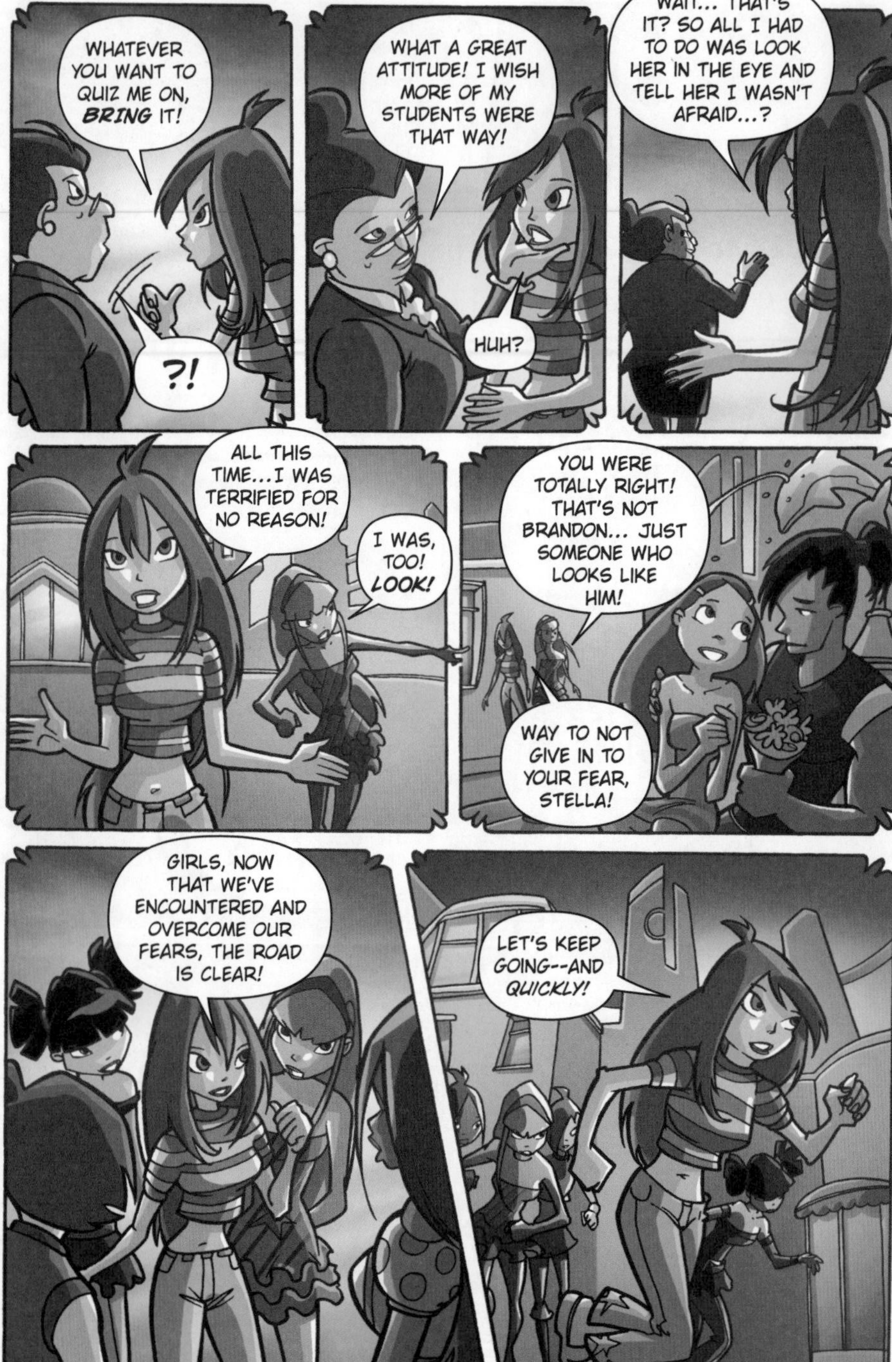
WHATEVER YOU WANT TO QUIZ ME ON, *BRING* IT!
?!
WHAT A GREAT ATTITUDE! I WISH MORE OF MY STUDENTS WERE THAT WAY!
HUH?
WAIT... THAT'S IT? SO ALL I HAD TO DO WAS LOOK HER IN THE EYE AND TELL HER I WASN'T AFRAID...?
ALL THIS TIME...I WAS TERRIFIED FOR NO REASON!
I WAS, TOO! *LOOK!*
YOU WERE TOTALLY RIGHT! THAT'S NOT BRANDON... JUST SOMEONE WHO LOOKS LIKE HIM!
WAY TO NOT GIVE IN TO YOUR FEAR, STELLA!
GIRLS, NOW THAT WE'VE ENCOUNTERED AND OVERCOME OUR FEARS, THE ROAD IS CLEAR!
LET'S KEEP GOING--AND *QUICKLY!*

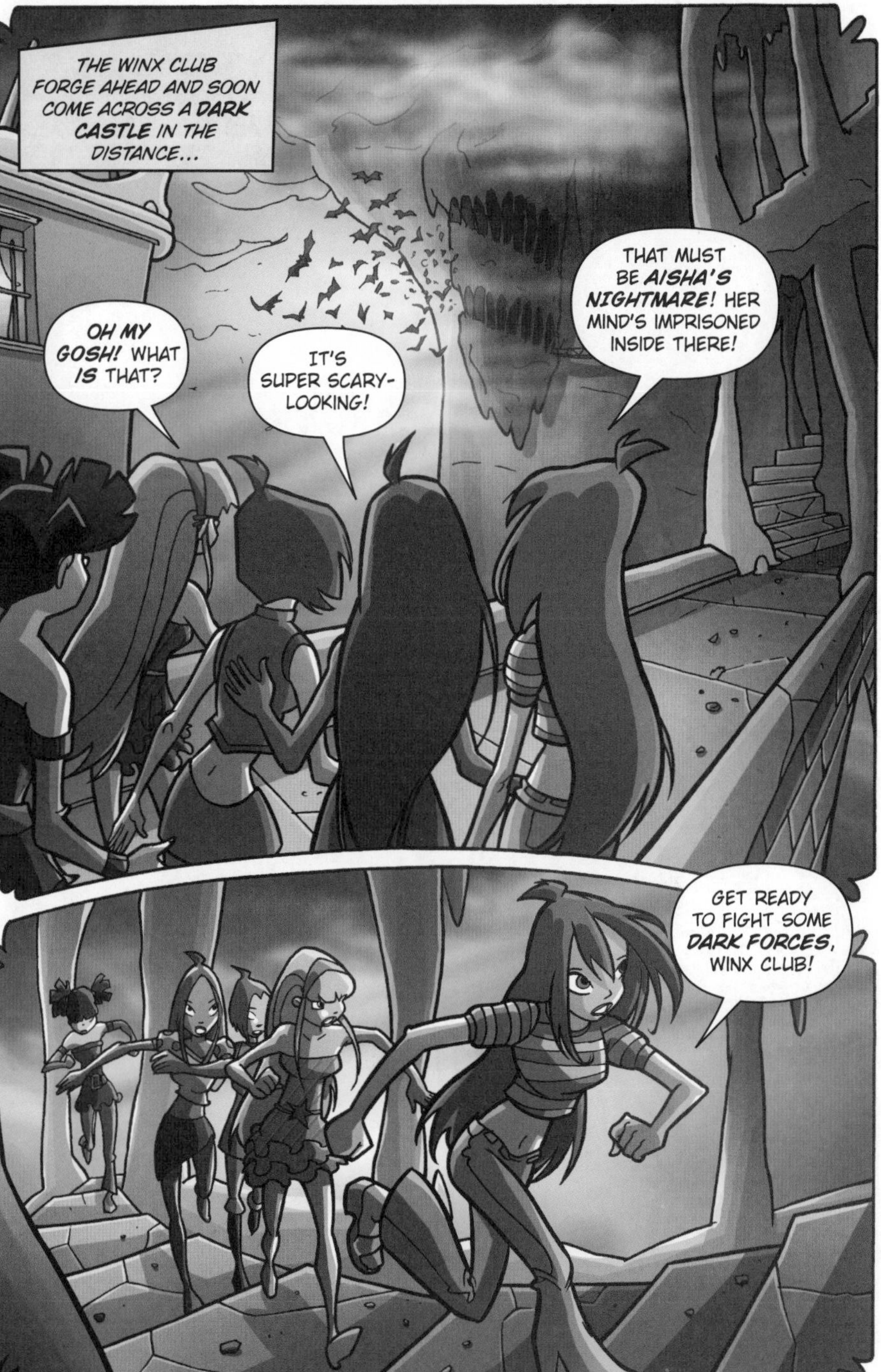
THE WINX CLUB FORGE AHEAD AND SOON COME ACROSS A DARK CASTLE IN THE DISTANCE...
OH MY GOSH! WHAT IS THAT?
IT'S SUPER SCARY-LOOKING!
THAT MUST BE AISHA'S NIGHTMARE! HER MIND'S IMPRISONED INSIDE THERE!
GET READY TO FIGHT SOME DARK FORCES, WINX CLUB!

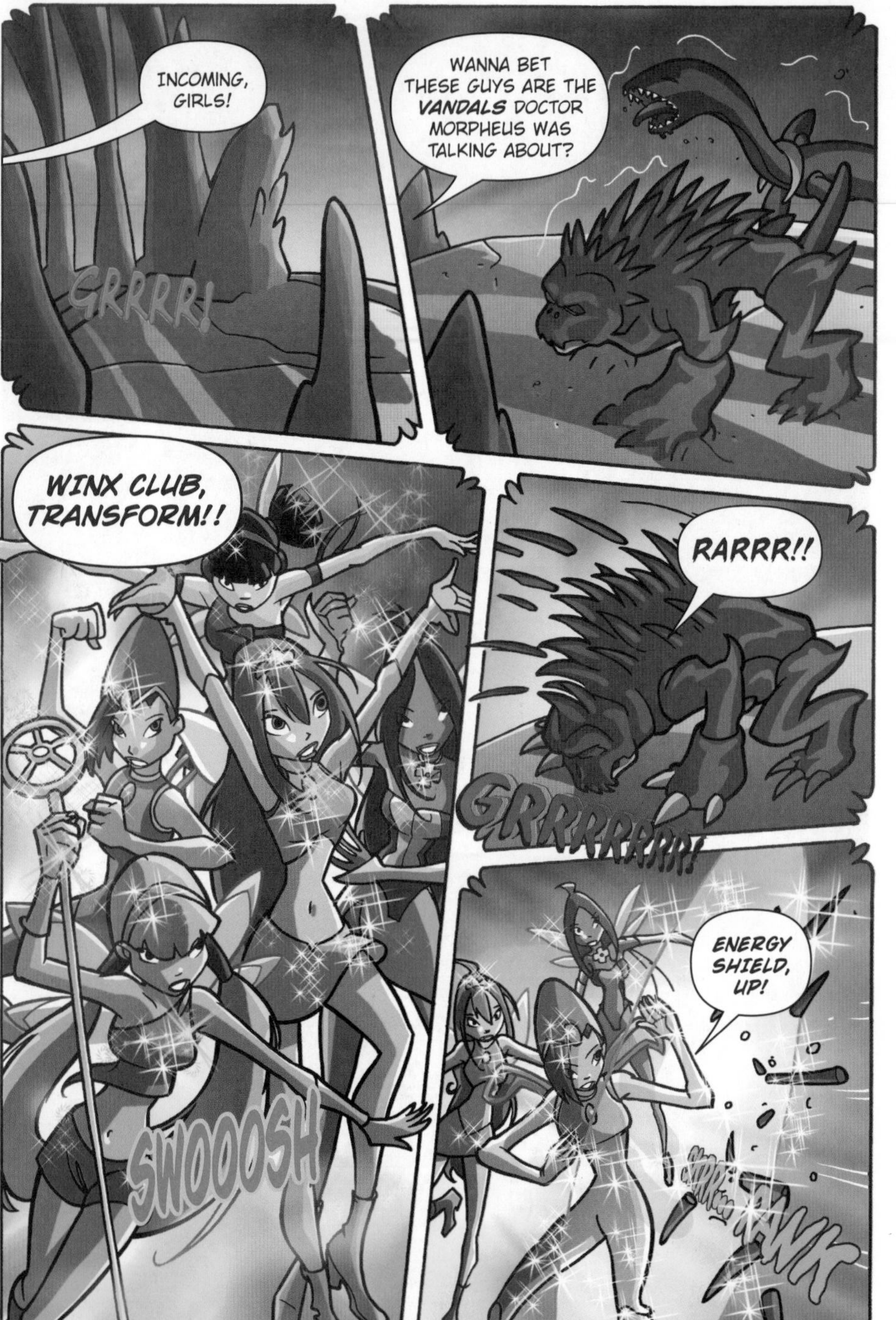
INCOMING, GIRLS!
GRRRR!
WANNA BET THESE GUYS ARE THE **VANDALS** DOCTOR MORPHEUS WAS TALKING ABOUT?
WINX CLUB, TRANSFORM!!
SWOOSH
RARRR!!
GRRRRRRRR!
ENERGY SHIELD, UP!

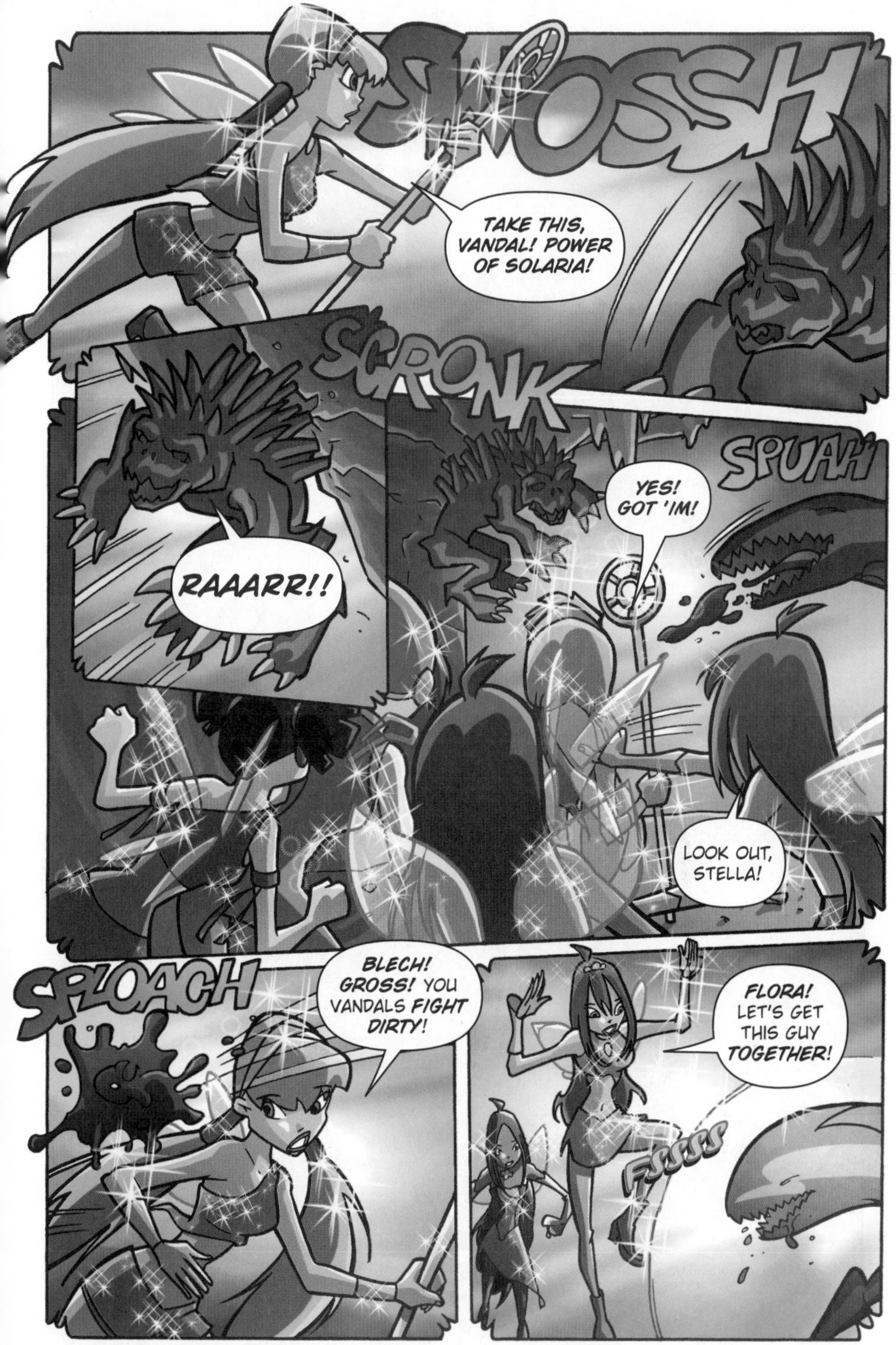
SPWOSSH
TAKE THIS, VANDAL! POWER OF SOLARIA!
SCRONK
RAAARR!!
YES! GOT 'IM!
SPUAH
LOOK OUT, STELLA!
SPLOACH
BLECH! GROSS! YOU VANDALS FIGHT DIRTY!
FLORA! LET'S GET THIS GUY TOGETHER!
FSSSSS

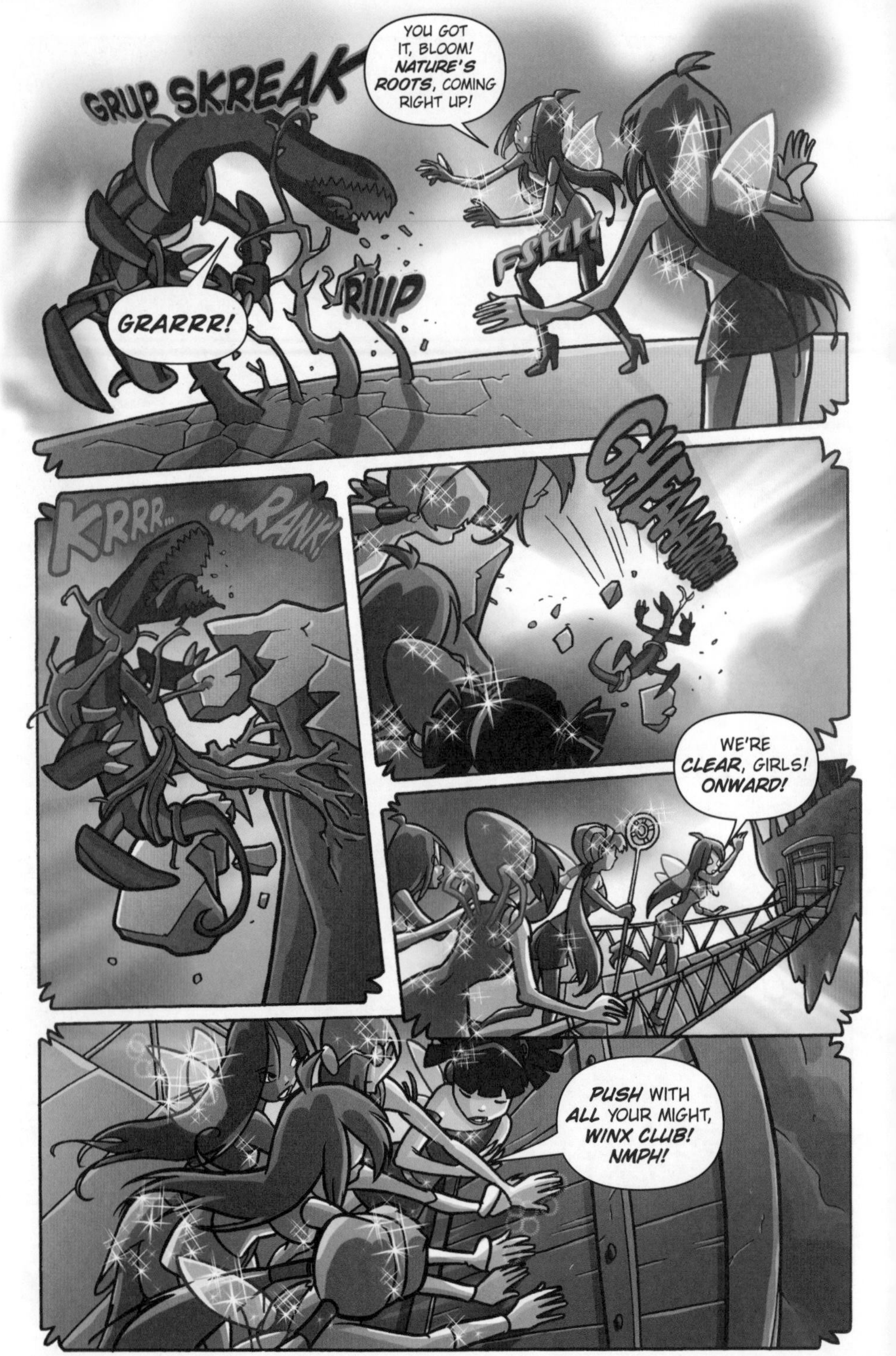
GRUP SKREAK
YOU GOT IT, BLOOM! NATURE'S ROOTS, COMING RIGHT UP!
FSHH
GRARRR!
RIIIP
KRRR... ...RANK!
GHEAAAAAAA
WE'RE CLEAR, GIRLS! ONWARD!
PUSH WITH ALL YOUR MIGHT, WINX CLUB! NMPH!

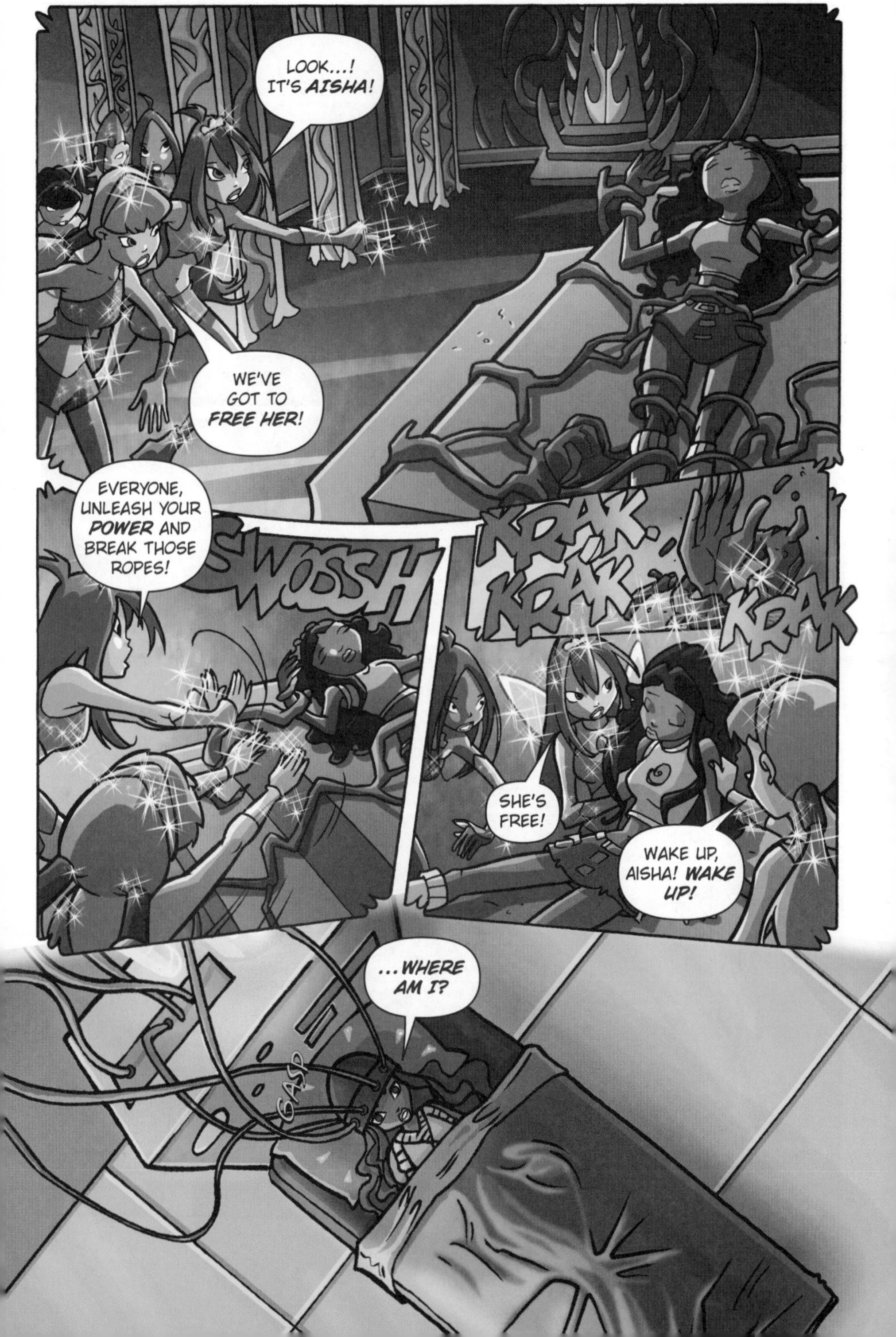
LOOK...! IT'S AISHA!
WE'VE GOT TO FREE HER!
EVERYONE, UNLEASH YOUR POWER AND BREAK THOSE ROPES!
SWOSSH
KRAK KRAK KRAK
SHE'S FREE!
WAKE UP, AISHA! WAKE UP!
...WHERE AM I?
GASP

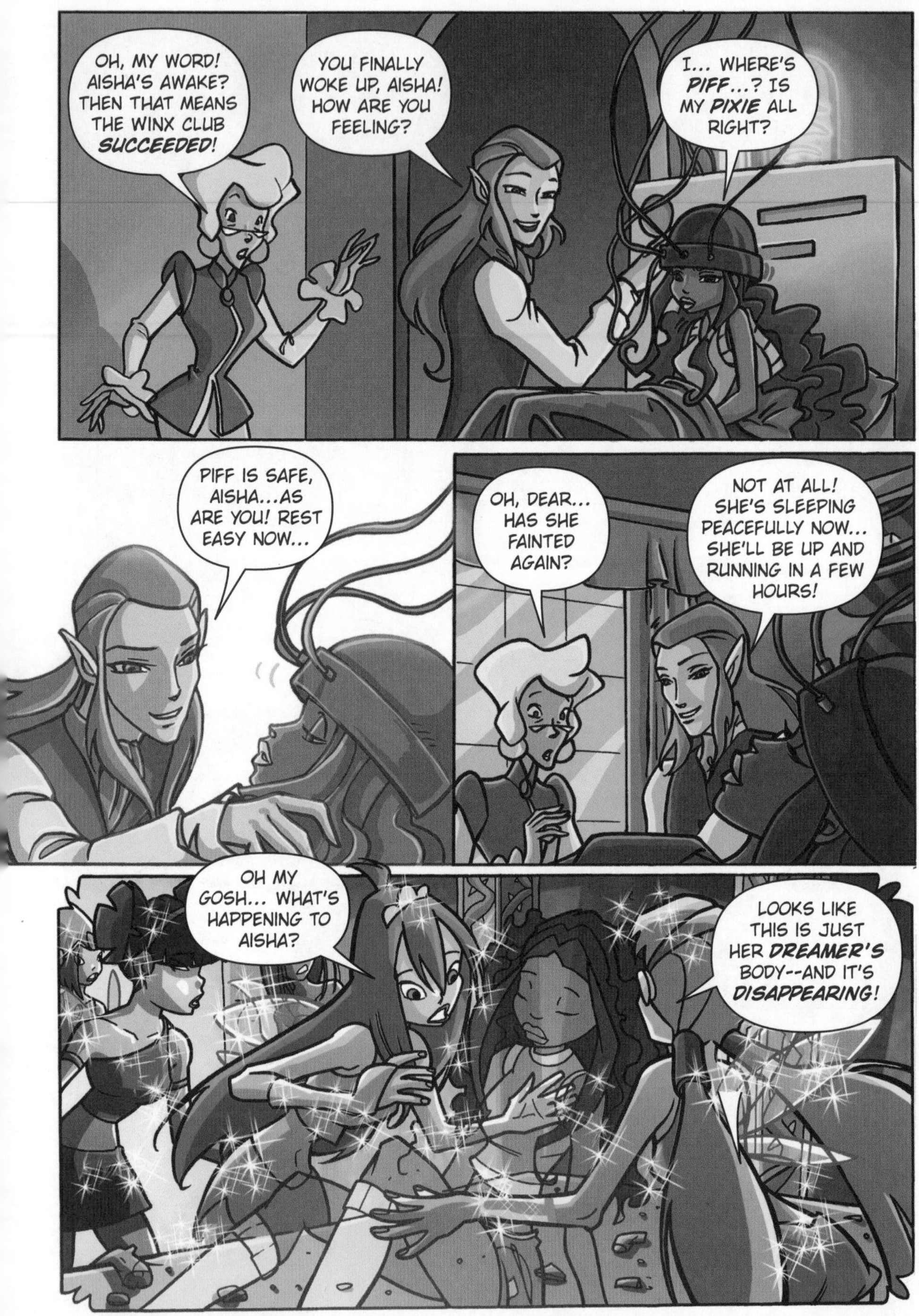
OH, MY WORD! AISHA'S AWAKE? THEN THAT MEANS THE WINX CLUB **SUCCEEDED**!
YOU FINALLY WOKE UP, AISHA! HOW ARE YOU FEELING?
I... WHERE'S **PIFF**...? IS MY **PIXIE** ALL RIGHT?
PIFF IS SAFE, AISHA...AS ARE YOU! REST EASY NOW...
OH, DEAR... HAS SHE FAINTED AGAIN?
NOT AT ALL! SHE'S SLEEPING PEACEFULLY NOW... SHE'LL BE UP AND RUNNING IN A FEW HOURS!
OH MY GOSH... WHAT'S HAPPENING TO AISHA?
LOOKS LIKE THIS IS JUST HER **DREAMER'S** BODY--AND IT'S **DISAPPEARING**!

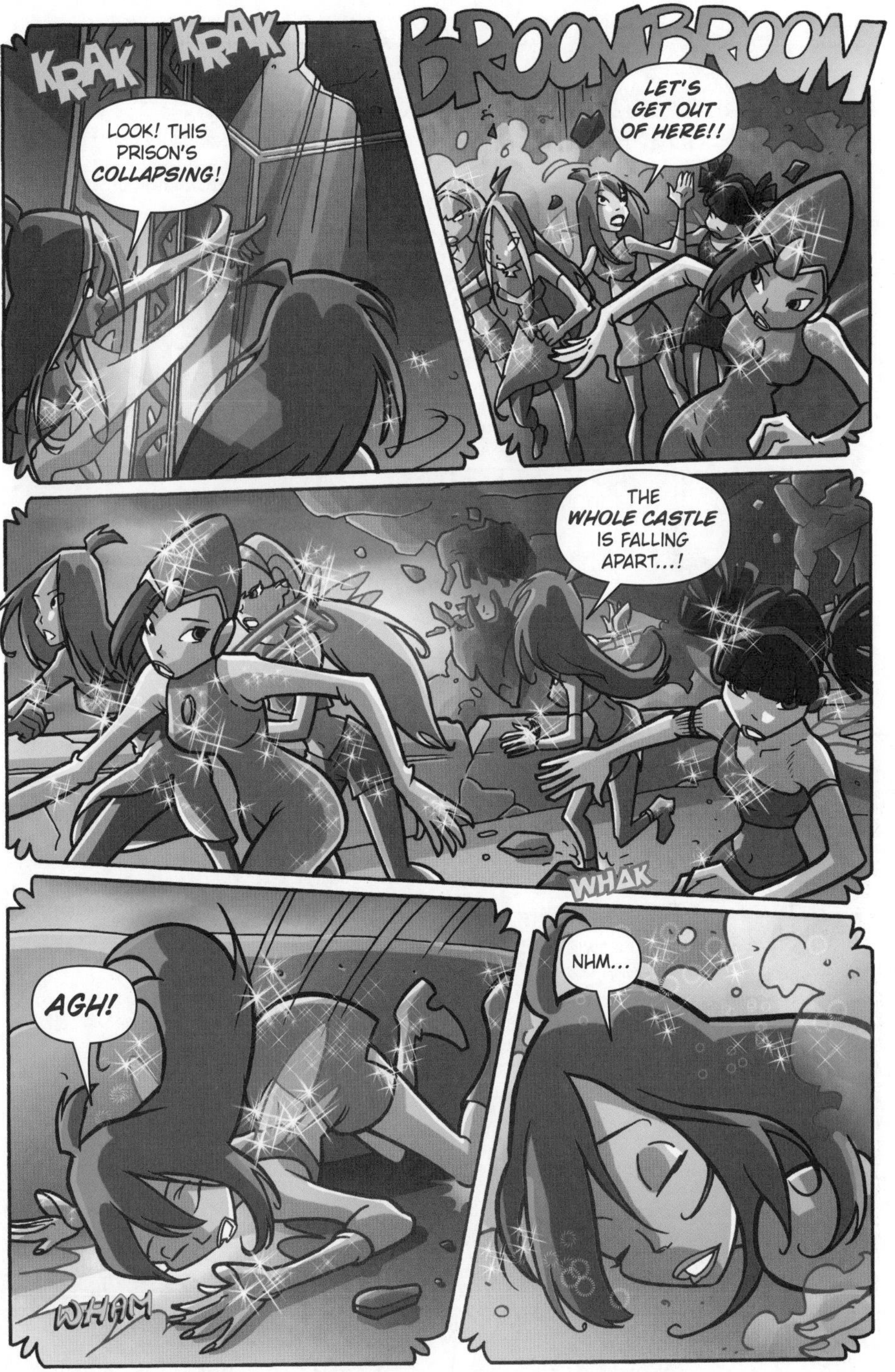
KRAK KRAK
LOOK! THIS PRISON'S COLLAPSING!
BROOM BROOM
LET'S GET OUT OF HERE!!
THE WHOLE CASTLE IS FALLING APART...!
WHAK
AGH!
WHAM
NHM...

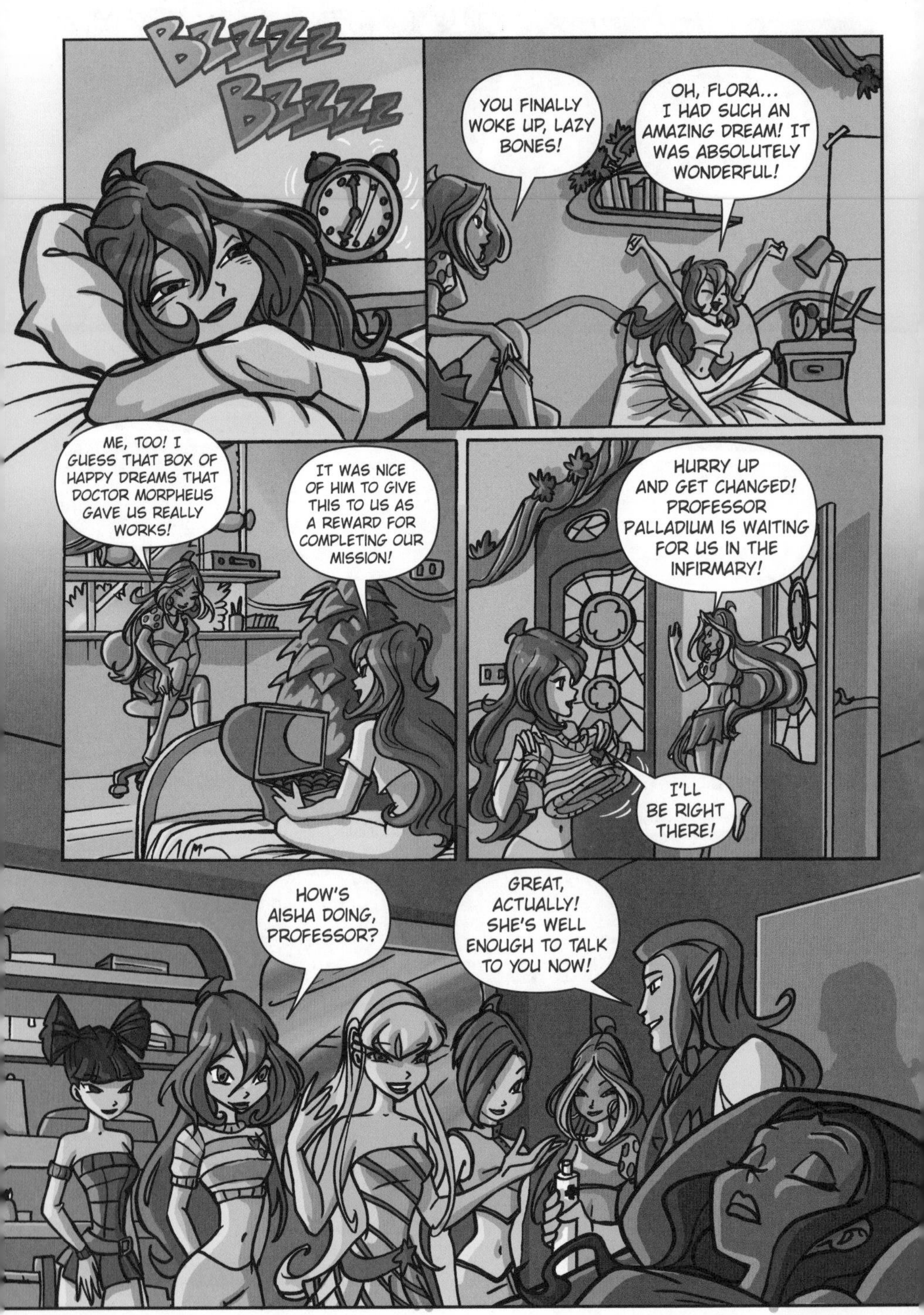
BZZZZ BZZZZ
YOU FINALLY WOKE UP, LAZY BONES!
OH, FLORA... I HAD SUCH AN AMAZING DREAM! IT WAS ABSOLUTELY WONDERFUL!
ME, TOO! I GUESS THAT BOX OF HAPPY DREAMS THAT DOCTOR MORPHEUS GAVE US REALLY WORKS!
IT WAS NICE OF HIM TO GIVE THIS TO US AS A REWARD FOR COMPLETING OUR MISSION!
HURRY UP AND GET CHANGED! PROFESSOR PALLADIUM IS WAITING FOR US IN THE INFIRMARY!
I'LL BE RIGHT THERE!
HOW'S AISHA DOING, PROFESSOR?
GREAT, ACTUALLY! SHE'S WELL ENOUGH TO TALK TO YOU NOW!

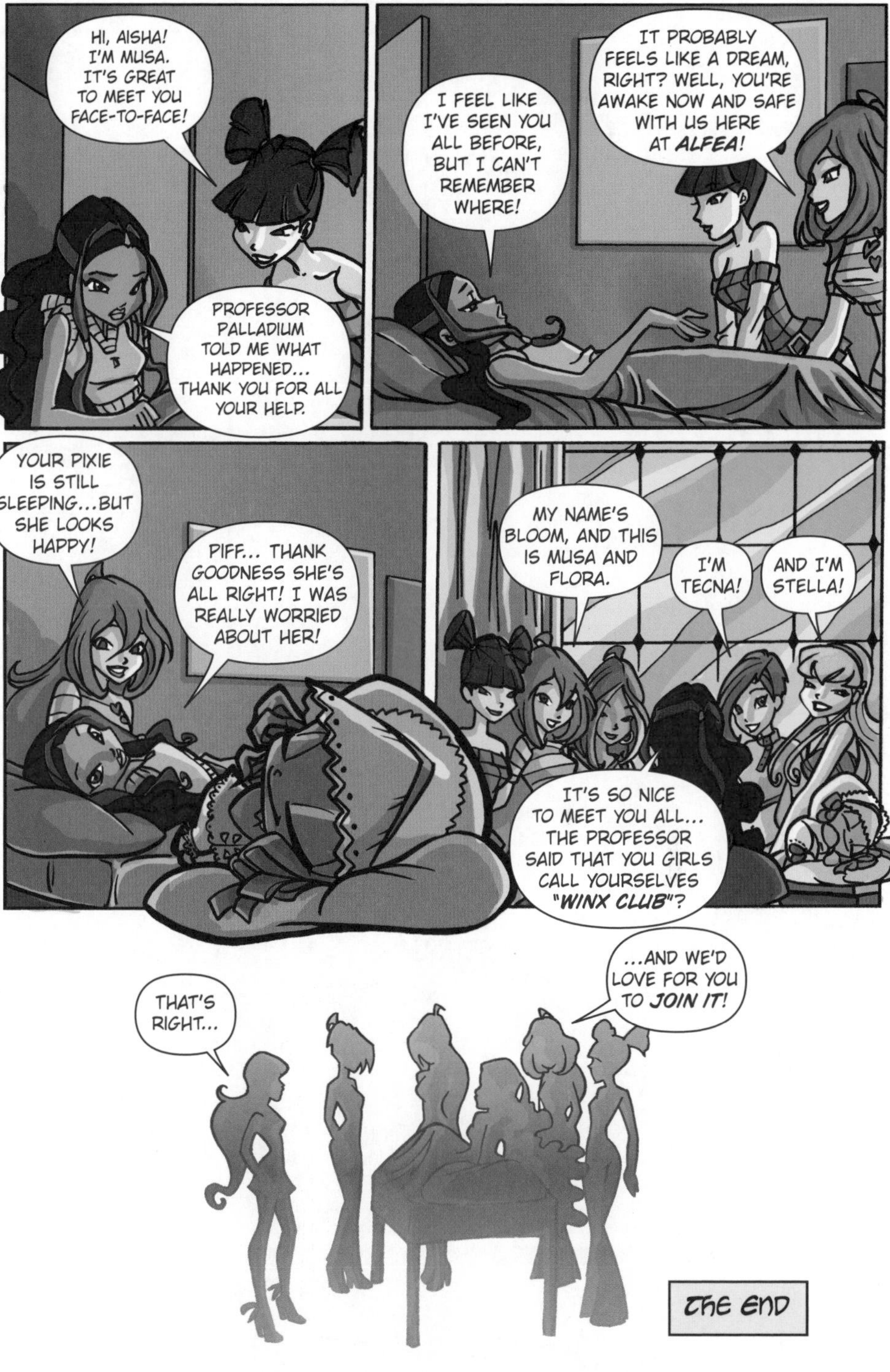
HI, AISHA! I'M MUSA. IT'S GREAT TO MEET YOU FACE-TO-FACE!
PROFESSOR PALLADIUM TOLD ME WHAT HAPPENED... THANK YOU FOR ALL YOUR HELP.
I FEEL LIKE I'VE SEEN YOU ALL BEFORE, BUT I CAN'T REMEMBER WHERE!
IT PROBABLY FEELS LIKE A DREAM, RIGHT? WELL, YOU'RE AWAKE NOW AND SAFE WITH US HERE AT ALFEA!
YOUR PIXIE IS STILL SLEEPING...BUT SHE LOOKS HAPPY!
PIFF... THANK GOODNESS SHE'S ALL RIGHT! I WAS REALLY WORRIED ABOUT HER!
MY NAME'S BLOOM, AND THIS IS MUSA AND FLORA.
I'M TECNA!
AND I'M STELLA!
IT'S SO NICE TO MEET YOU ALL... THE PROFESSOR SAID THAT YOU GIRLS CALL YOURSELVES "WINX CLUB"?
THAT'S RIGHT...
...AND WE'D LOVE FOR YOU TO JOIN IT!
THE END

An Evil
Wind

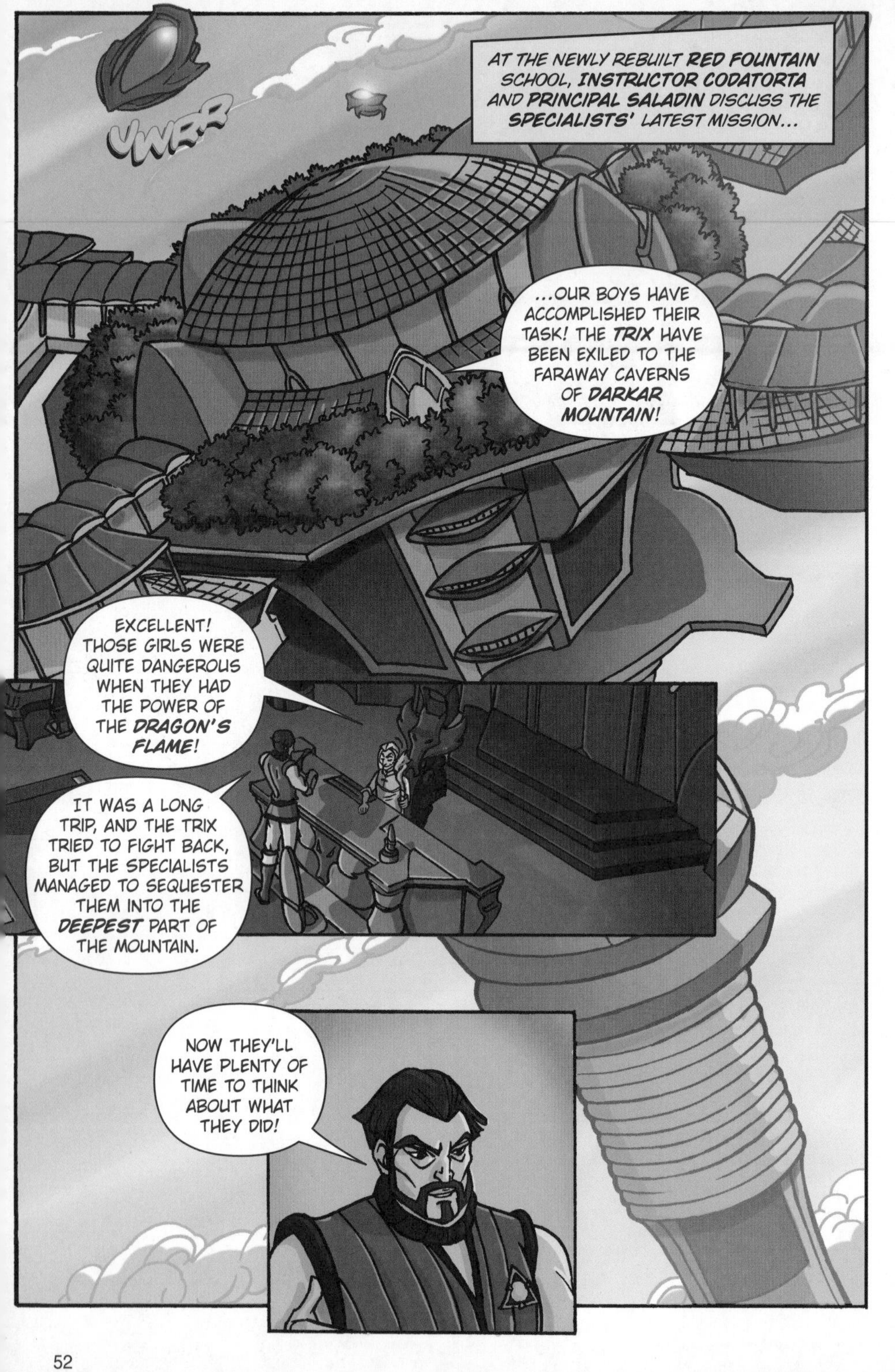
UWRR
AT THE NEWLY REBUILT RED FOUNTAIN SCHOOL, INSTRUCTOR CODATORTA AND PRINCIPAL SALADIN DISCUSS THE SPECIALISTS' LATEST MISSION...
...OUR BOYS HAVE ACCOMPLISHED THEIR TASK! THE TRIX HAVE BEEN EXILED TO THE FARAWAY CAVERNS OF DARKAR MOUNTAIN!
EXCELLENT! THOSE GIRLS WERE QUITE DANGEROUS WHEN THEY HAD THE POWER OF THE DRAGON'S FLAME!
IT WAS A LONG TRIP, AND THE TRIX TRIED TO FIGHT BACK, BUT THE SPECIALISTS MANAGED TO SEQUESTER THEM INTO THE DEEPEST PART OF THE MOUNTAIN.
NOW THEY'LL HAVE PLENTY OF TIME TO THINK ABOUT WHAT THEY DID!

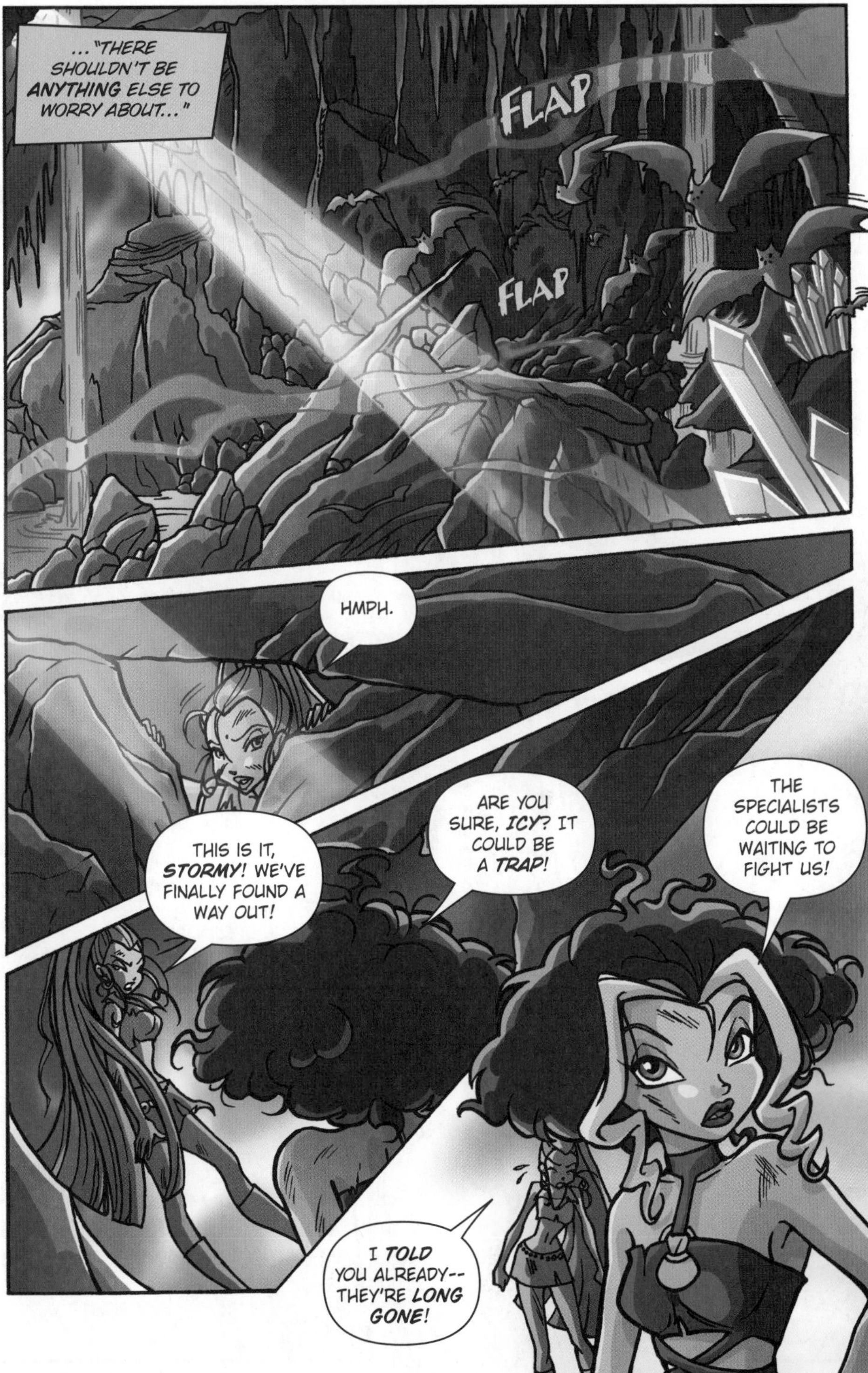
..."THERE SHOULDN'T BE ANYTHING ELSE TO WORRY ABOUT..."
FLAP
FLAP
HMPH.
THIS IS IT, STORMY! WE'VE FINALLY FOUND A WAY OUT!
ARE YOU SURE, ICY? IT COULD BE A TRAP!
THE SPECIALISTS COULD BE WAITING TO FIGHT US!
I TOLD YOU ALREADY-- THEY'RE LONG GONE!

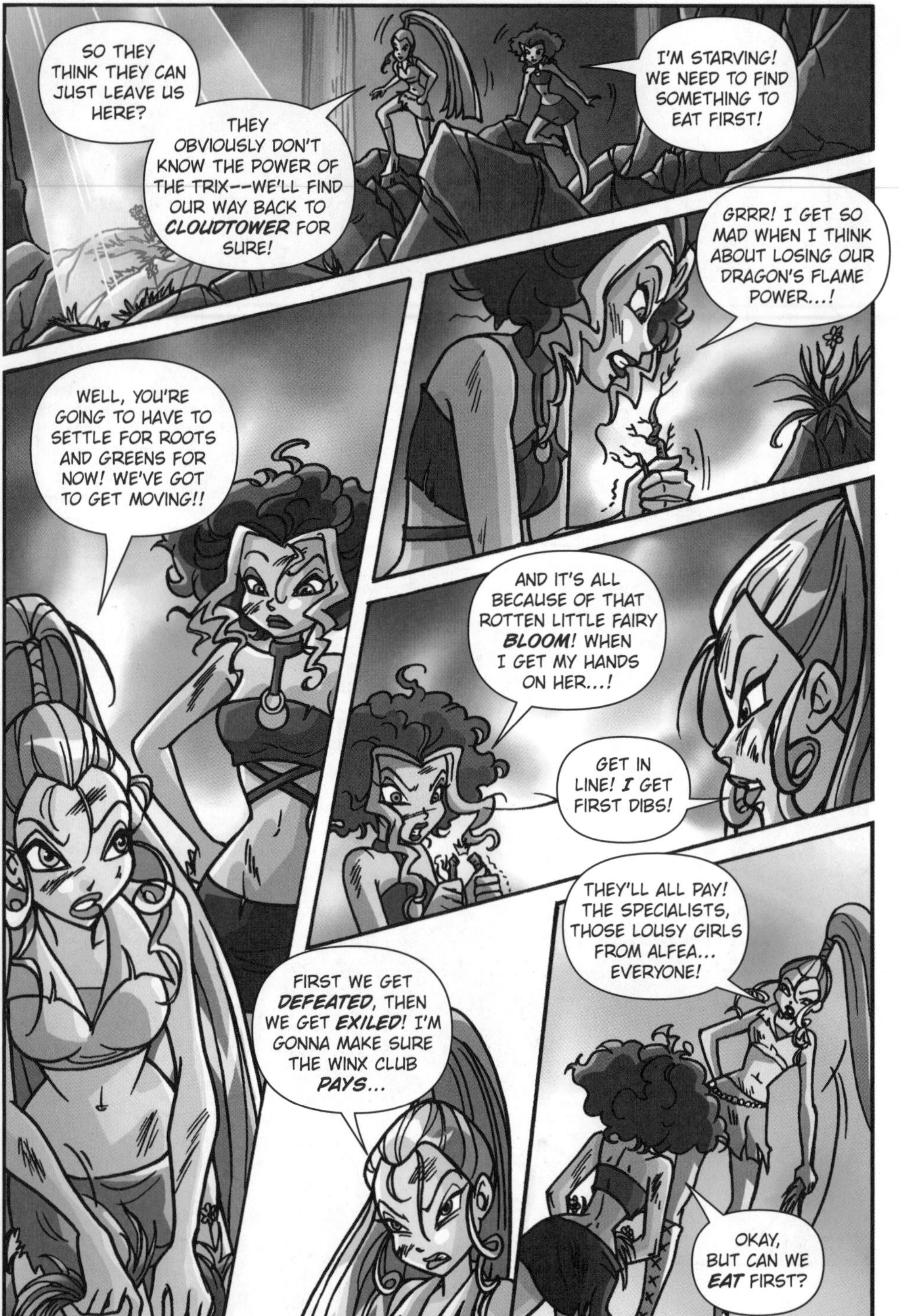
SO THEY THINK THEY CAN JUST LEAVE US HERE?
THEY OBVIOUSLY DON'T KNOW THE POWER OF THE TRIX--WE'LL FIND OUR WAY BACK TO CLOUDTOWER FOR SURE!
I'M STARVING! WE NEED TO FIND SOMETHING TO EAT FIRST!
GRRR! I GET SO MAD WHEN I THINK ABOUT LOSING OUR DRAGON'S FLAME POWER...!
WELL, YOU'RE GOING TO HAVE TO SETTLE FOR ROOTS AND GREENS FOR NOW! WE'VE GOT TO GET MOVING!!
AND IT'S ALL BECAUSE OF THAT ROTTEN LITTLE FAIRY BLOOM! WHEN I GET MY HANDS ON HER...!
GET IN LINE! I GET FIRST DIBS!
THEY'LL ALL PAY! THE SPECIALISTS, THOSE LOUSY GIRLS FROM ALFEA... EVERYONE!
FIRST WE GET DEFEATED, THEN WE GET EXILED! I'M GONNA MAKE SURE THE WINX CLUB PAYS...
OKAY, BUT CAN WE EAT FIRST?

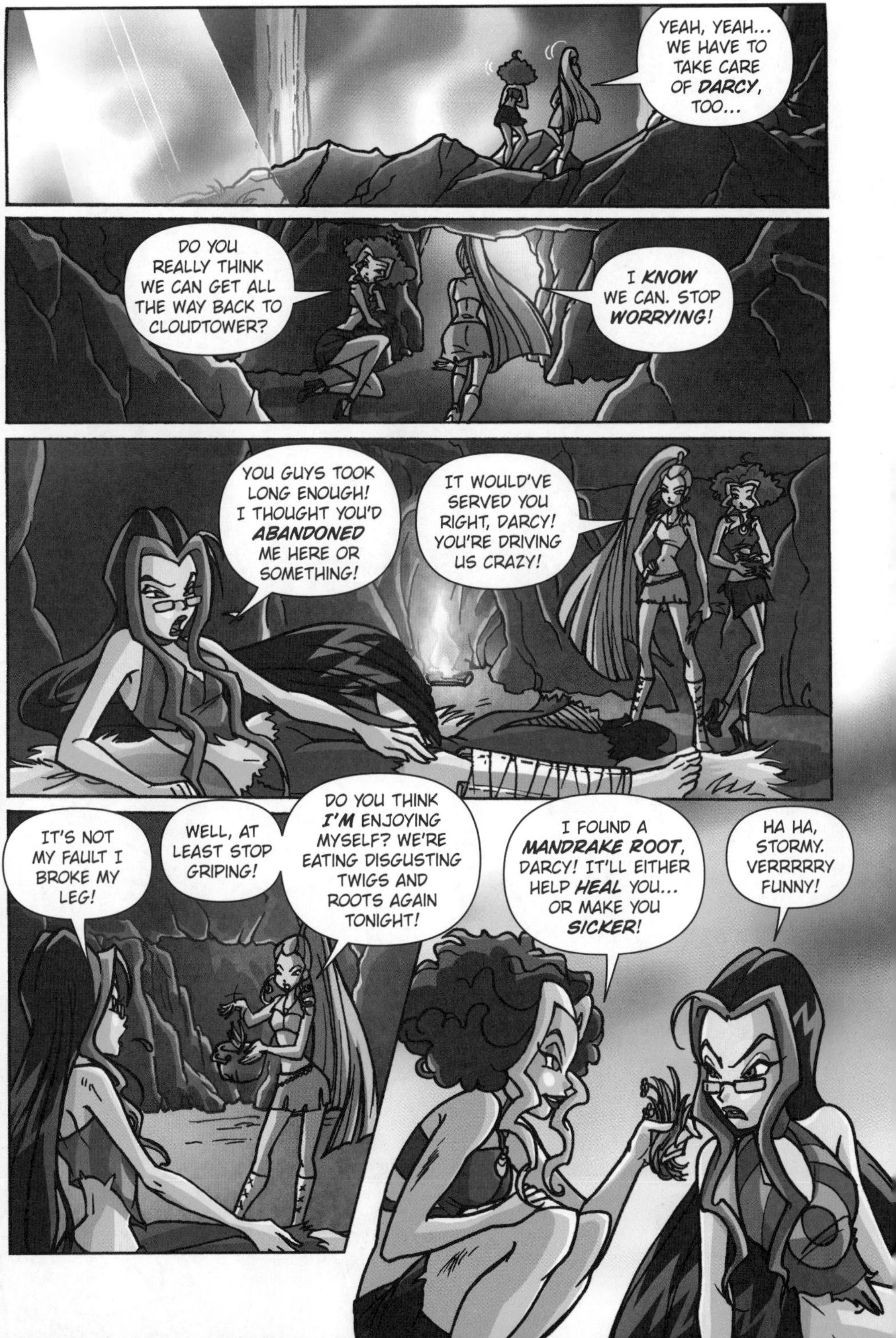
YEAH, YEAH... WE HAVE TO TAKE CARE OF **DARCY**, TOO...
DO YOU REALLY THINK WE CAN GET ALL THE WAY BACK TO CLOUDTOWER?
I **KNOW** WE CAN. STOP **WORRYING**!
YOU GUYS TOOK LONG ENOUGH! I THOUGHT YOU'D **ABANDONED** ME HERE OR SOMETHING!
IT WOULD'VE SERVED YOU RIGHT, DARCY! YOU'RE DRIVING US CRAZY!
IT'S NOT MY FAULT I BROKE MY LEG!
WELL, AT LEAST STOP GRIPING!
DO YOU THINK **I'M** ENJOYING MYSELF? WE'RE EATING DISGUSTING TWIGS AND ROOTS AGAIN TONIGHT!
I FOUND A **MANDRAKE ROOT**, DARCY! IT'LL EITHER HELP **HEAL** YOU... OR MAKE YOU **SICKER**!
HA HA, STORMY. VERRRRRY FUNNY!

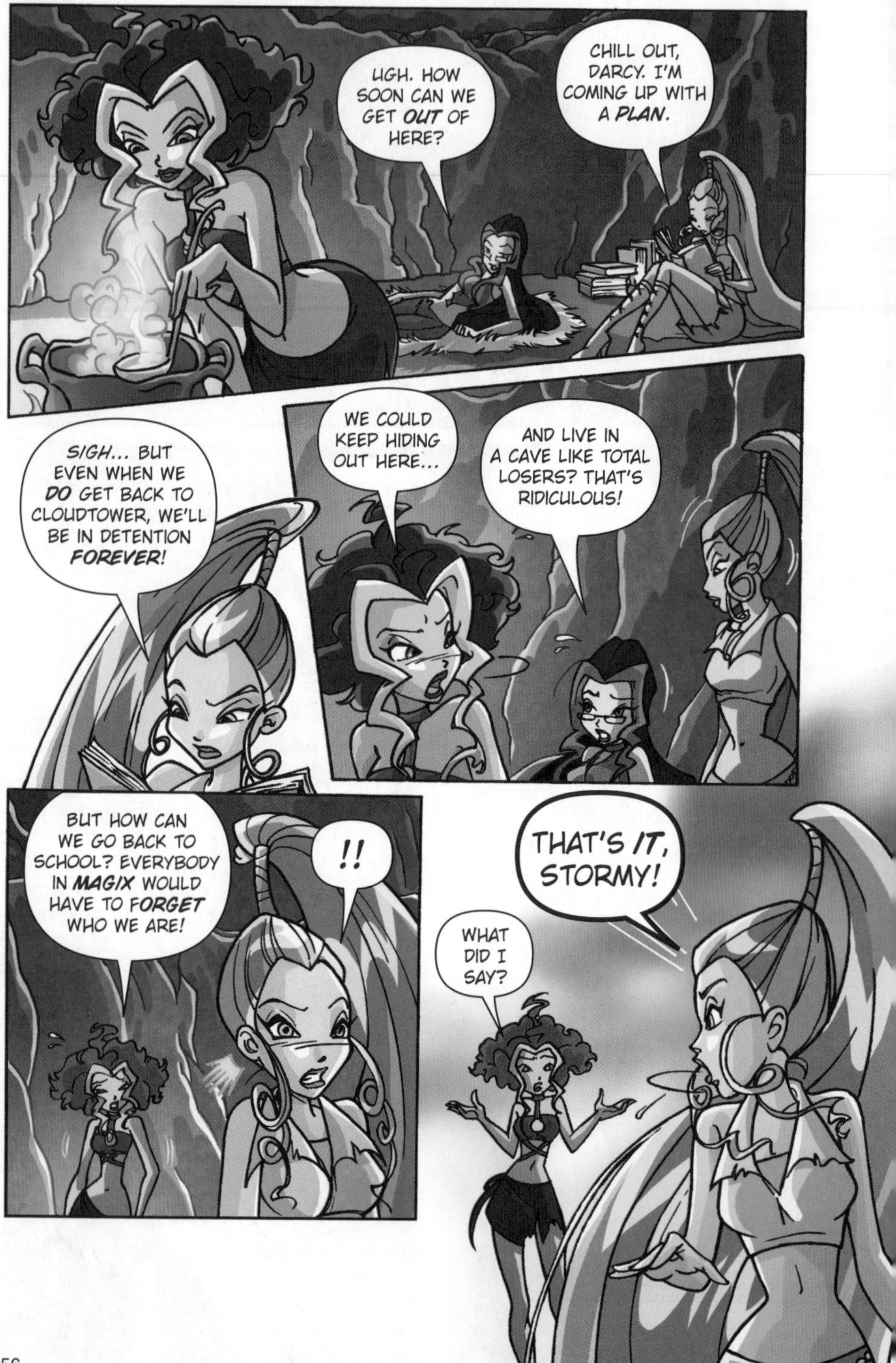
UGH. HOW SOON CAN WE GET OUT OF HERE?
CHILL OUT, DARCY. I'M COMING UP WITH A PLAN.
SIGH... BUT EVEN WHEN WE DO GET BACK TO CLOUDTOWER, WE'LL BE IN DETENTION FOREVER!
WE COULD KEEP HIDING OUT HERE...
AND LIVE IN A CAVE LIKE TOTAL LOSERS? THAT'S RIDICULOUS!
BUT HOW CAN WE GO BACK TO SCHOOL? EVERYBODY IN MAGIX WOULD HAVE TO FORGET WHO WE ARE!
!!
THAT'S IT, STORMY!
WHAT DID I SAY?

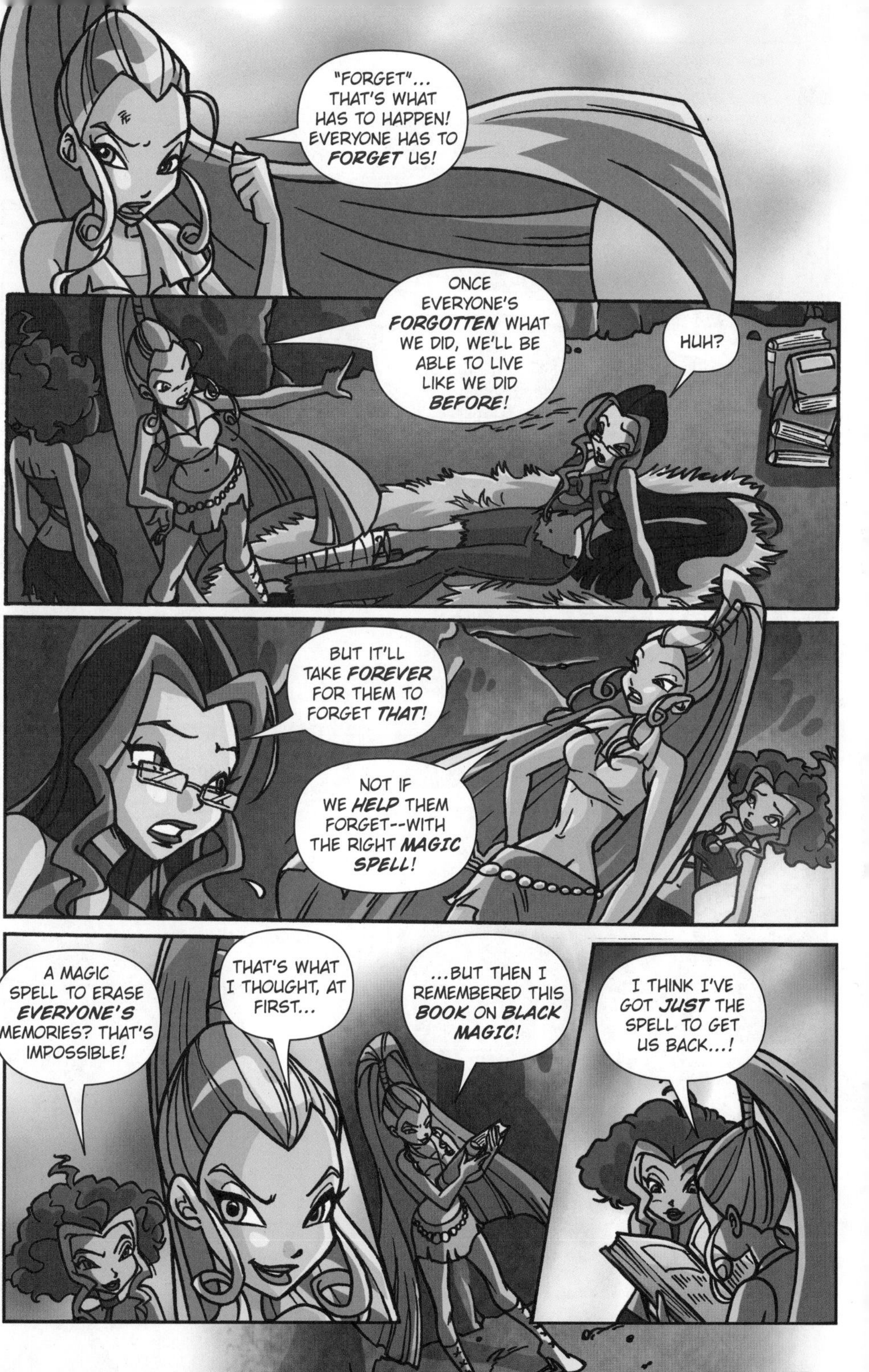
"FORGET"... THAT'S WHAT HAS TO HAPPEN! EVERYONE HAS TO *FORGET* US!
ONCE EVERYONE'S *FORGOTTEN* WHAT WE DID, WE'LL BE ABLE TO LIVE LIKE WE DID *BEFORE*!
HUH?
BUT IT'LL TAKE *FOREVER* FOR THEM TO FORGET *THAT*!
NOT IF WE *HELP* THEM FORGET--WITH THE RIGHT *MAGIC SPELL*!
A MAGIC SPELL TO ERASE *EVERYONE'S* MEMORIES? THAT'S IMPOSSIBLE!
THAT'S WHAT I THOUGHT, AT FIRST...
...BUT THEN I REMEMBERED THIS *BOOK* ON *BLACK MAGIC*!
I THINK I'VE GOT *JUST* THE SPELL TO GET US BACK...!

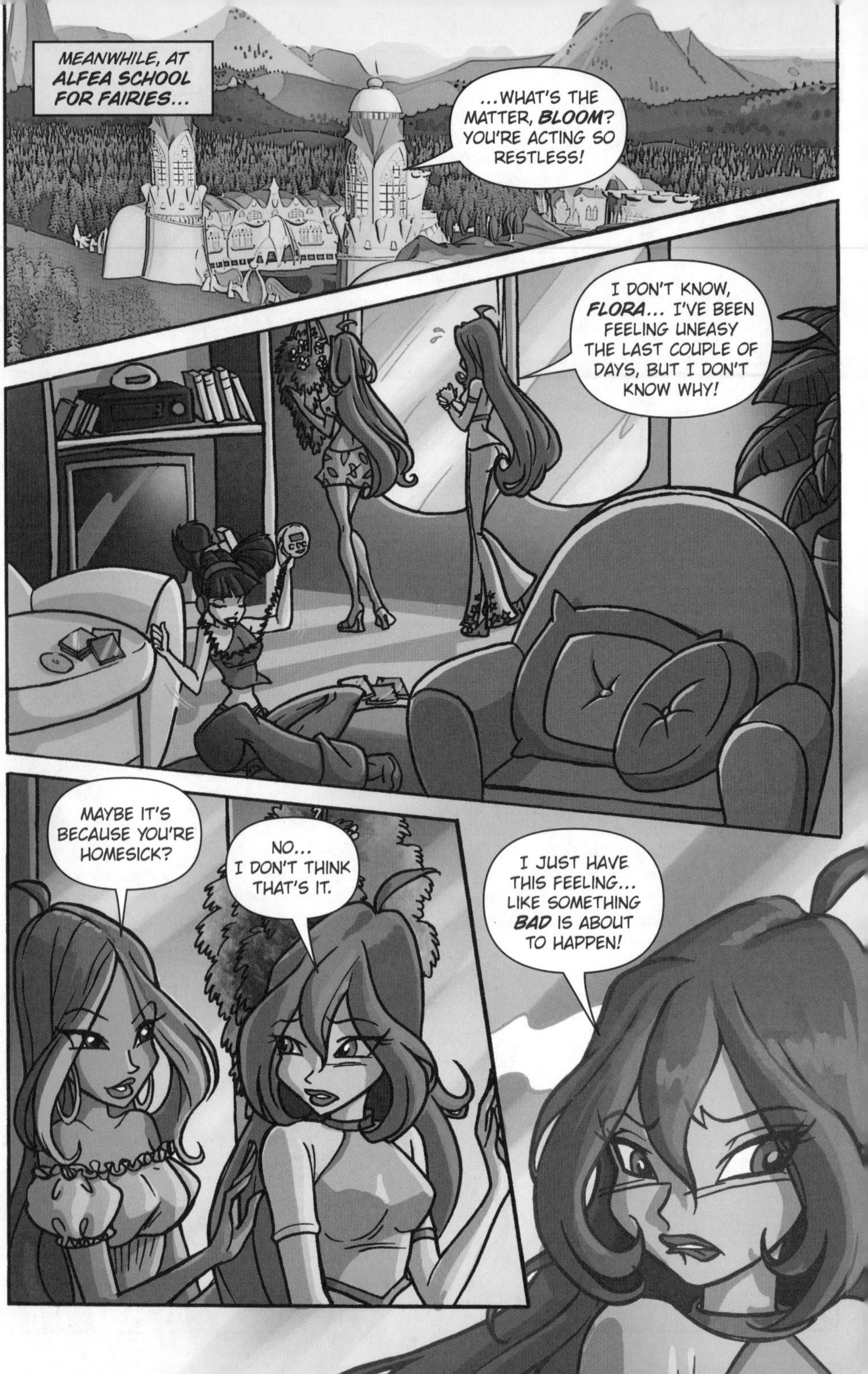
MEANWHILE, AT ALFEA SCHOOL FOR FAIRIES...
...WHAT'S THE MATTER, BLOOM? YOU'RE ACTING SO RESTLESS!
I DON'T KNOW, FLORA... I'VE BEEN FEELING UNEASY THE LAST COUPLE OF DAYS, BUT I DON'T KNOW WHY!
MAYBE IT'S BECAUSE YOU'RE HOMESICK?
NO... I DON'T THINK THAT'S IT.
I JUST HAVE THIS FEELING... LIKE SOMETHING BAD IS ABOUT TO HAPPEN!

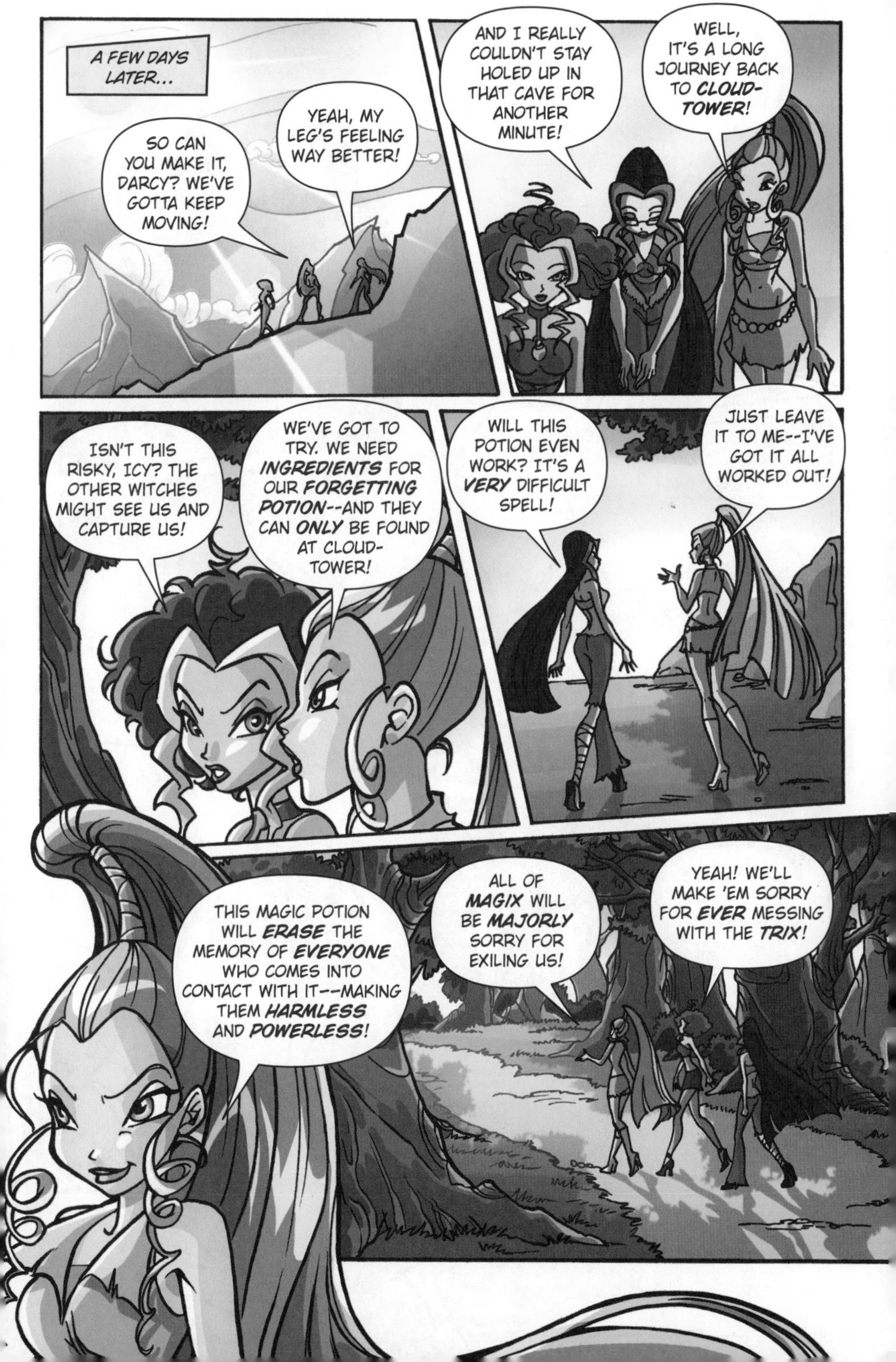
A FEW DAYS LATER...
SO CAN YOU MAKE IT, DARCY? WE'VE GOTTA KEEP MOVING!
YEAH, MY LEG'S FEELING WAY BETTER!
AND I REALLY COULDN'T STAY HOLED UP IN THAT CAVE FOR ANOTHER MINUTE!
WELL, IT'S A LONG JOURNEY BACK TO CLOUD-TOWER!
ISN'T THIS RISKY, ICY? THE OTHER WITCHES MIGHT SEE US AND CAPTURE US!
WE'VE GOT TO TRY. WE NEED INGREDIENTS FOR OUR FORGETTING POTION--AND THEY CAN ONLY BE FOUND AT CLOUD-TOWER!
WILL THIS POTION EVEN WORK? IT'S A VERY DIFFICULT SPELL!
JUST LEAVE IT TO ME--I'VE GOT IT ALL WORKED OUT!
THIS MAGIC POTION WILL ERASE THE MEMORY OF EVERYONE WHO COMES INTO CONTACT WITH IT--MAKING THEM HARMLESS AND POWERLESS!
ALL OF MAGIX WILL BE MAJORLY SORRY FOR EXILING US!
YEAH! WE'LL MAKE 'EM SORRY FOR EVER MESSING WITH THE TRIX!

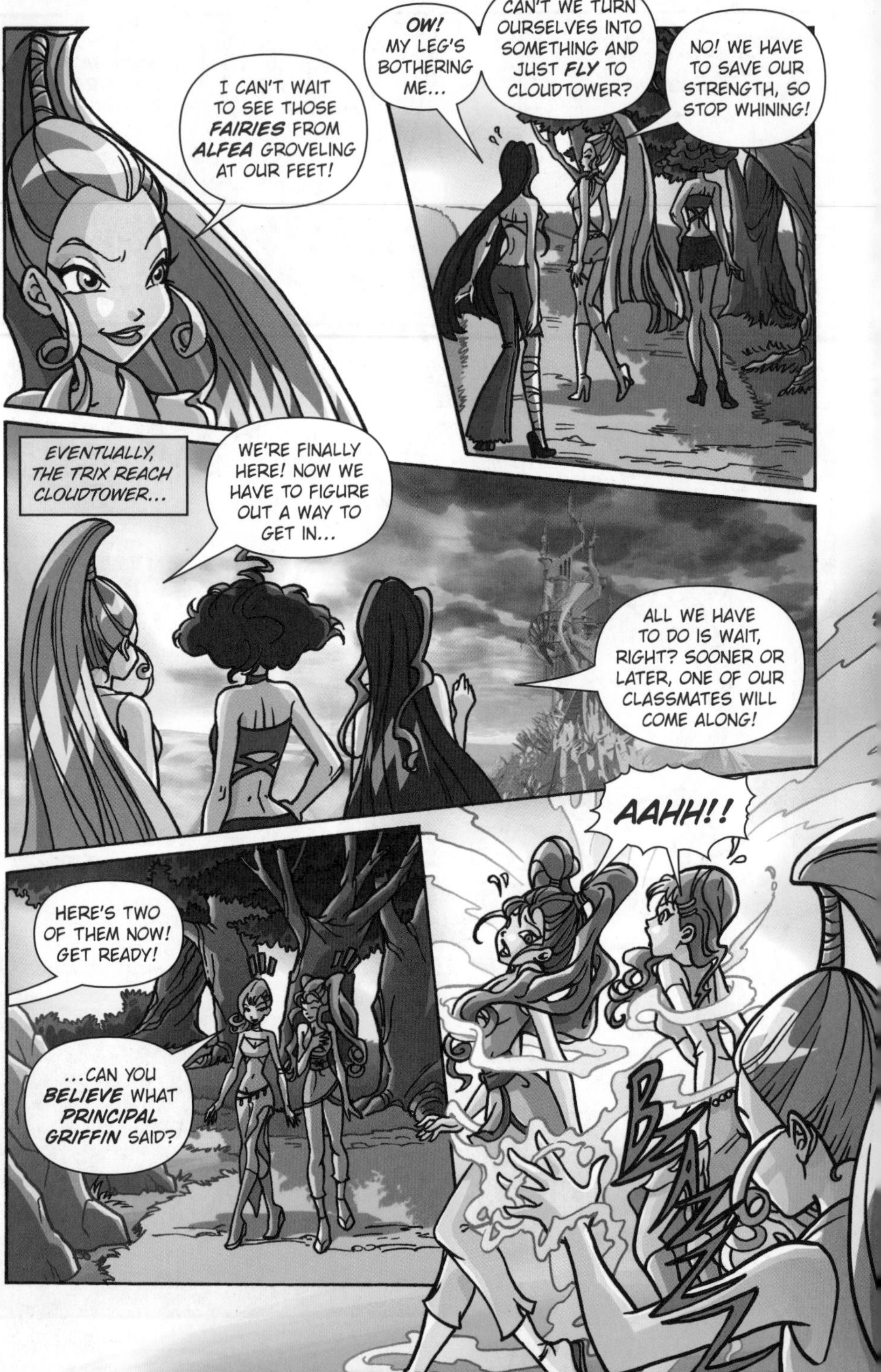
I CAN'T WAIT TO SEE THOSE FAIRIES FROM ALFEA GROVELING AT OUR FEET!
OW! MY LEG'S BOTHERING ME...
CAN'T WE TURN OURSELVES INTO SOMETHING AND JUST FLY TO CLOUDTOWER?
NO! WE HAVE TO SAVE OUR STRENGTH, SO STOP WHINING!
EVENTUALLY, THE TRIX REACH CLOUDTOWER...
WE'RE FINALLY HERE! NOW WE HAVE TO FIGURE OUT A WAY TO GET IN...
ALL WE HAVE TO DO IS WAIT, RIGHT? SOONER OR LATER, ONE OF OUR CLASSMATES WILL COME ALONG!
HERE'S TWO OF THEM NOW! GET READY!
...CAN YOU BELIEVE WHAT PRINCIPAL GRIFFIN SAID?
AAHH!!

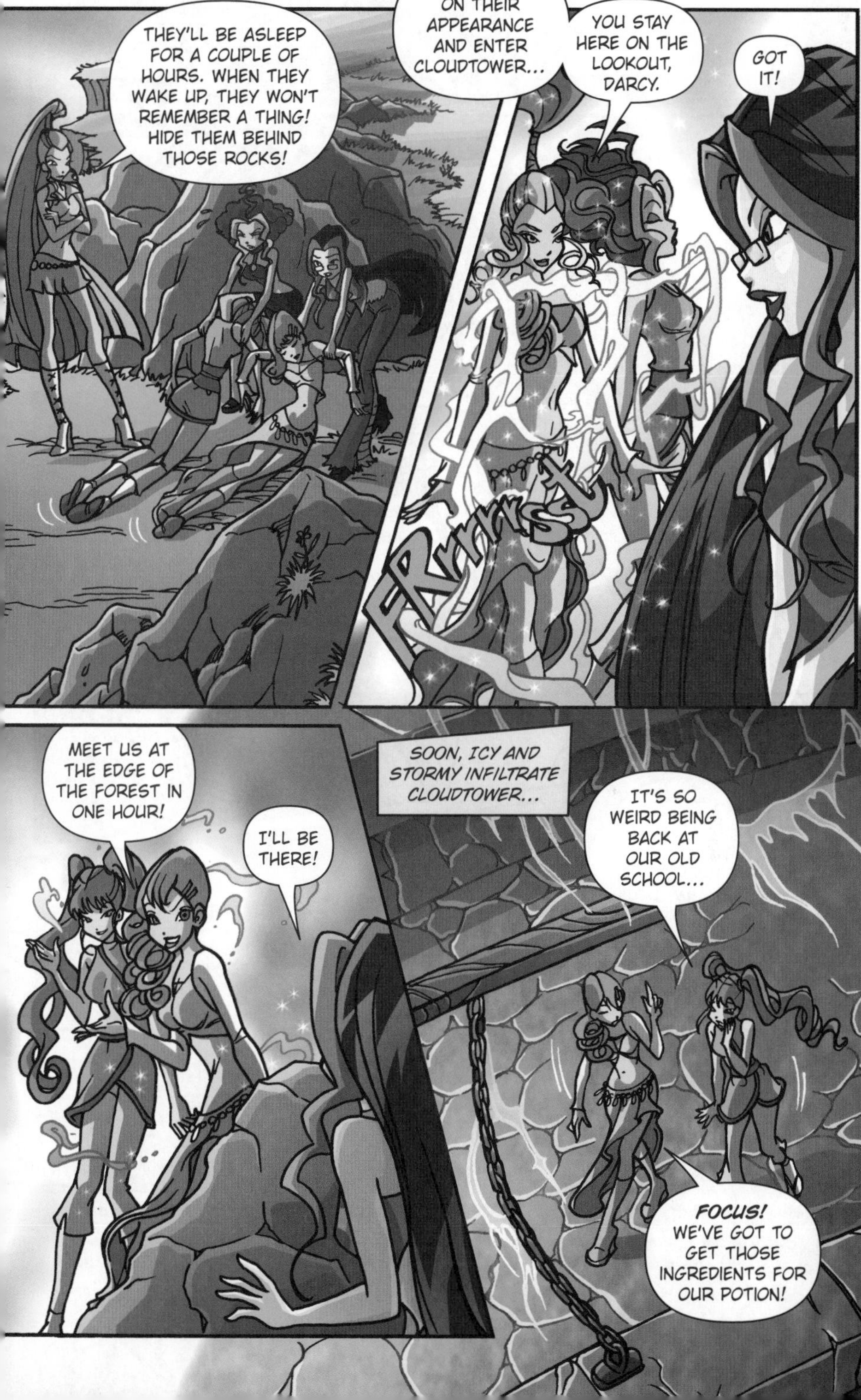
THEY'LL BE ASLEEP FOR A COUPLE OF HOURS. WHEN THEY WAKE UP, THEY WON'T REMEMBER A THING! HIDE THEM BEHIND THOSE ROCKS!
WE'LL TAKE ON THEIR APPEARANCE AND ENTER CLOUDTOWER...
YOU STAY HERE ON THE LOOKOUT, DARCY.
GOT IT!
FRRRRSST
MEET US AT THE EDGE OF THE FOREST IN ONE HOUR!
I'LL BE THERE!
SOON, ICY AND STORMY INFILTRATE CLOUDTOWER...
IT'S SO WEIRD BEING BACK AT OUR OLD SCHOOL...
FOCUS! WE'VE GOT TO GET THOSE INGREDIENTS FOR OUR POTION!

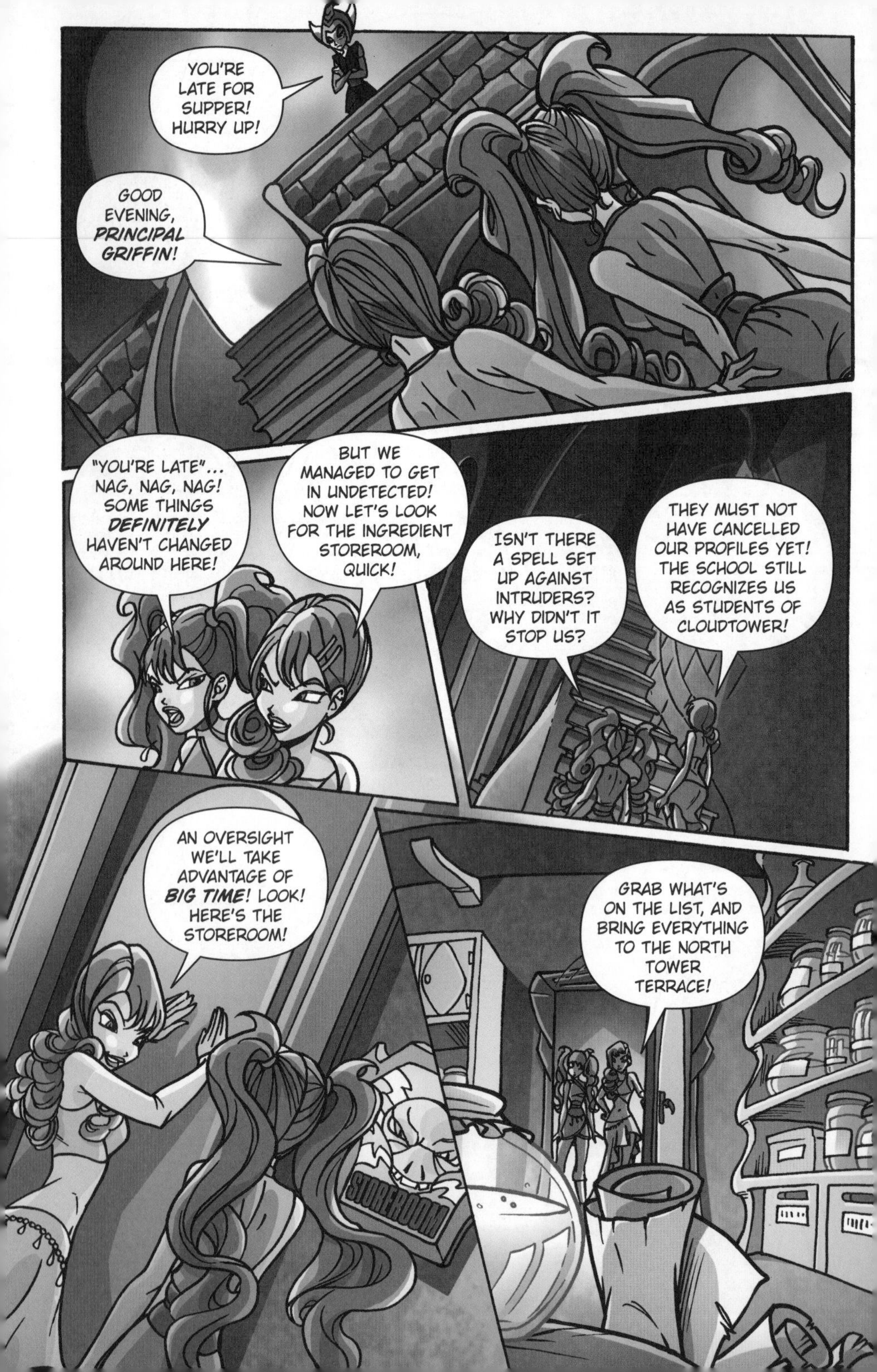
YOU'RE LATE FOR SUPPER! HURRY UP!
GOOD EVENING, PRINCIPAL GRIFFIN!
"YOU'RE LATE"... NAG, NAG, NAG! SOME THINGS DEFINITELY HAVEN'T CHANGED AROUND HERE!
BUT WE MANAGED TO GET IN UNDETECTED! NOW LET'S LOOK FOR THE INGREDIENT STOREROOM, QUICK!
ISN'T THERE A SPELL SET UP AGAINST INTRUDERS? WHY DIDN'T IT STOP US?
THEY MUST NOT HAVE CANCELLED OUR PROFILES YET! THE SCHOOL STILL RECOGNIZES US AS STUDENTS OF CLOUDTOWER!
AN OVERSIGHT WE'LL TAKE ADVANTAGE OF BIG TIME! LOOK! HERE'S THE STOREROOM!
STOREROOM
GRAB WHAT'S ON THE LIST, AND BRING EVERYTHING TO THE NORTH TOWER TERRACE!

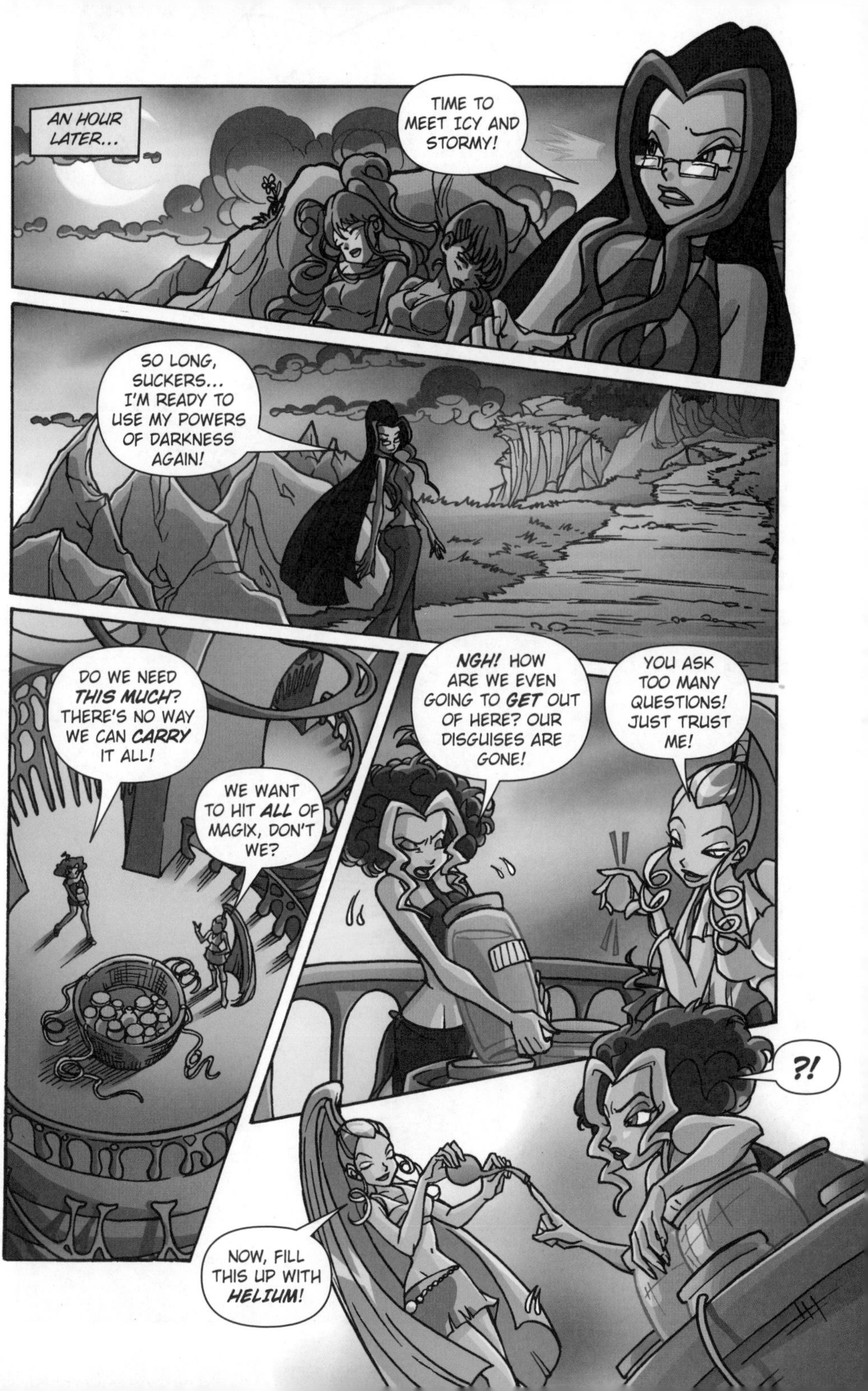
AN HOUR LATER...
TIME TO MEET ICY AND STORMY!
SO LONG, SUCKERS... I'M READY TO USE MY POWERS OF DARKNESS AGAIN!
DO WE NEED THIS MUCH? THERE'S NO WAY WE CAN CARRY IT ALL!
WE WANT TO HIT ALL OF MAGIX, DON'T WE?
NGH! HOW ARE WE EVEN GOING TO GET OUT OF HERE? OUR DISGUISES ARE GONE!
YOU ASK TOO MANY QUESTIONS! JUST TRUST ME!
?!
NOW, FILL THIS UP WITH HELIUM!

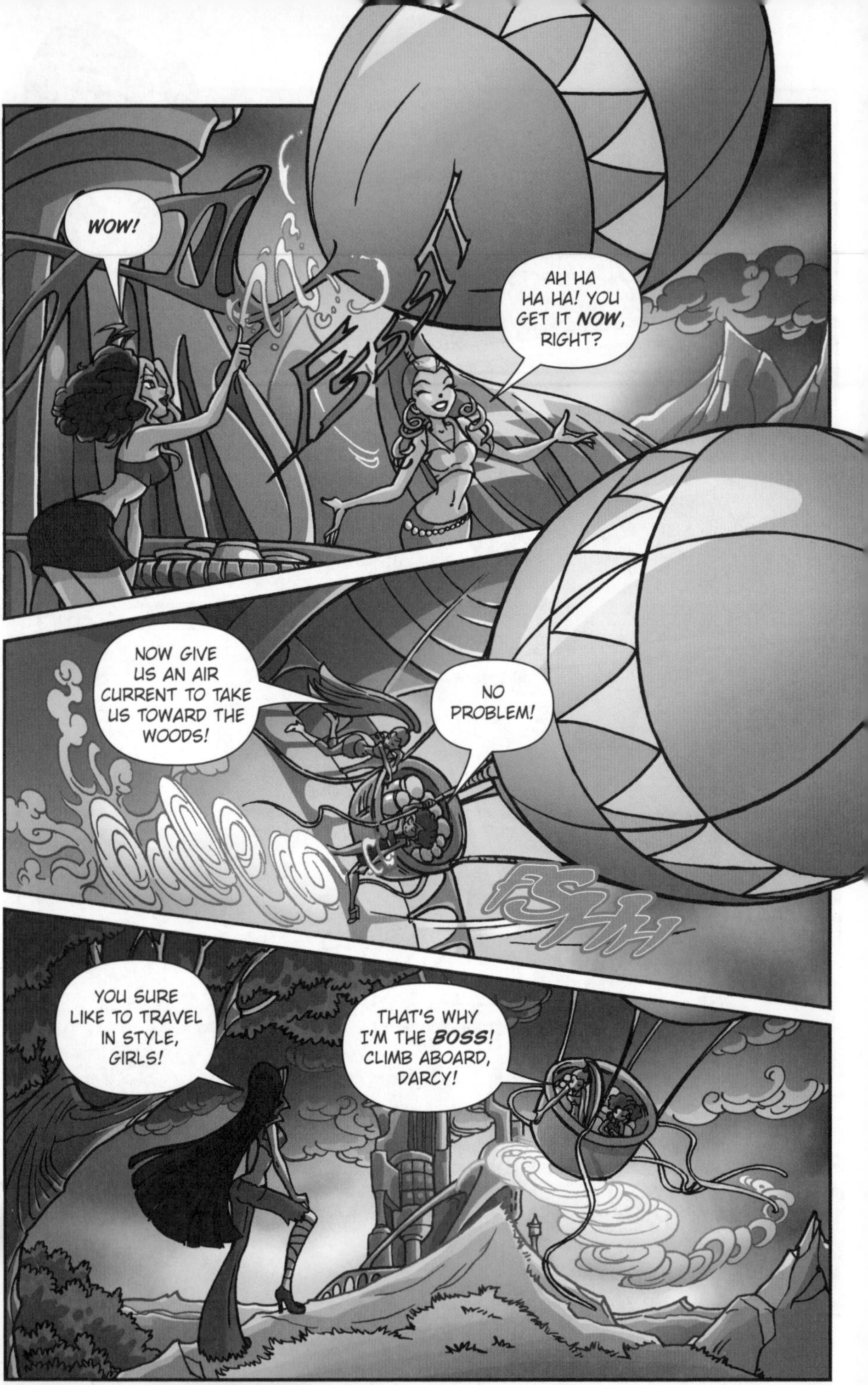
WOW!
FSSST
AH HA HA HA! YOU GET IT NOW, RIGHT?
NOW GIVE US AN AIR CURRENT TO TAKE US TOWARD THE WOODS!
NO PROBLEM!
FSHH
YOU SURE LIKE TO TRAVEL IN STYLE, GIRLS!
THAT'S WHY I'M THE BOSS! CLIMB ABOARD, DARCY!

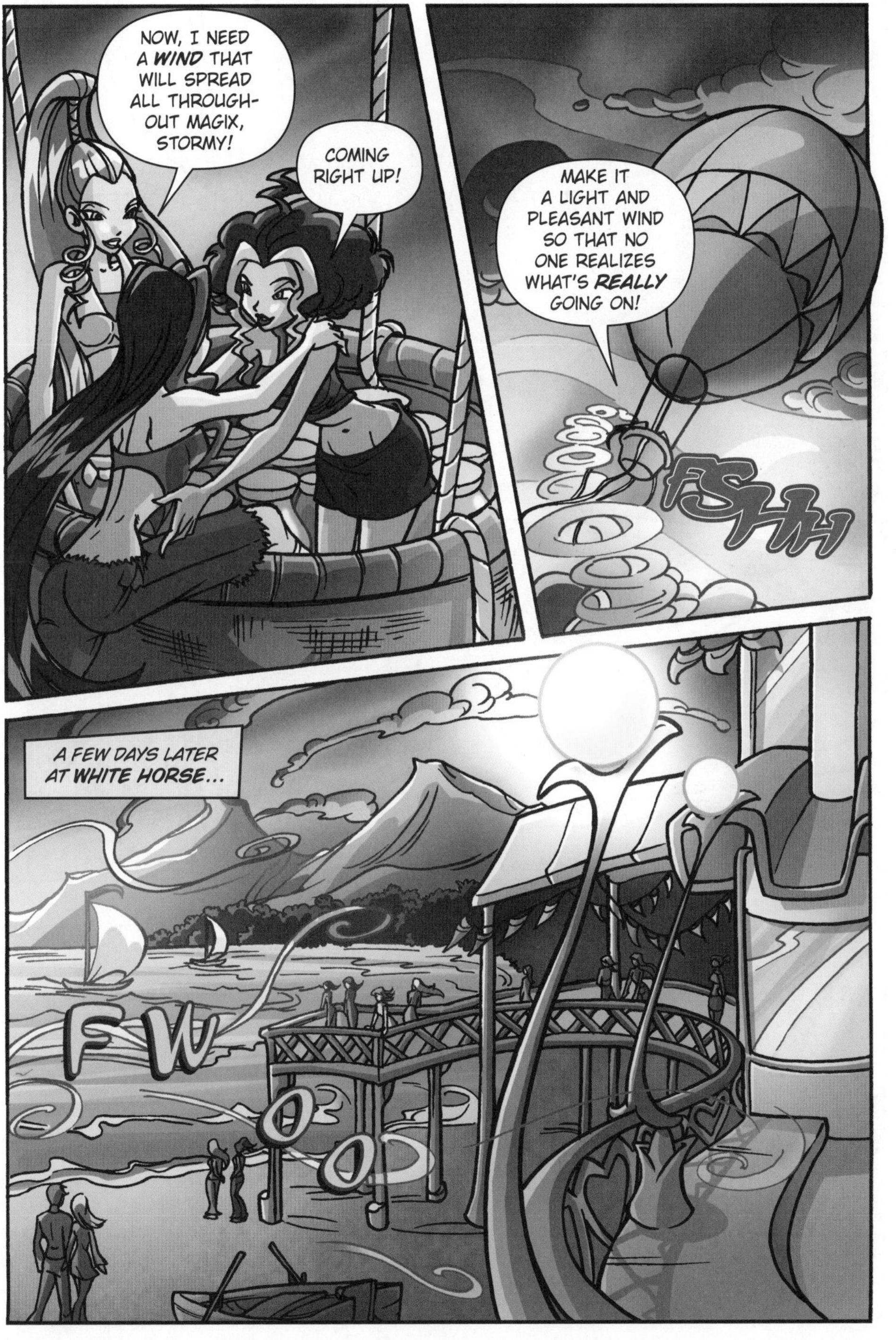
NOW, I NEED A WIND THAT WILL SPREAD ALL THROUGH-OUT MAGIX, STORMY!
COMING RIGHT UP!
MAKE IT A LIGHT AND PLEASANT WIND SO THAT NO ONE REALIZES WHAT'S REALLY GOING ON!
FSHH
A FEW DAYS LATER AT WHITE HORSE...
FWOO

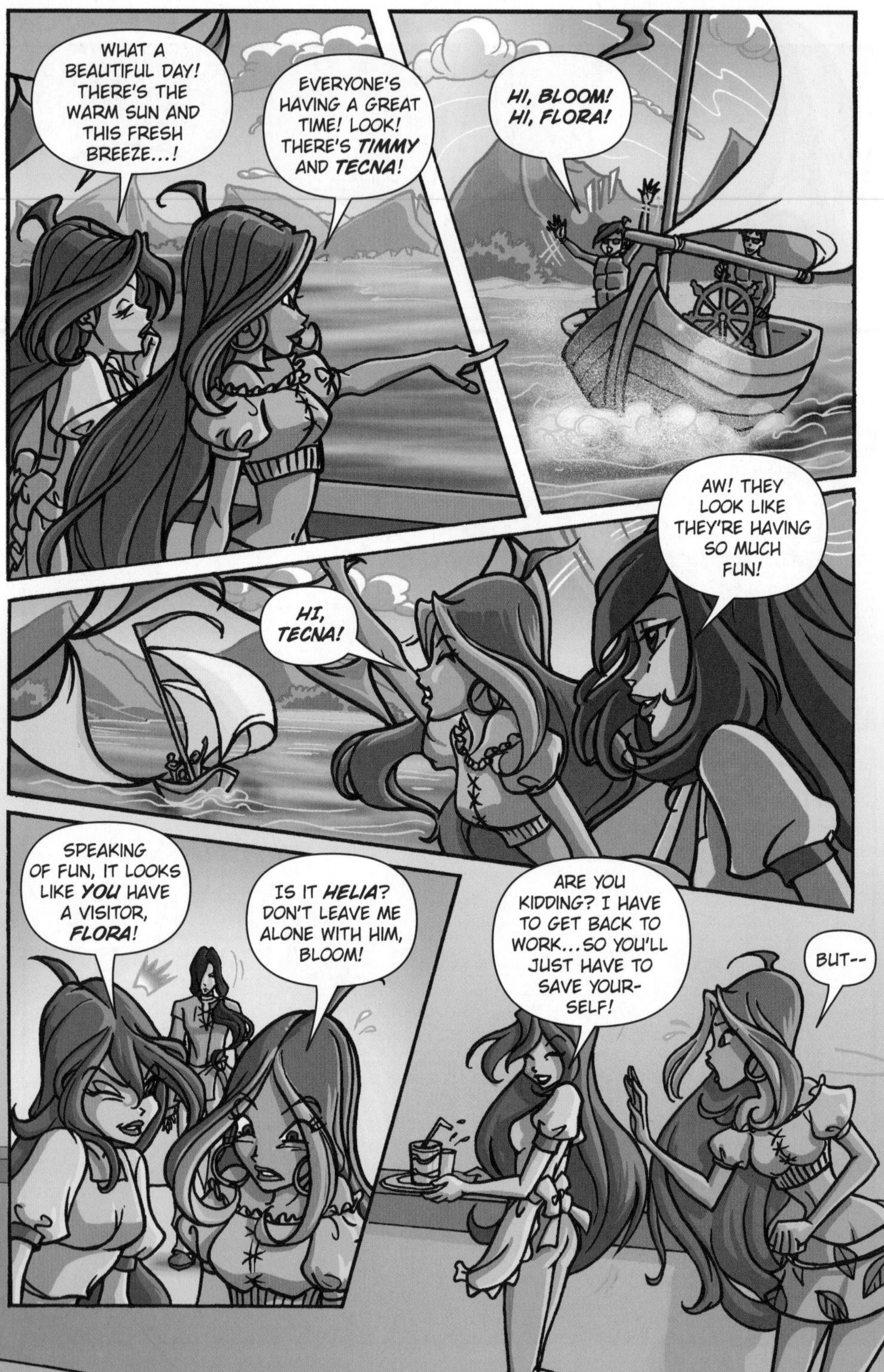
WHAT A BEAUTIFUL DAY! THERE'S THE WARM SUN AND THIS FRESH BREEZE...!
EVERYONE'S HAVING A GREAT TIME! LOOK! THERE'S TIMMY AND TECNA!
HI, BLOOM! HI, FLORA!
AW! THEY LOOK LIKE THEY'RE HAVING SO MUCH FUN!
HI, TECNA!
SPEAKING OF FUN, IT LOOKS LIKE YOU HAVE A VISITOR, FLORA!
IS IT HELIA? DON'T LEAVE ME ALONE WITH HIM, BLOOM!
ARE YOU KIDDING? I HAVE TO GET BACK TO WORK...SO YOU'LL JUST HAVE TO SAVE YOURSELF!
BUT--

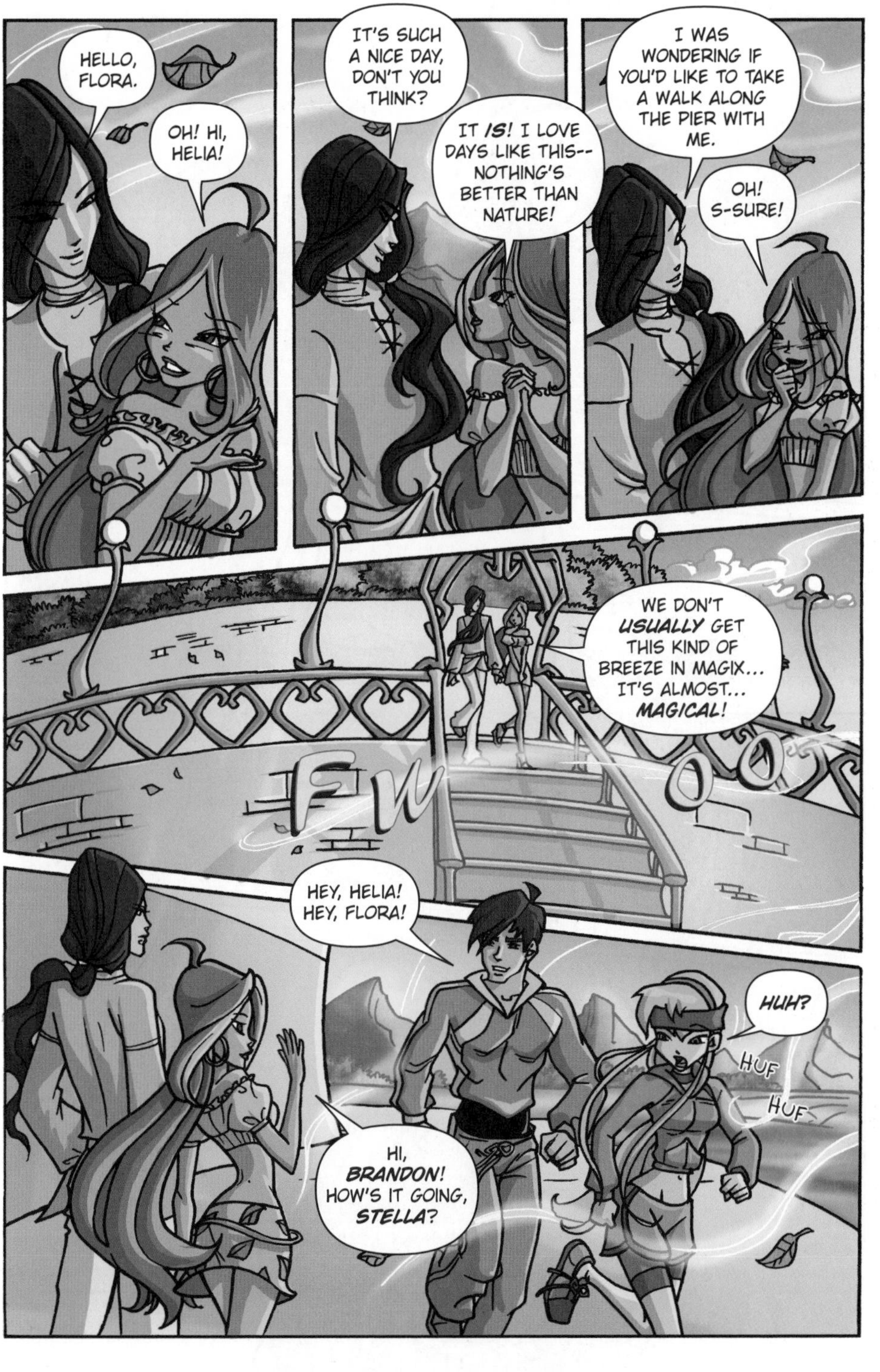
HELLO, FLORA.
OH! HI, HELIA!
IT'S SUCH A NICE DAY, DON'T YOU THINK?
IT IS! I LOVE DAYS LIKE THIS-- NOTHING'S BETTER THAN NATURE!
I WAS WONDERING IF YOU'D LIKE TO TAKE A WALK ALONG THE PIER WITH ME.
OH! S-SURE!
WE DON'T USUALLY GET THIS KIND OF BREEZE IN MAGIX... IT'S ALMOST... MAGICAL!
FWOOO
HEY, HELIA! HEY, FLORA!
HUH?
HUF
HUF
HI, BRANDON! HOW'S IT GOING, STELLA?

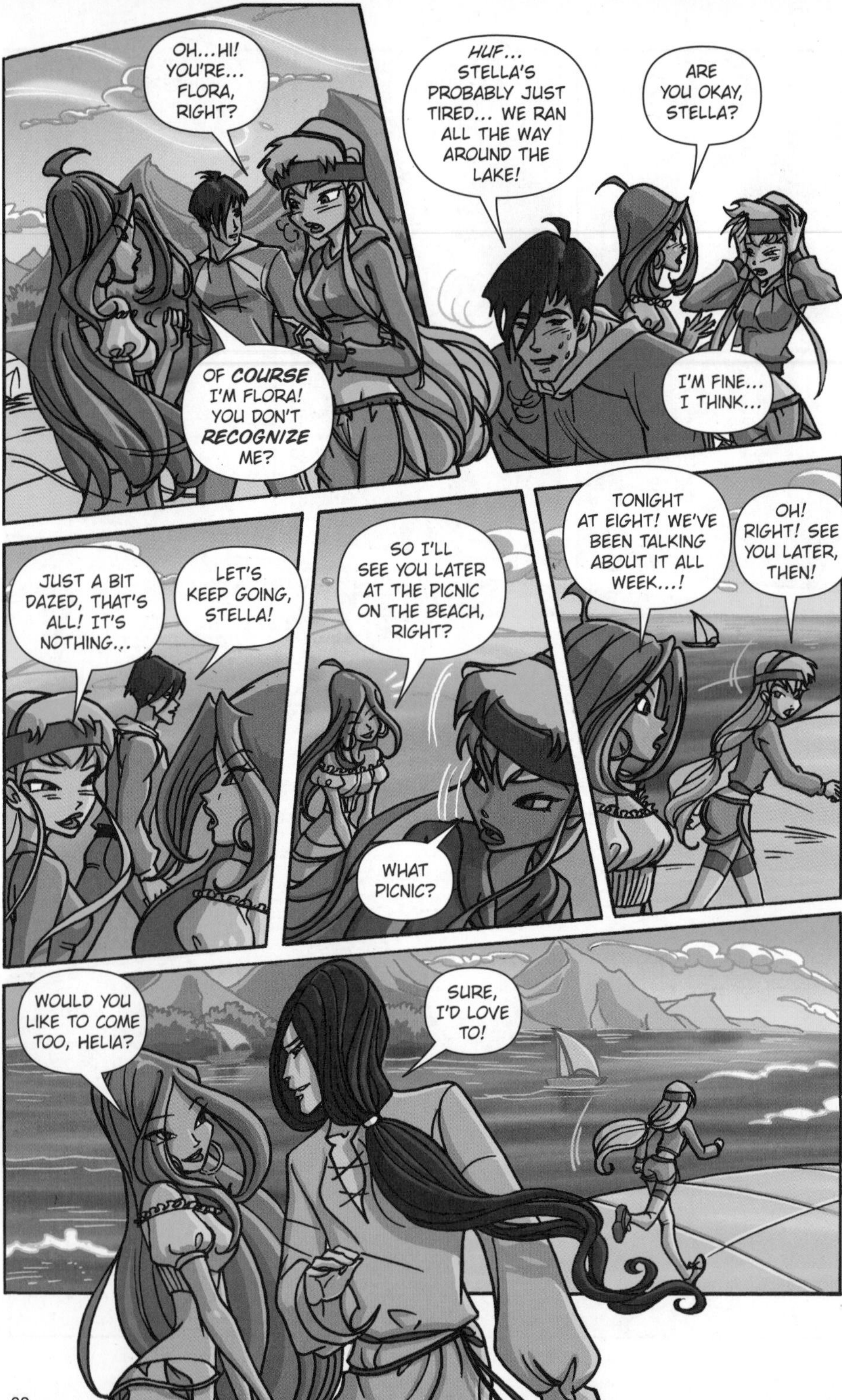
OH...HI! YOU'RE... FLORA, RIGHT?
OF COURSE I'M FLORA! YOU DON'T RECOGNIZE ME?
HUF... STELLA'S PROBABLY JUST TIRED... WE RAN ALL THE WAY AROUND THE LAKE!
ARE YOU OKAY, STELLA?
I'M FINE... I THINK...
JUST A BIT DAZED, THAT'S ALL! IT'S NOTHING...
LET'S KEEP GOING, STELLA!
SO I'LL SEE YOU LATER AT THE PICNIC ON THE BEACH, RIGHT?
WHAT PICNIC?
TONIGHT AT EIGHT! WE'VE BEEN TALKING ABOUT IT ALL WEEK...!
OH! RIGHT! SEE YOU LATER, THEN!
WOULD YOU LIKE TO COME TOO, HELIA?
SURE, I'D LOVE TO!

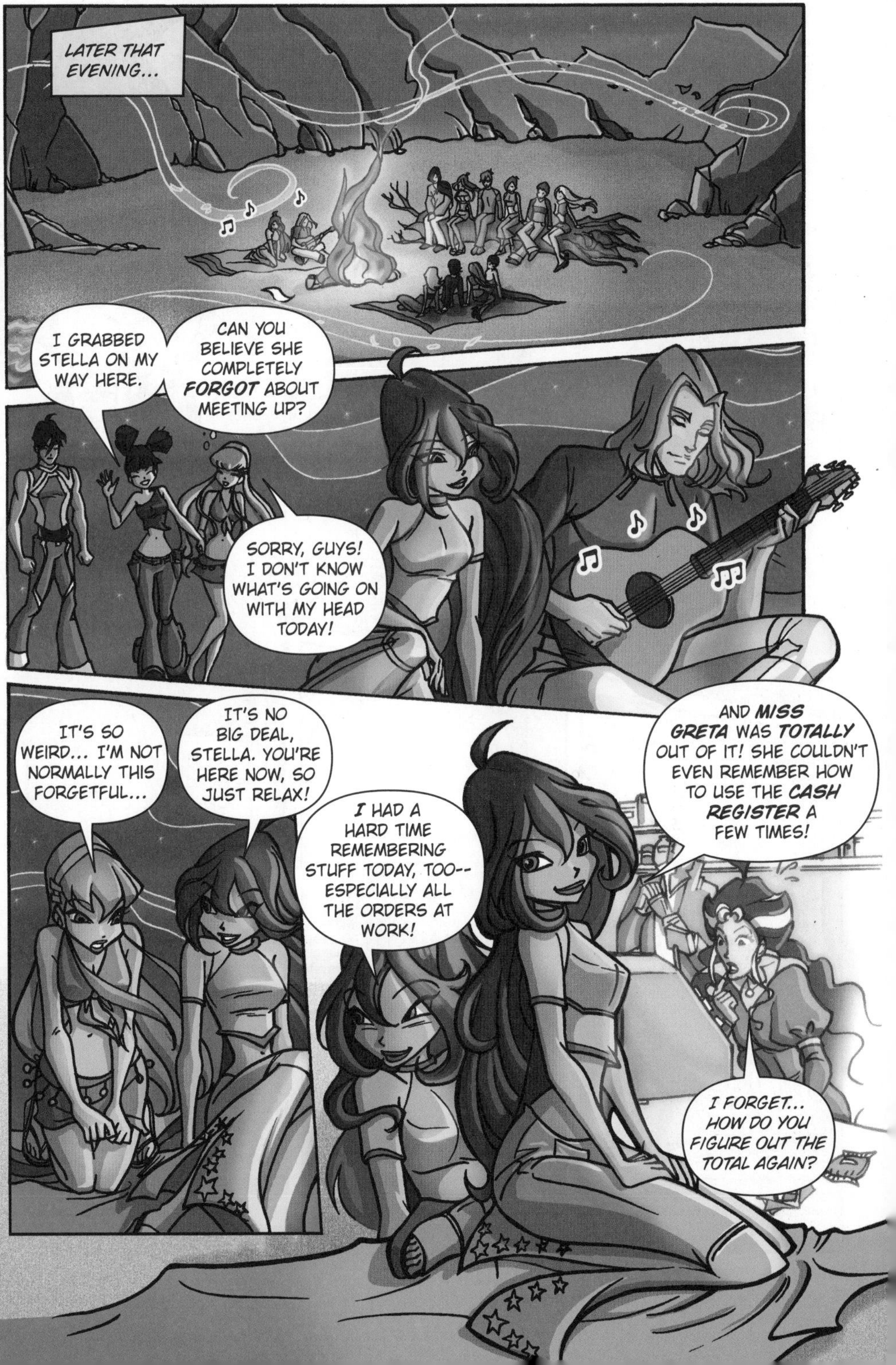
LATER THAT EVENING...
I GRABBED STELLA ON MY WAY HERE.
CAN YOU BELIEVE SHE COMPLETELY FORGOT ABOUT MEETING UP?
SORRY, GUYS! I DON'T KNOW WHAT'S GOING ON WITH MY HEAD TODAY!
IT'S SO WEIRD... I'M NOT NORMALLY THIS FORGETFUL...
IT'S NO BIG DEAL, STELLA. YOU'RE HERE NOW, SO JUST RELAX!
I HAD A HARD TIME REMEMBERING STUFF TODAY, TOO-- ESPECIALLY ALL THE ORDERS AT WORK!
AND MISS GRETA WAS TOTALLY OUT OF IT! SHE COULDN'T EVEN REMEMBER HOW TO USE THE CASH REGISTER A FEW TIMES!
I FORGET... HOW DO YOU FIGURE OUT THE TOTAL AGAIN?

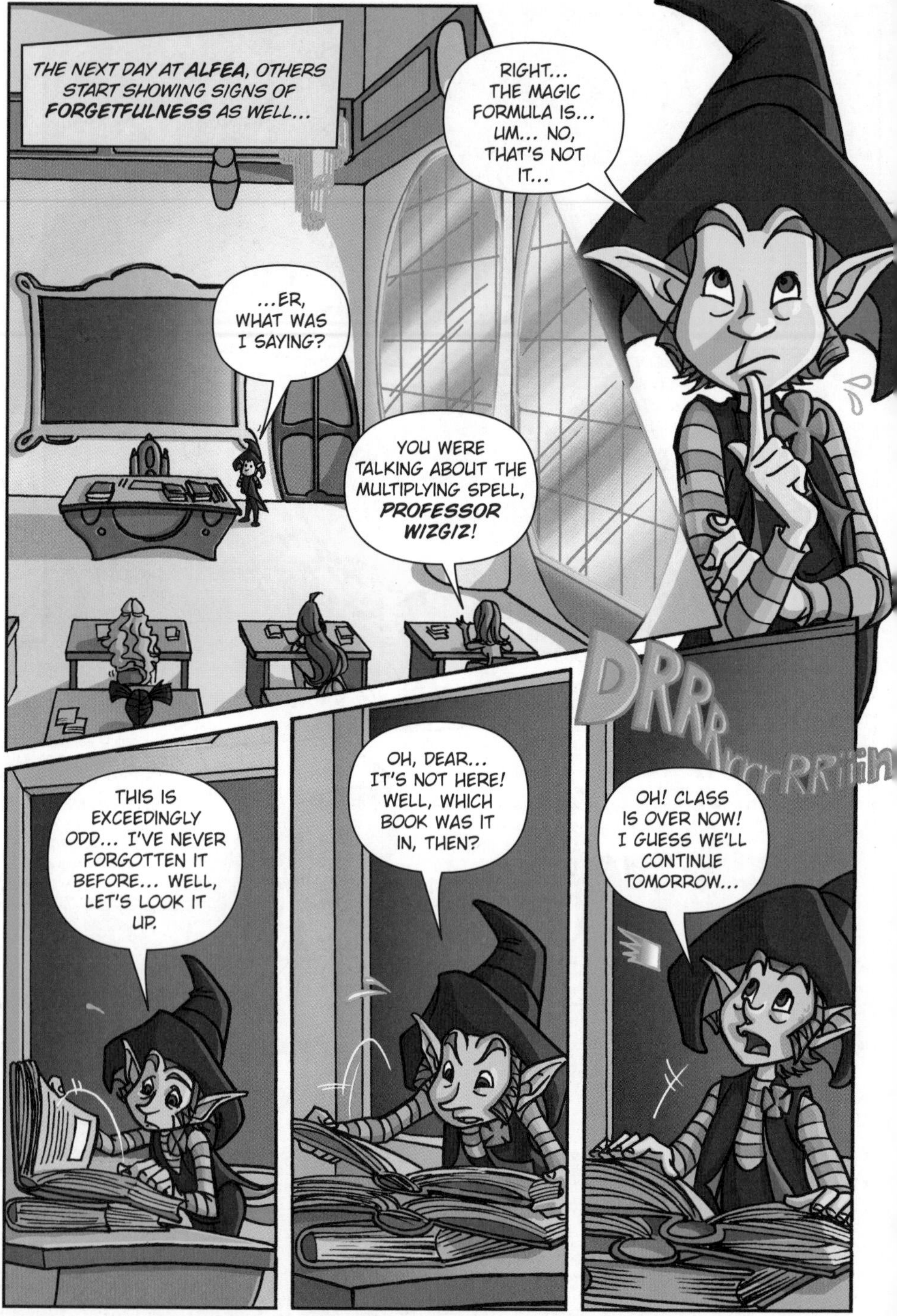
THE NEXT DAY AT ALFEA, OTHERS START SHOWING SIGNS OF FORGETFULNESS AS WELL...
RIGHT... THE MAGIC FORMULA IS... UM... NO, THAT'S NOT IT...
...ER, WHAT WAS I SAYING?
YOU WERE TALKING ABOUT THE MULTIPLYING SPELL, PROFESSOR WIZGIZ!
DRRRrrrrRRiiin
THIS IS EXCEEDINGLY ODD... I'VE NEVER FORGOTTEN IT BEFORE... WELL, LET'S LOOK IT UP.
OH, DEAR... IT'S NOT HERE! WELL, WHICH BOOK WAS IT IN, THEN?
OH! CLASS IS OVER NOW! I GUESS WE'LL CONTINUE TOMORROW...

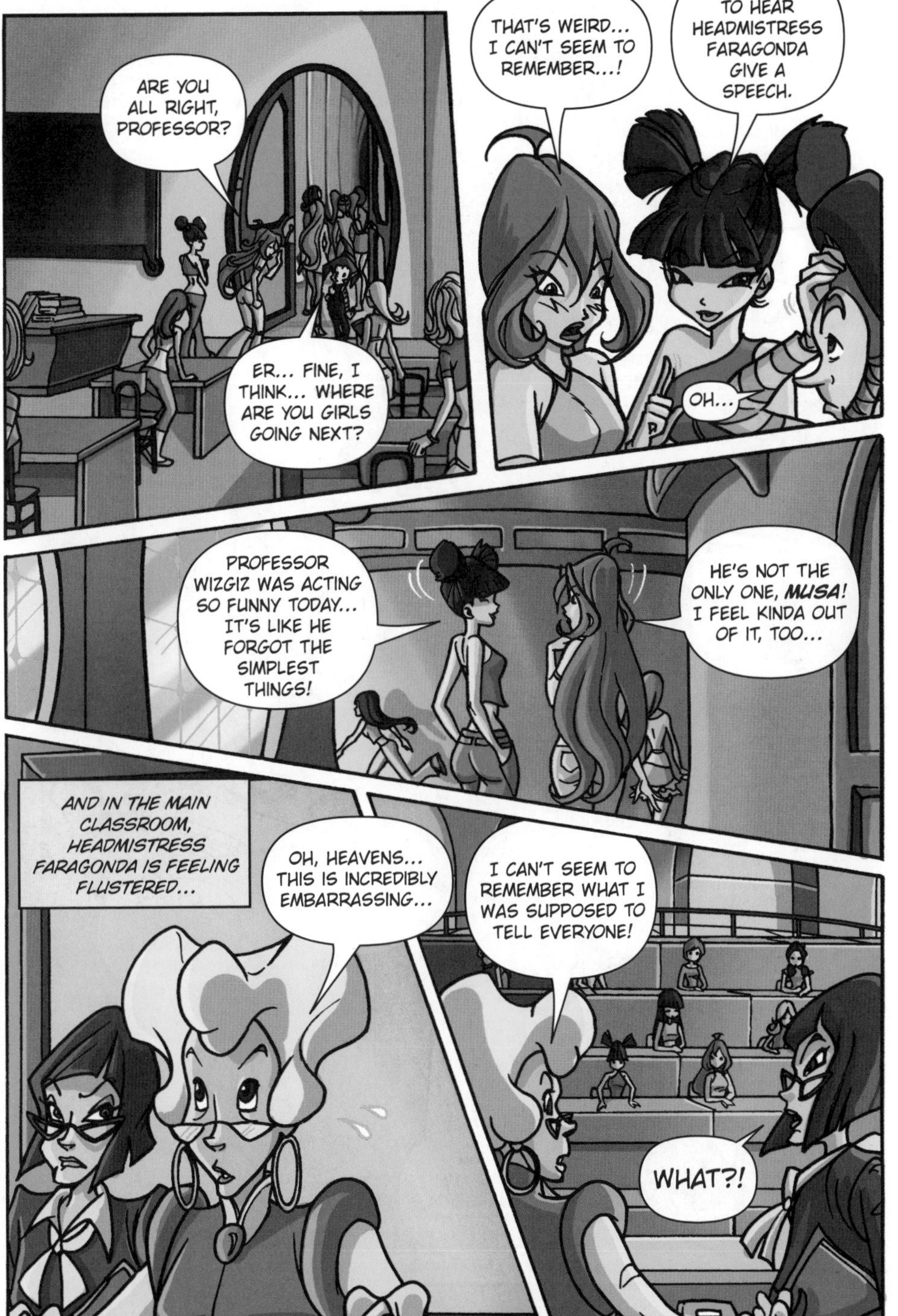
ARE YOU ALL RIGHT, PROFESSOR?
ER... FINE, I THINK... WHERE ARE YOU GIRLS GOING NEXT?
THAT'S WEIRD... I CAN'T SEEM TO REMEMBER...!
WE'RE OFF TO HEAR HEADMISTRESS FARAGONDA GIVE A SPEECH.
OH...
PROFESSOR WIZGIZ WAS ACTING SO FUNNY TODAY... IT'S LIKE HE FORGOT THE SIMPLEST THINGS!
HE'S NOT THE ONLY ONE, MUSA! I FEEL KINDA OUT OF IT, TOO...
AND IN THE MAIN CLASSROOM, HEADMISTRESS FARAGONDA IS FEELING FLUSTERED...
OH, HEAVENS... THIS IS INCREDIBLY EMBARRASSING...
I CAN'T SEEM TO REMEMBER WHAT I WAS SUPPOSED TO TELL EVERYONE!
WHAT?!

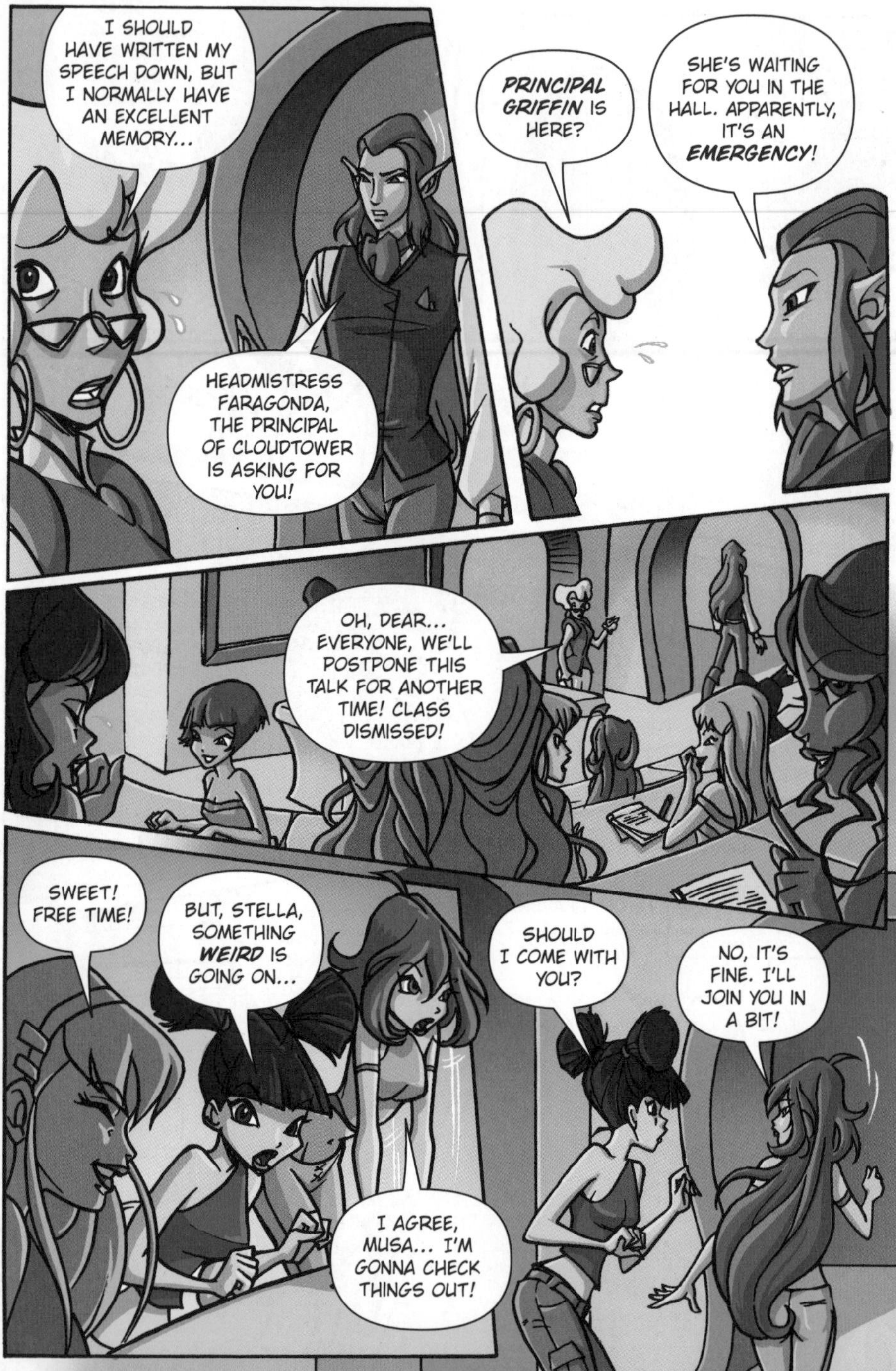
I SHOULD HAVE WRITTEN MY SPEECH DOWN, BUT I NORMALLY HAVE AN EXCELLENT MEMORY...
HEADMISTRESS FARAGONDA, THE PRINCIPAL OF CLOUDTOWER IS ASKING FOR YOU!
PRINCIPAL GRIFFIN IS HERE?
SHE'S WAITING FOR YOU IN THE HALL. APPARENTLY, IT'S AN EMERGENCY!
OH, DEAR... EVERYONE, WE'LL POSTPONE THIS TALK FOR ANOTHER TIME! CLASS DISMISSED!
SWEET! FREE TIME!
BUT, STELLA, SOMETHING WEIRD IS GOING ON...
I AGREE, MUSA... I'M GONNA CHECK THINGS OUT!
SHOULD I COME WITH YOU?
NO, IT'S FINE. I'LL JOIN YOU IN A BIT!

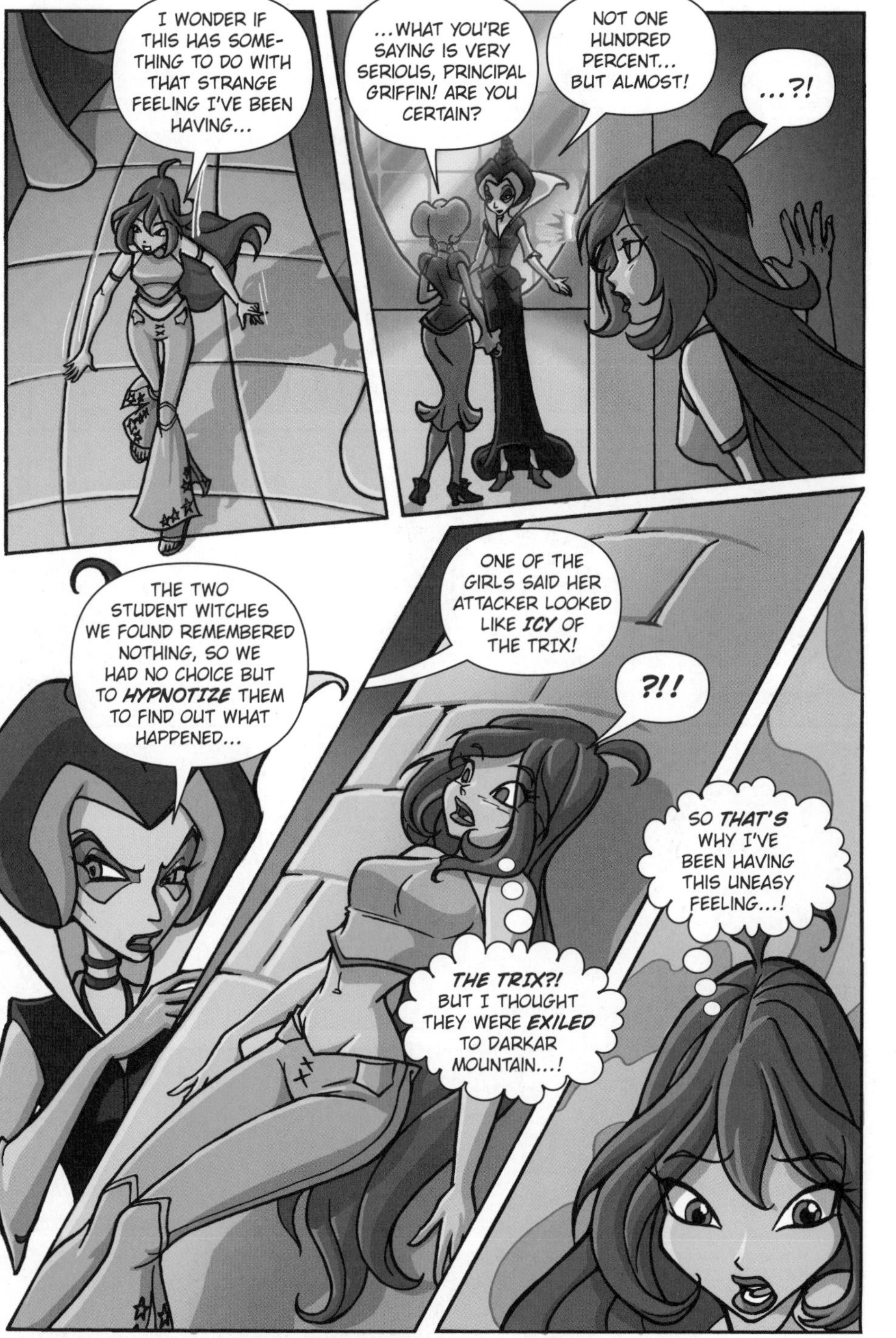
I WONDER IF THIS HAS SOME-THING TO DO WITH THAT STRANGE FEELING I'VE BEEN HAVING...
...WHAT YOU'RE SAYING IS VERY SERIOUS, PRINCIPAL GRIFFIN! ARE YOU CERTAIN?
NOT ONE HUNDRED PERCENT... BUT ALMOST!
...?!
THE TWO STUDENT WITCHES WE FOUND REMEMBERED NOTHING, SO WE HAD NO CHOICE BUT TO HYPNOTIZE THEM TO FIND OUT WHAT HAPPENED...
ONE OF THE GIRLS SAID HER ATTACKER LOOKED LIKE ICY OF THE TRIX!
?!!
THE TRIX?! BUT I THOUGHT THEY WERE EXILED TO DARKAR MOUNTAIN...!
SO THAT'S WHY I'VE BEEN HAVING THIS UNEASY FEELING...!

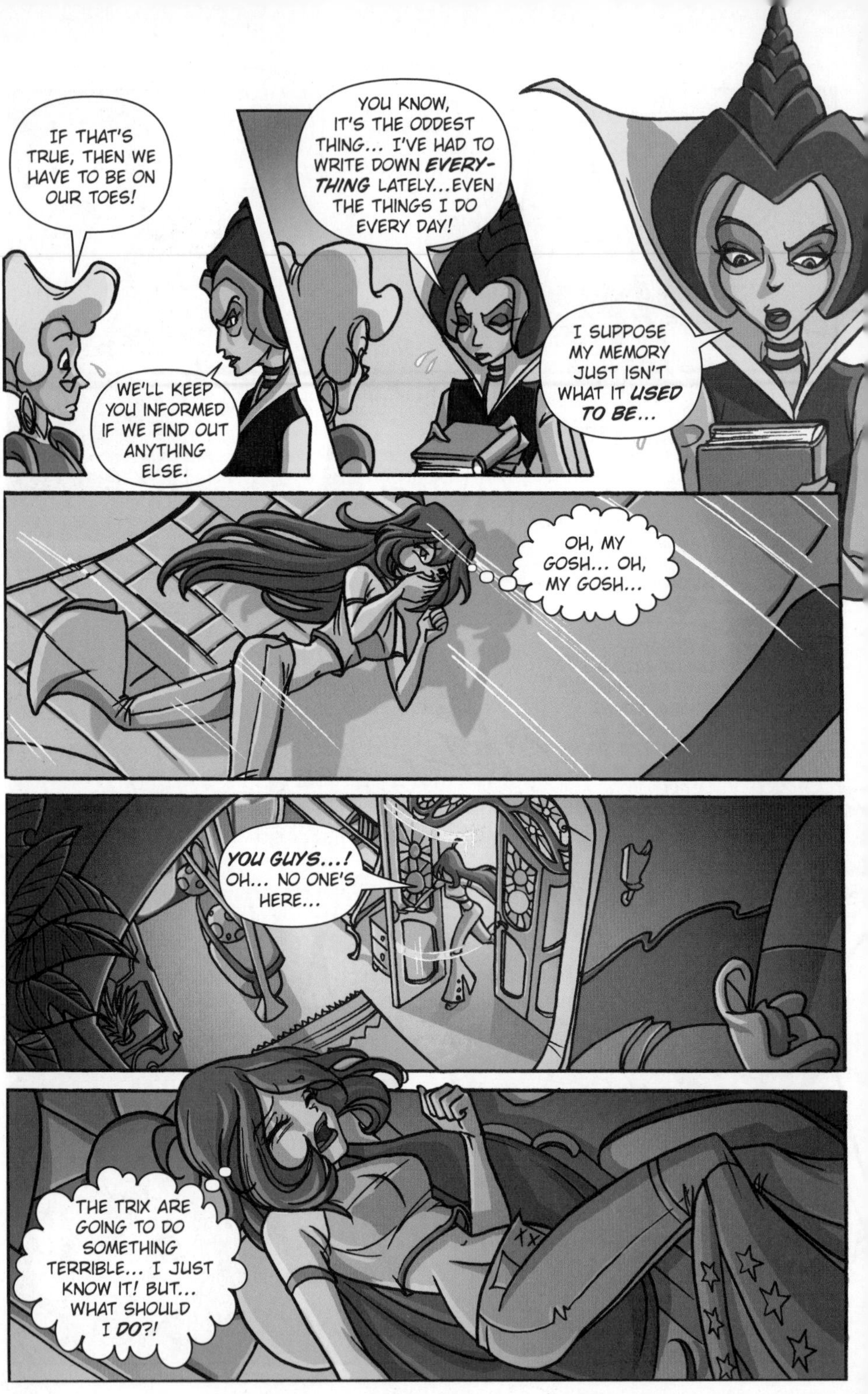
IF THAT'S TRUE, THEN WE HAVE TO BE ON OUR TOES!
WE'LL KEEP YOU INFORMED IF WE FIND OUT ANYTHING ELSE.
YOU KNOW, IT'S THE ODDEST THING... I'VE HAD TO WRITE DOWN EVERY-THING LATELY...EVEN THE THINGS I DO EVERY DAY!
I SUPPOSE MY MEMORY JUST ISN'T WHAT IT USED TO BE...
OH, MY GOSH... OH, MY GOSH...
YOU GUYS...! OH... NO ONE'S HERE...
THE TRIX ARE GOING TO DO SOMETHING TERRIBLE... I JUST KNOW IT! BUT... WHAT SHOULD I DO?!

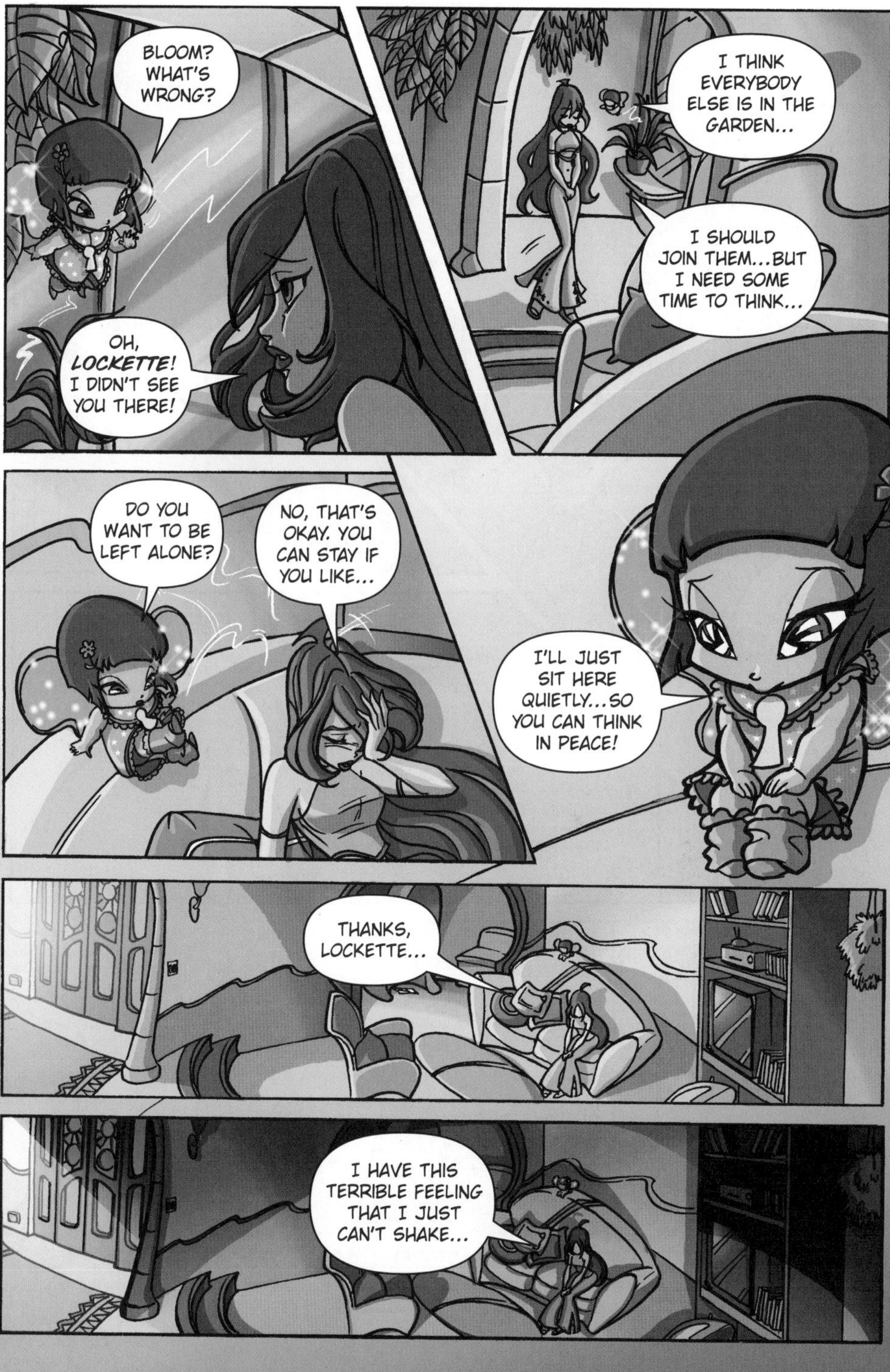
BLOOM? WHAT'S WRONG?
OH, LOCKETTE! I DIDN'T SEE YOU THERE!
I THINK EVERYBODY ELSE IS IN THE GARDEN...
I SHOULD JOIN THEM...BUT I NEED SOME TIME TO THINK...
DO YOU WANT TO BE LEFT ALONE?
NO, THAT'S OKAY. YOU CAN STAY IF YOU LIKE...
I'LL JUST SIT HERE QUIETLY...SO YOU CAN THINK IN PEACE!
THANKS, LOCKETTE...
I HAVE THIS TERRIBLE FEELING THAT I JUST CAN'T SHAKE...

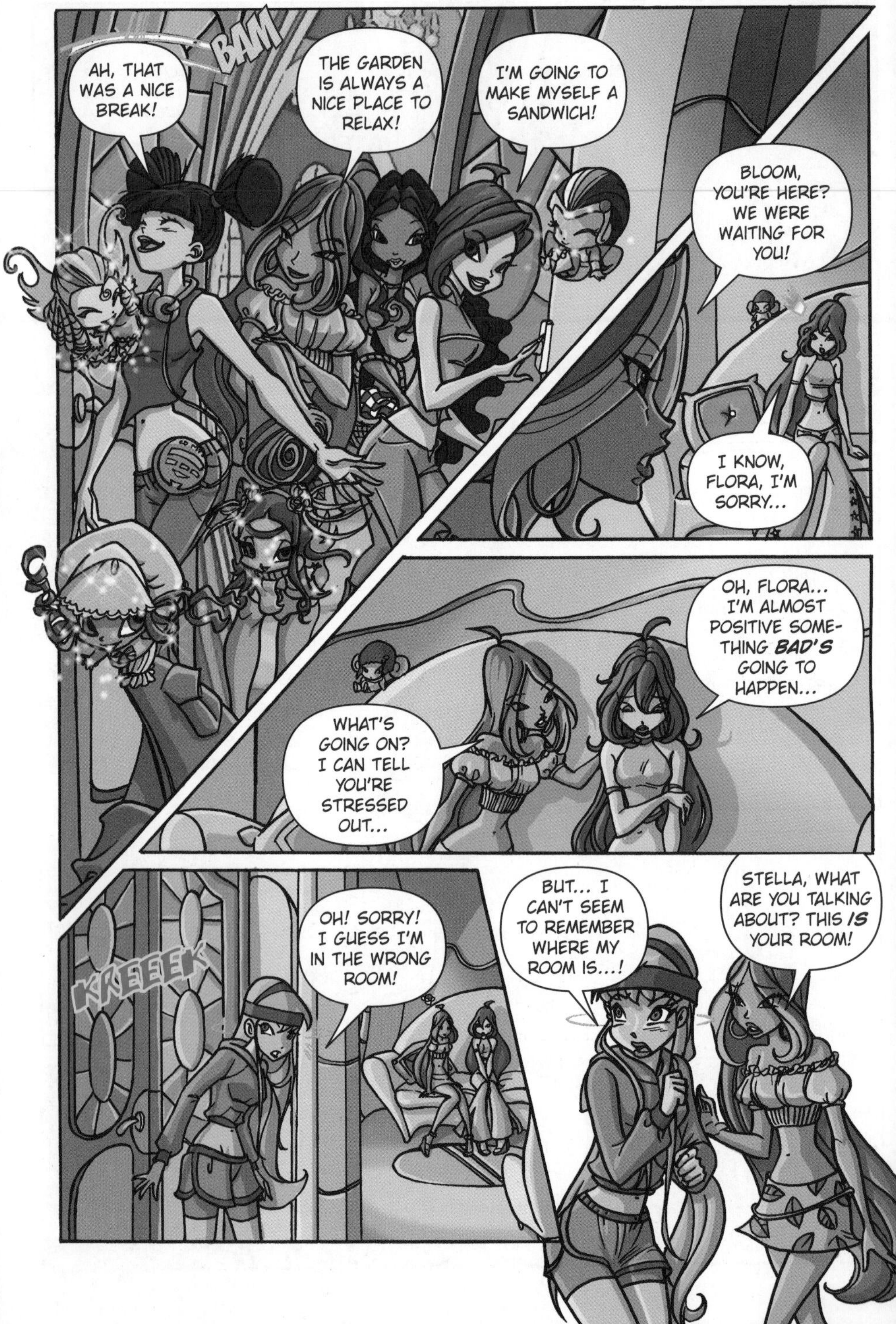
BAM
AH, THAT WAS A NICE BREAK!
THE GARDEN IS ALWAYS A NICE PLACE TO RELAX!
I'M GOING TO MAKE MYSELF A SANDWICH!
BLOOM, YOU'RE HERE? WE WERE WAITING FOR YOU!
I KNOW, FLORA, I'M SORRY...
OH, FLORA... I'M ALMOST POSITIVE SOME-THING BAD'S GOING TO HAPPEN...
WHAT'S GOING ON? I CAN TELL YOU'RE STRESSED OUT...
KREEEK
OH! SORRY! I GUESS I'M IN THE WRONG ROOM!
BUT... I CAN'T SEEM TO REMEMBER WHERE MY ROOM IS...!
STELLA, WHAT ARE YOU TALKING ABOUT? THIS IS YOUR ROOM!

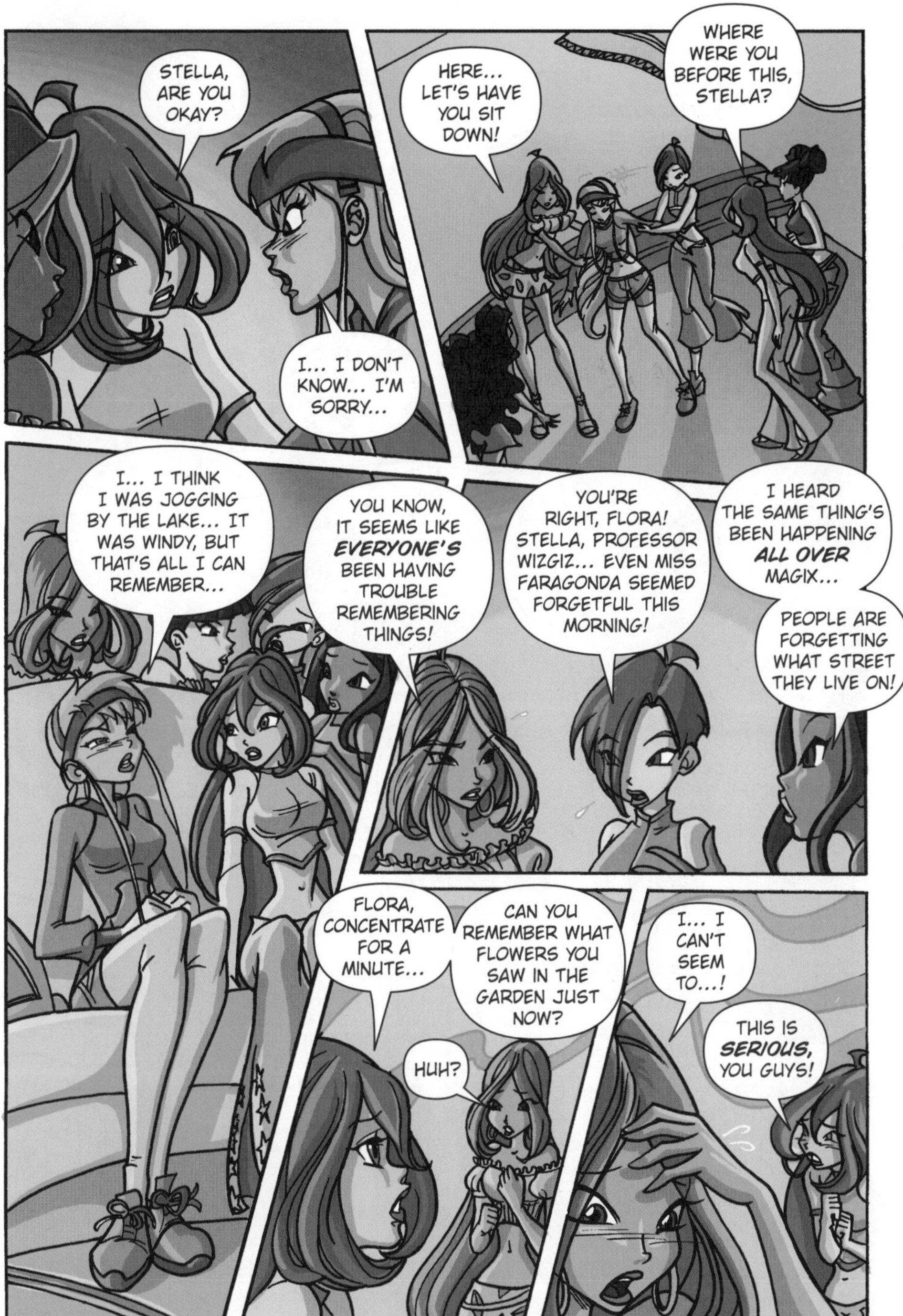
STELLA, ARE YOU OKAY?
I... I DON'T KNOW... I'M SORRY...
HERE... LET'S HAVE YOU SIT DOWN!
WHERE WERE YOU BEFORE THIS, STELLA?
I... I THINK I WAS JOGGING BY THE LAKE... IT WAS WINDY, BUT THAT'S ALL I CAN REMEMBER...
YOU KNOW, IT SEEMS LIKE EVERYONE'S BEEN HAVING TROUBLE REMEMBERING THINGS!
YOU'RE RIGHT, FLORA! STELLA, PROFESSOR WIZGIZ... EVEN MISS FARAGONDA SEEMED FORGETFUL THIS MORNING!
I HEARD THE SAME THING'S BEEN HAPPENING ALL OVER MAGIX...
PEOPLE ARE FORGETTING WHAT STREET THEY LIVE ON!
FLORA, CONCENTRATE FOR A MINUTE...
CAN YOU REMEMBER WHAT FLOWERS YOU SAW IN THE GARDEN JUST NOW?
HUH?
I... I CAN'T SEEM TO...!
THIS IS SERIOUS, YOU GUYS!

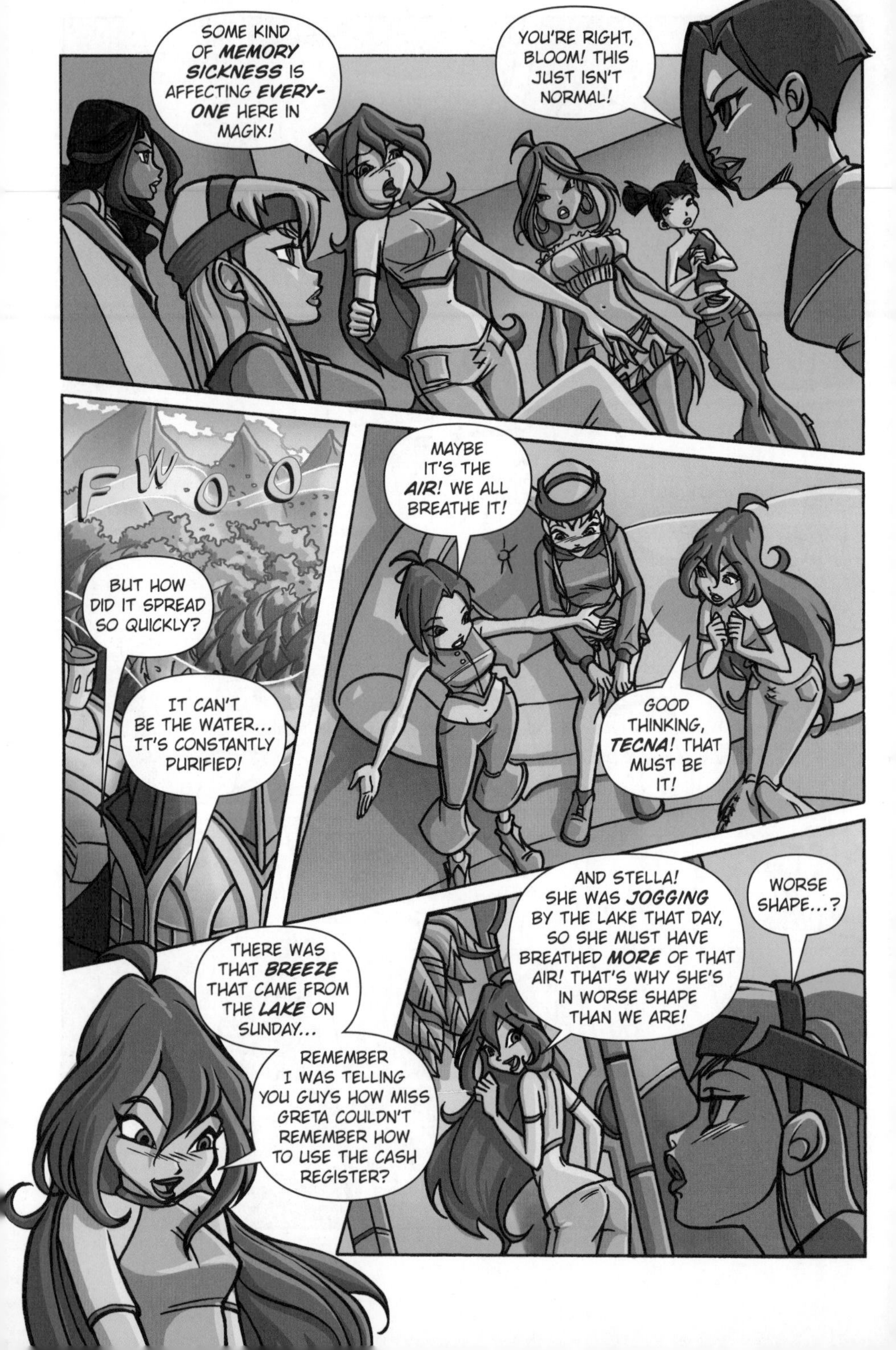

SOME KIND OF MEMORY SICKNESS IS AFFECTING EVERY-ONE HERE IN MAGIX!
YOU'RE RIGHT, BLOOM! THIS JUST ISN'T NORMAL!
FWOO
BUT HOW DID IT SPREAD SO QUICKLY?
IT CAN'T BE THE WATER... IT'S CONSTANTLY PURIFIED!
MAYBE IT'S THE AIR! WE ALL BREATHE IT!
GOOD THINKING, TECNA! THAT MUST BE IT!
THERE WAS THAT BREEZE THAT CAME FROM THE LAKE ON SUNDAY...
REMEMBER I WAS TELLING YOU GUYS HOW MISS GRETA COULDN'T REMEMBER HOW TO USE THE CASH REGISTER?
AND STELLA! SHE WAS JOGGING BY THE LAKE THAT DAY, SO SHE MUST HAVE BREATHED MORE OF THAT AIR! THAT'S WHY SHE'S IN WORSE SHAPE THAN WE ARE!
WORSE SHAPE...?

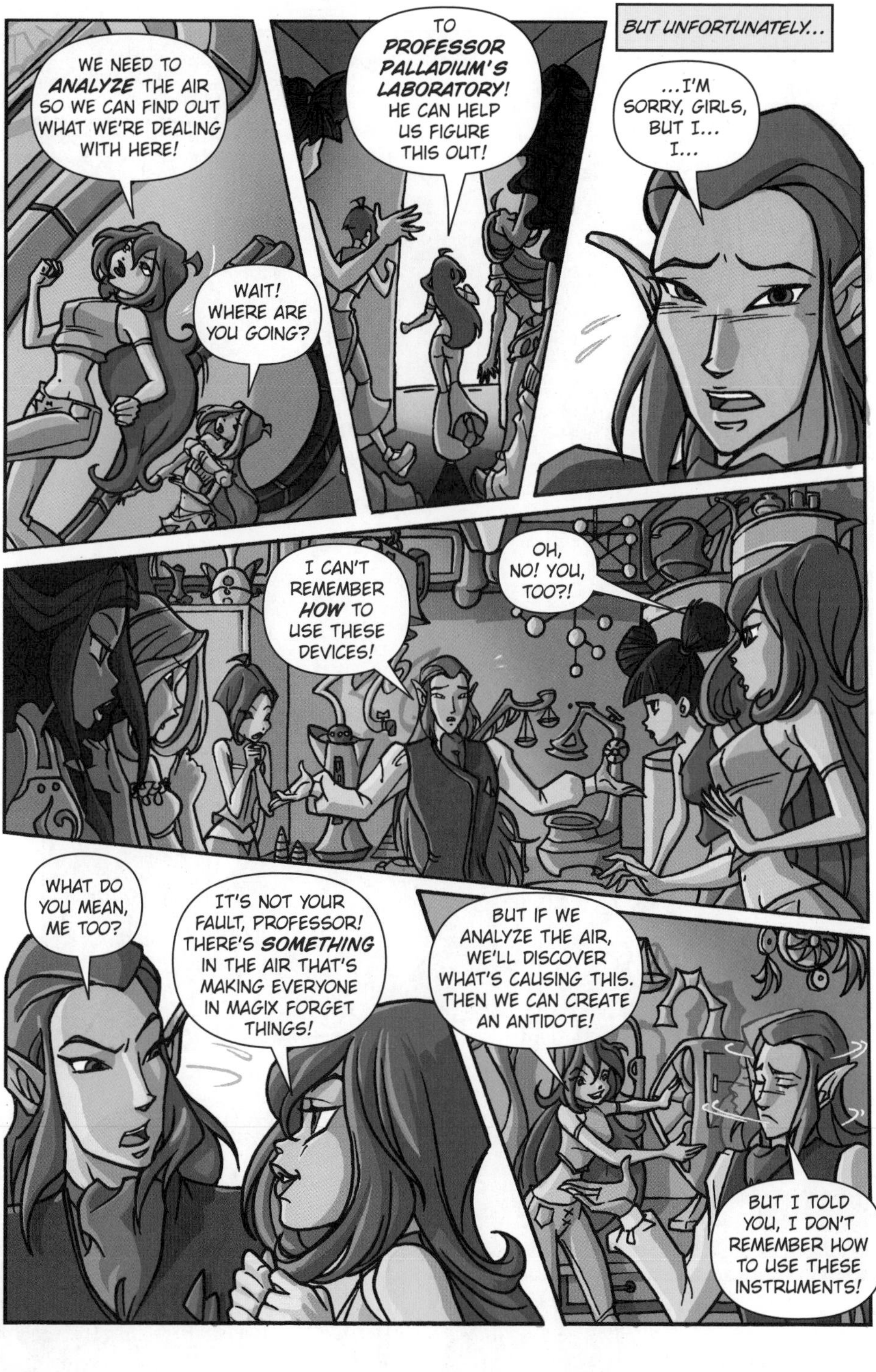
WE NEED TO ANALYZE THE AIR SO WE CAN FIND OUT WHAT WE'RE DEALING WITH HERE!
WAIT! WHERE ARE YOU GOING?
TO PROFESSOR PALLADIUM'S LABORATORY! HE CAN HELP US FIGURE THIS OUT!
BUT UNFORTUNATELY...
...I'M SORRY, GIRLS, BUT I... I...
I CAN'T REMEMBER HOW TO USE THESE DEVICES!
OH, NO! YOU, TOO?!
WHAT DO YOU MEAN, ME TOO?
IT'S NOT YOUR FAULT, PROFESSOR! THERE'S SOMETHING IN THE AIR THAT'S MAKING EVERYONE IN MAGIX FORGET THINGS!
BUT IF WE ANALYZE THE AIR, WE'LL DISCOVER WHAT'S CAUSING THIS. THEN WE CAN CREATE AN ANTIDOTE!
BUT I TOLD YOU, I DON'T REMEMBER HOW TO USE THESE INSTRUMENTS!

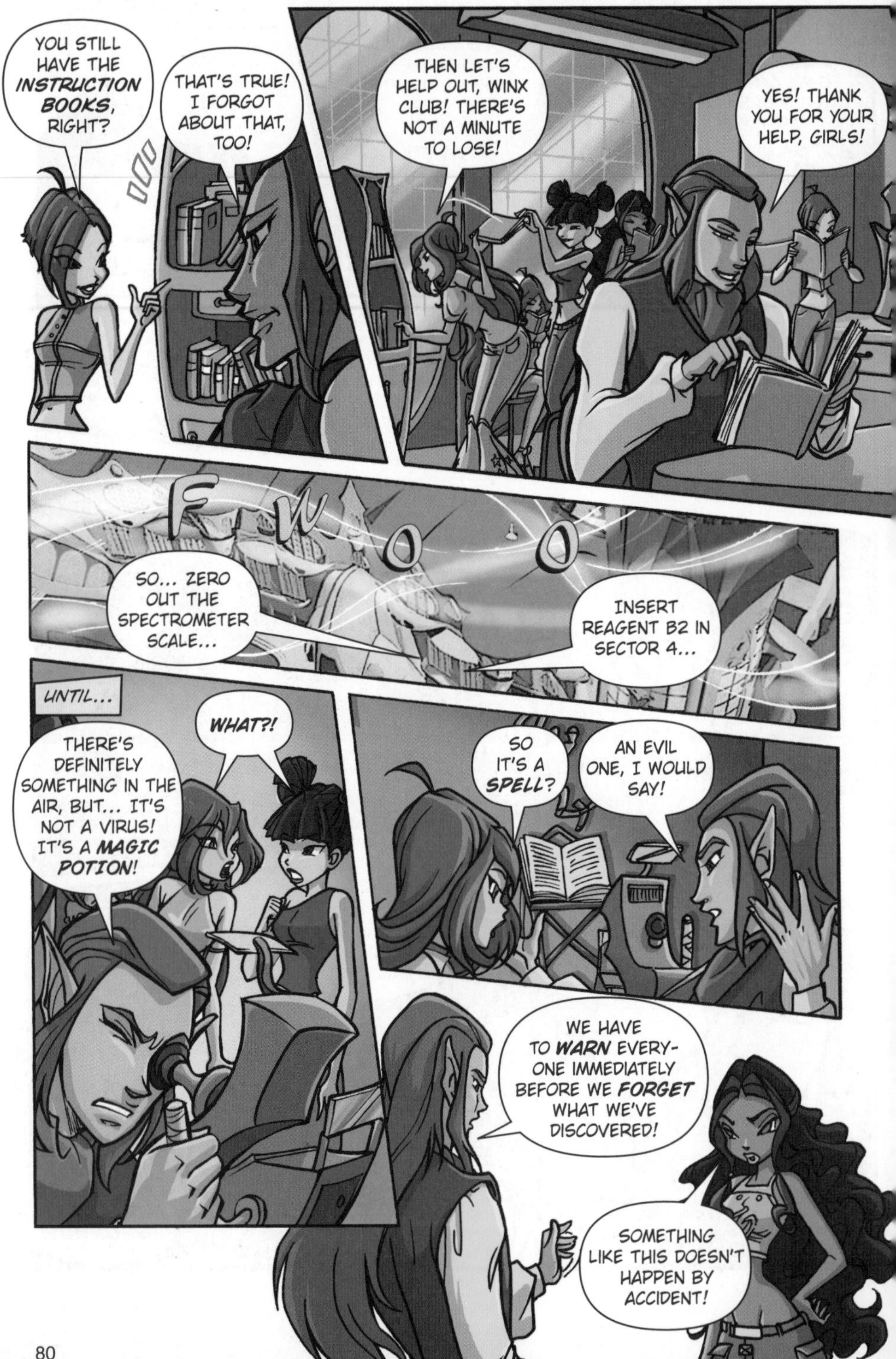
YOU STILL HAVE THE INSTRUCTION BOOKS, RIGHT?
THAT'S TRUE! I FORGOT ABOUT THAT, TOO!
THEN LET'S HELP OUT, WINX CLUB! THERE'S NOT A MINUTE TO LOSE!
YES! THANK YOU FOR YOUR HELP, GIRLS!
FWOO
SO... ZERO OUT THE SPECTROMETER SCALE...
INSERT REAGENT B2 IN SECTOR 4...
UNTIL...
THERE'S DEFINITELY SOMETHING IN THE AIR, BUT... IT'S NOT A VIRUS! IT'S A MAGIC POTION!
WHAT?!
SO IT'S A SPELL?
AN EVIL ONE, I WOULD SAY!
WE HAVE TO WARN EVERY-ONE IMMEDIATELY BEFORE WE FORGET WHAT WE'VE DISCOVERED!
SOMETHING LIKE THIS DOESN'T HAPPEN BY ACCIDENT!

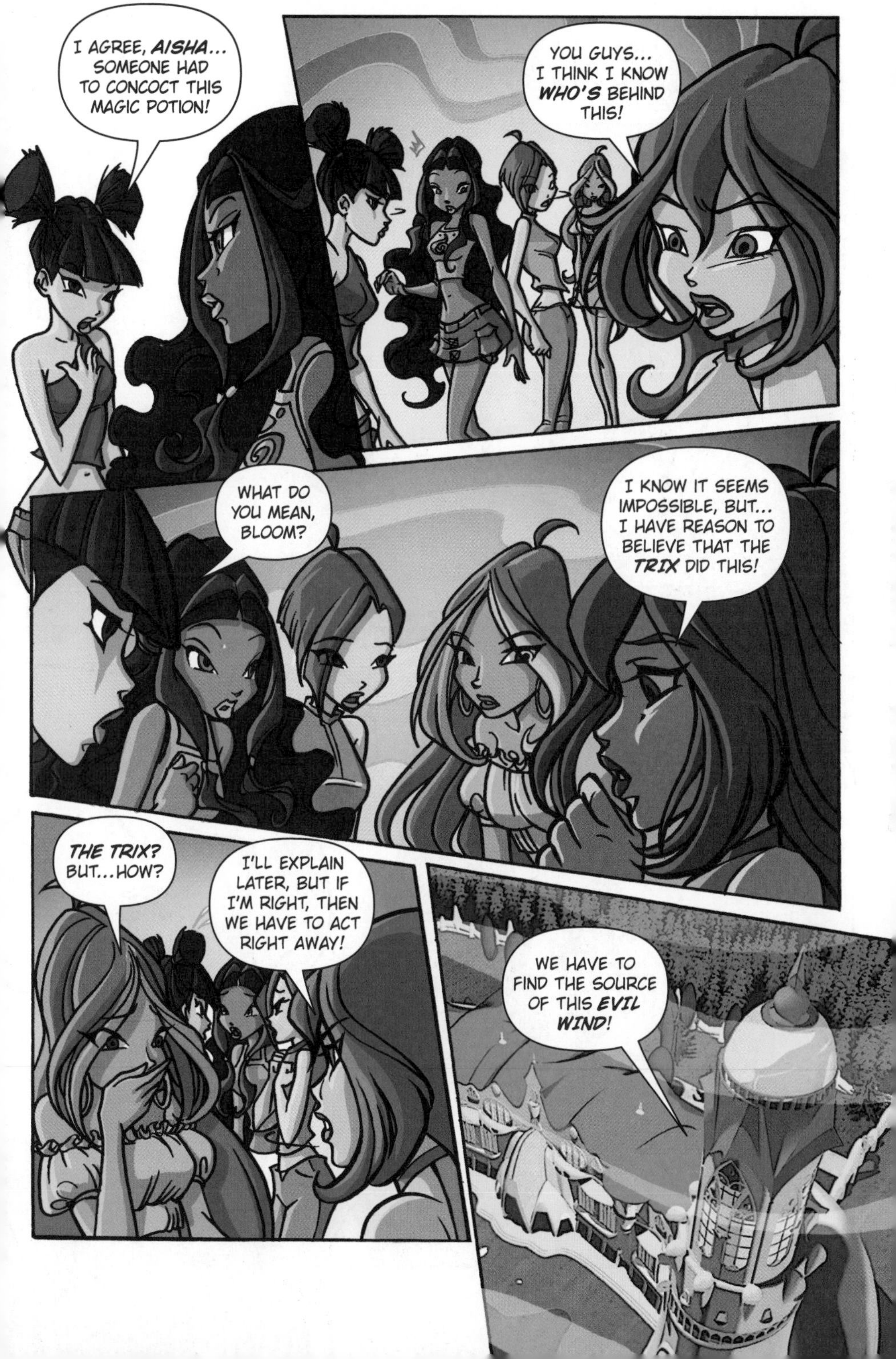

I AGREE, **AISHA...** SOMEONE HAD TO CONCOCT THIS MAGIC POTION!
YOU GUYS... I THINK I KNOW **WHO'S** BEHIND THIS!
WHAT DO YOU MEAN, BLOOM?
I KNOW IT SEEMS IMPOSSIBLE, BUT... I HAVE REASON TO BELIEVE THAT THE **TRIX** DID THIS!
THE TRIX? BUT...HOW?
I'LL EXPLAIN LATER, BUT IF I'M RIGHT, THEN WE HAVE TO ACT RIGHT AWAY!
WE HAVE TO FIND THE SOURCE OF THIS **EVIL WIND!**

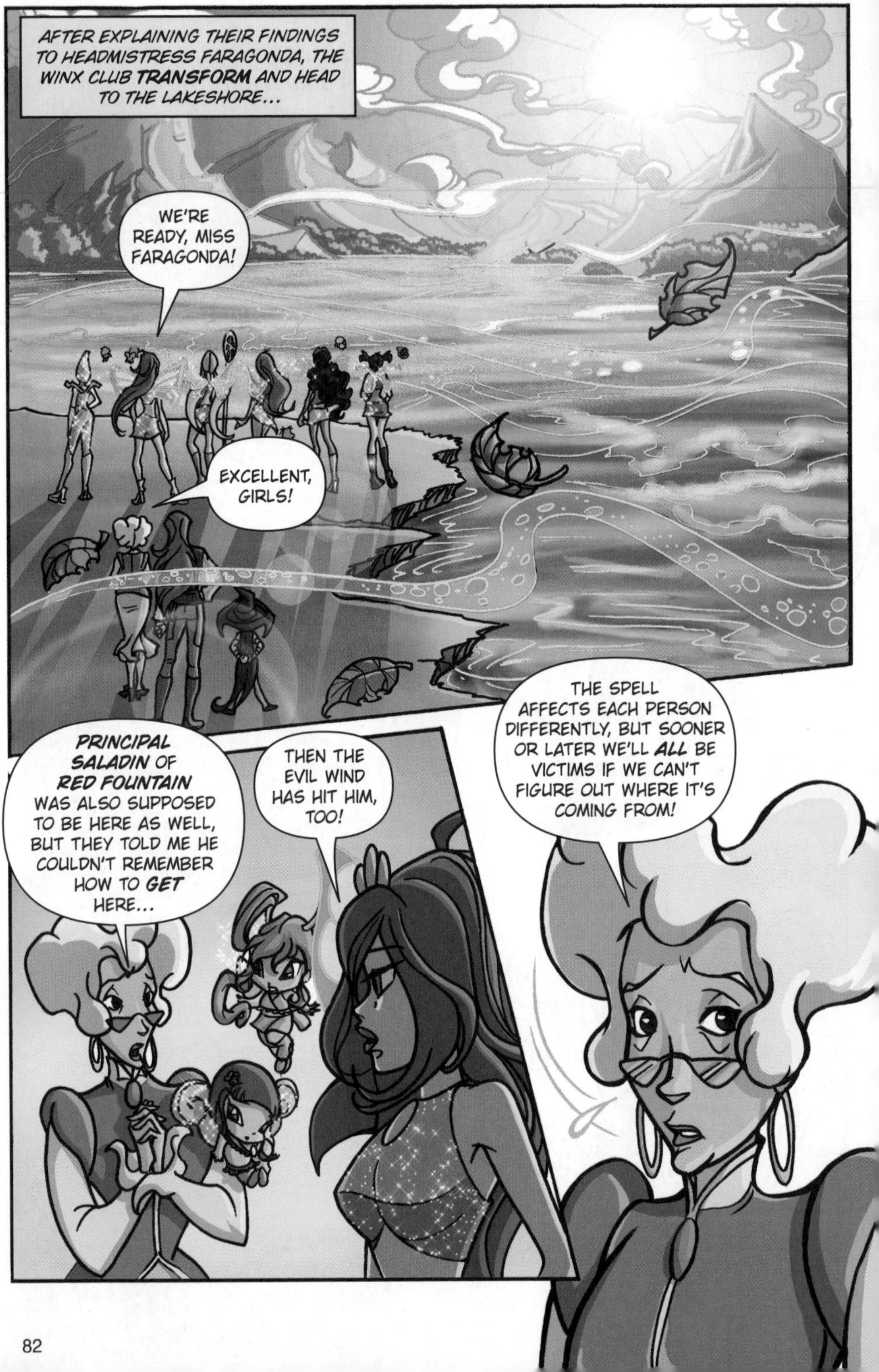
AFTER EXPLAINING THEIR FINDINGS TO HEADMISTRESS FARAGONDA, THE WINX CLUB **TRANSFORM** AND HEAD TO THE LAKESHORE...
WE'RE READY, MISS FARAGONDA!
EXCELLENT, GIRLS!
PRINCIPAL SALADIN OF **RED FOUNTAIN** WAS ALSO SUPPOSED TO BE HERE AS WELL, BUT THEY TOLD ME HE COULDN'T REMEMBER HOW TO **GET** HERE...
THEN THE EVIL WIND HAS HIT HIM, TOO!
THE SPELL AFFECTS EACH PERSON DIFFERENTLY, BUT SOONER OR LATER WE'LL **ALL** BE VICTIMS IF WE CAN'T FIGURE OUT WHERE IT'S COMING FROM!

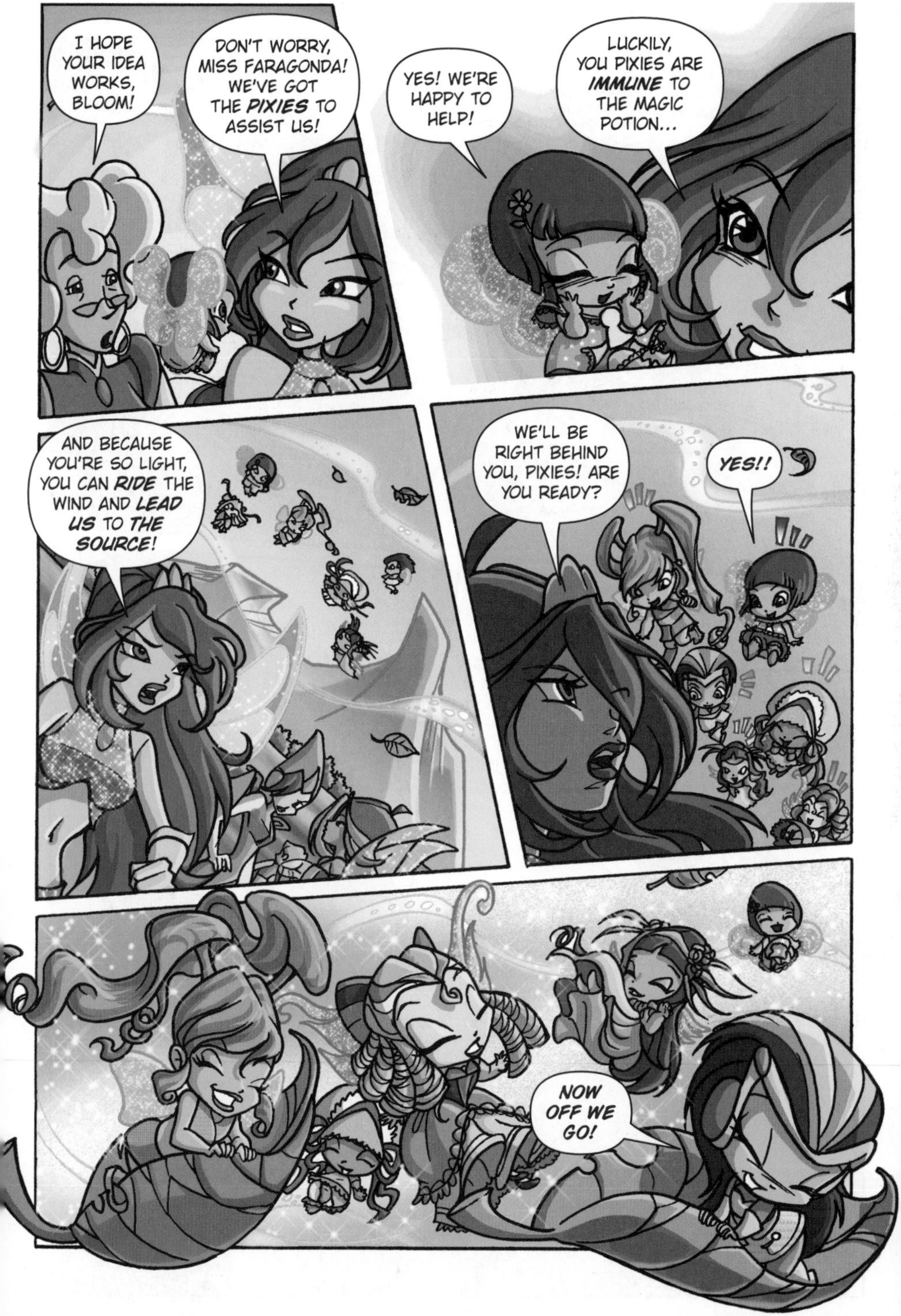
I HOPE YOUR IDEA WORKS, BLOOM!
DON'T WORRY, MISS FARAGONDA! WE'VE GOT THE PIXIES TO ASSIST US!
YES! WE'RE HAPPY TO HELP!
LUCKILY, YOU PIXIES ARE IMMUNE TO THE MAGIC POTION...
AND BECAUSE YOU'RE SO LIGHT, YOU CAN RIDE THE WIND AND LEAD US TO THE SOURCE!
WE'LL BE RIGHT BEHIND YOU, PIXIES! ARE YOU READY?
YES!!
NOW OFF WE GO!

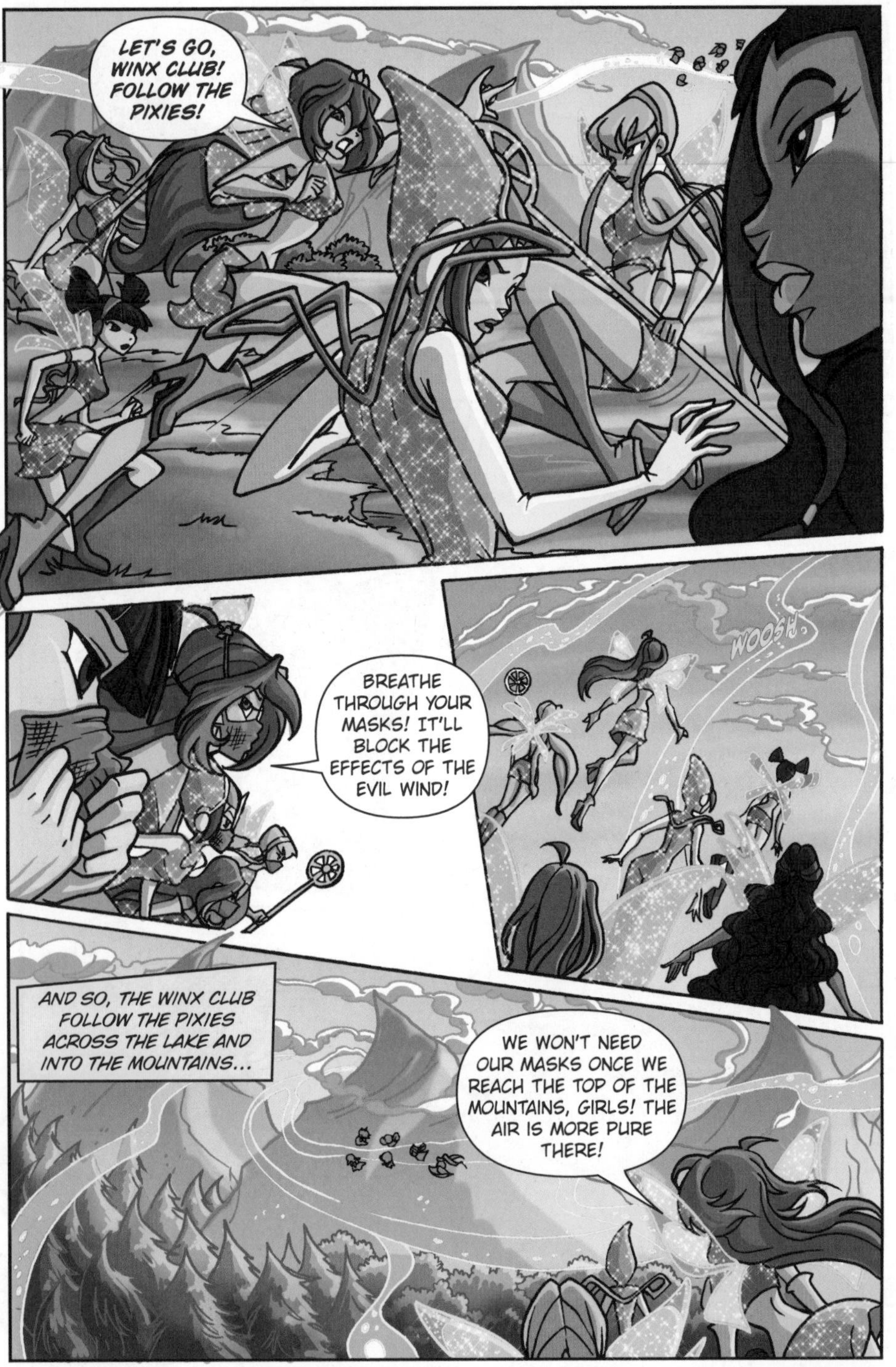
LET'S GO, WINX CLUB! FOLLOW THE PIXIES!
BREATHE THROUGH YOUR MASKS! IT'LL BLOCK THE EFFECTS OF THE EVIL WIND!
WOOSH
AND SO, THE WINX CLUB FOLLOW THE PIXIES ACROSS THE LAKE AND INTO THE MOUNTAINS...
WE WON'T NEED OUR MASKS ONCE WE REACH THE TOP OF THE MOUNTAINS, GIRLS! THE AIR IS MORE PURE THERE!

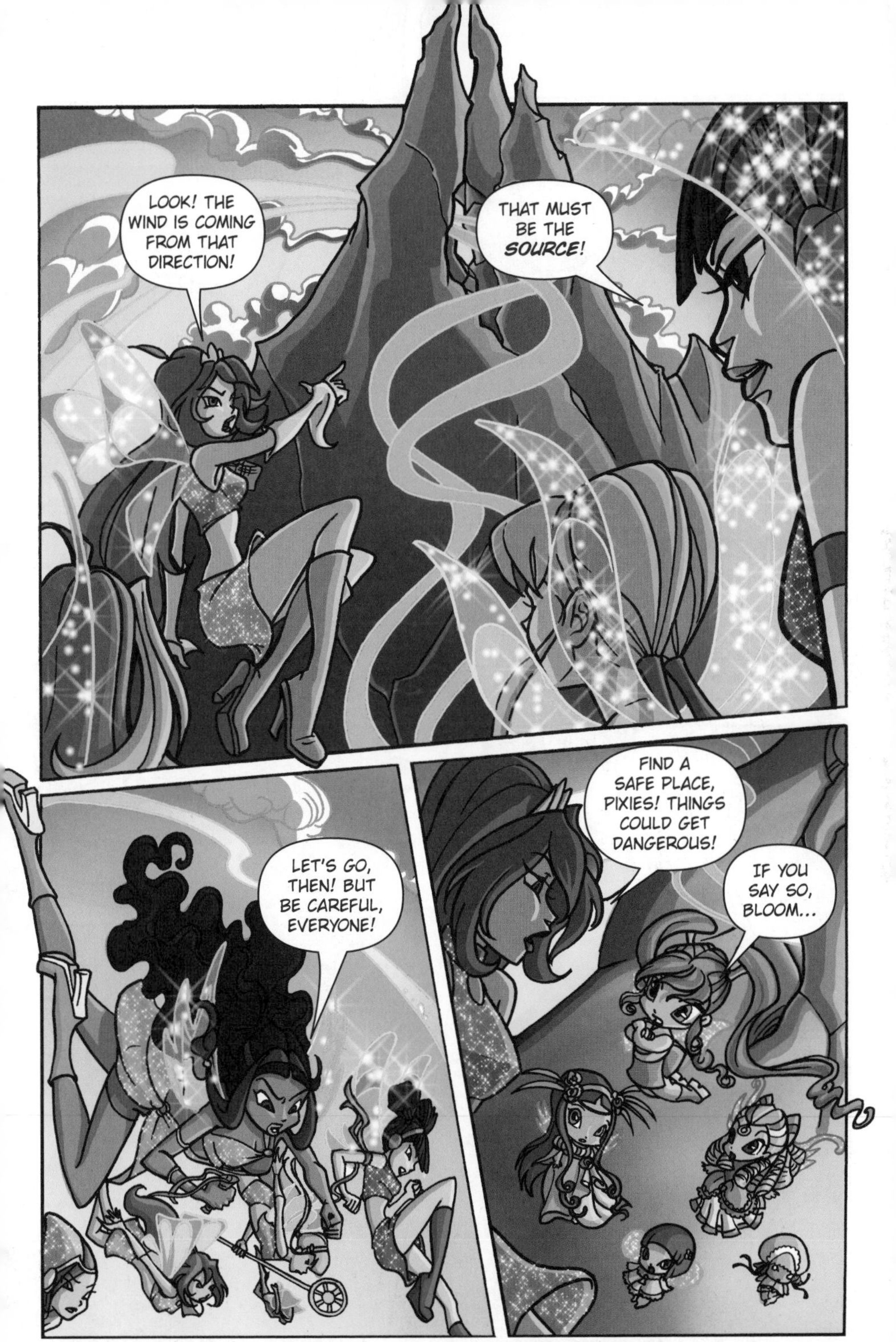
LOOK! THE WIND IS COMING FROM THAT DIRECTION!
THAT MUST BE THE SOURCE!
LET'S GO, THEN! BUT BE CAREFUL, EVERYONE!
FIND A SAFE PLACE, PIXIES! THINGS COULD GET DANGEROUS!
IF YOU SAY SO, BLOOM...

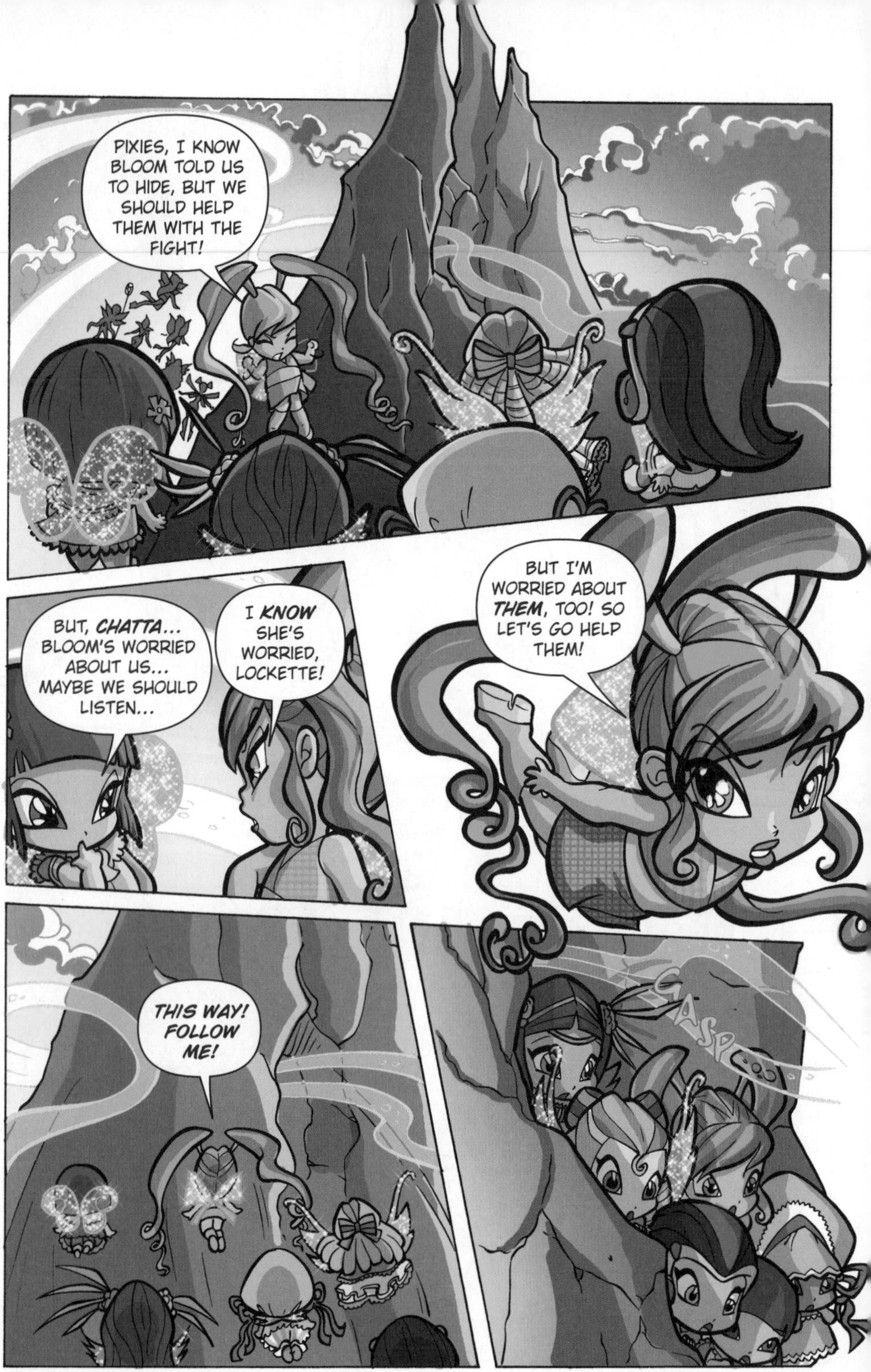
PIXIES, I KNOW BLOOM TOLD US TO HIDE, BUT WE SHOULD HELP THEM WITH THE FIGHT!
BUT, CHATTA... BLOOM'S WORRIED ABOUT US... MAYBE WE SHOULD LISTEN...
I KNOW SHE'S WORRIED, LOCKETTE!
BUT I'M WORRIED ABOUT THEM, TOO! SO LET'S GO HELP THEM!
THIS WAY! FOLLOW ME!
GASP

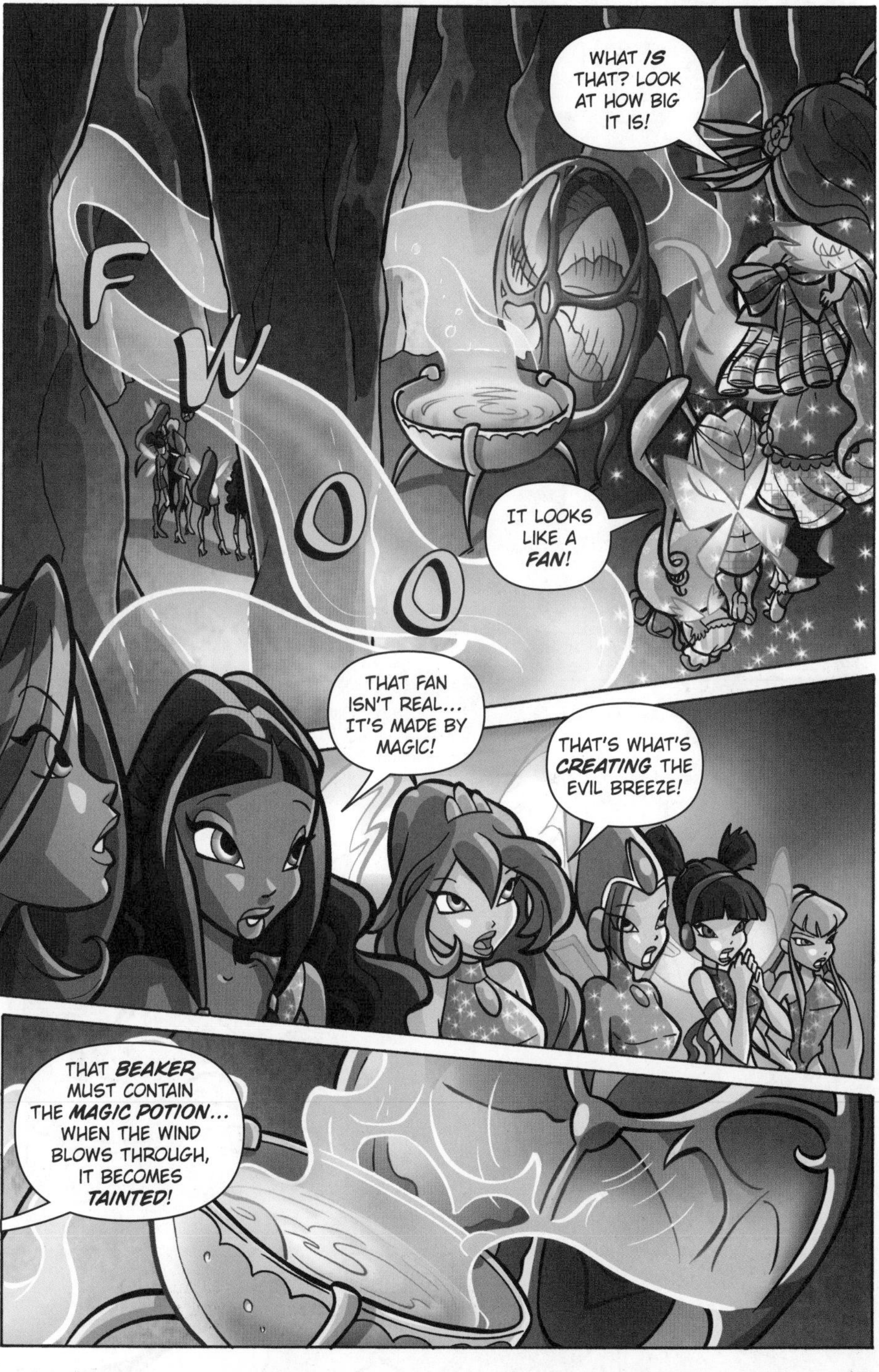
WHAT IS THAT? LOOK AT HOW BIG IT IS!
FWOOO
IT LOOKS LIKE A FAN!
THAT FAN ISN'T REAL... IT'S MADE BY MAGIC!
THAT'S WHAT'S CREATING THE EVIL BREEZE!
THAT BEAKER MUST CONTAIN THE MAGIC POTION... WHEN THE WIND BLOWS THROUGH, IT BECOMES TAINTED!

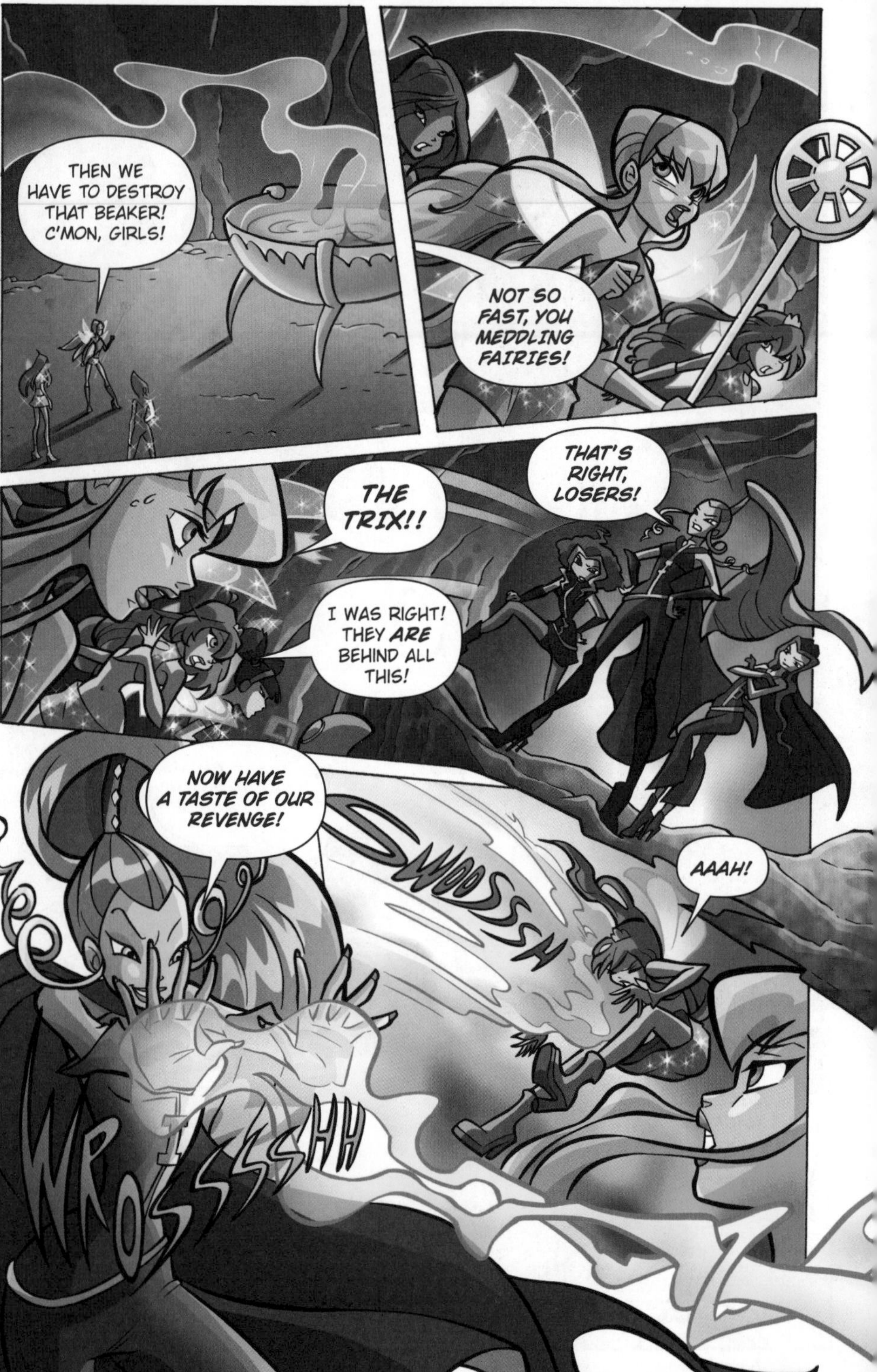

THEN WE HAVE TO DESTROY THAT BEAKER! C'MON, GIRLS!
NOT SO FAST, YOU MEDDLING FAIRIES!
THE TRIX!!
I WAS RIGHT! THEY *ARE* BEHIND ALL THIS!
THAT'S RIGHT, LOSERS!
NOW HAVE A TASTE OF OUR REVENGE!
SWOOOSSSH
AAAH!
WROSSSSHH

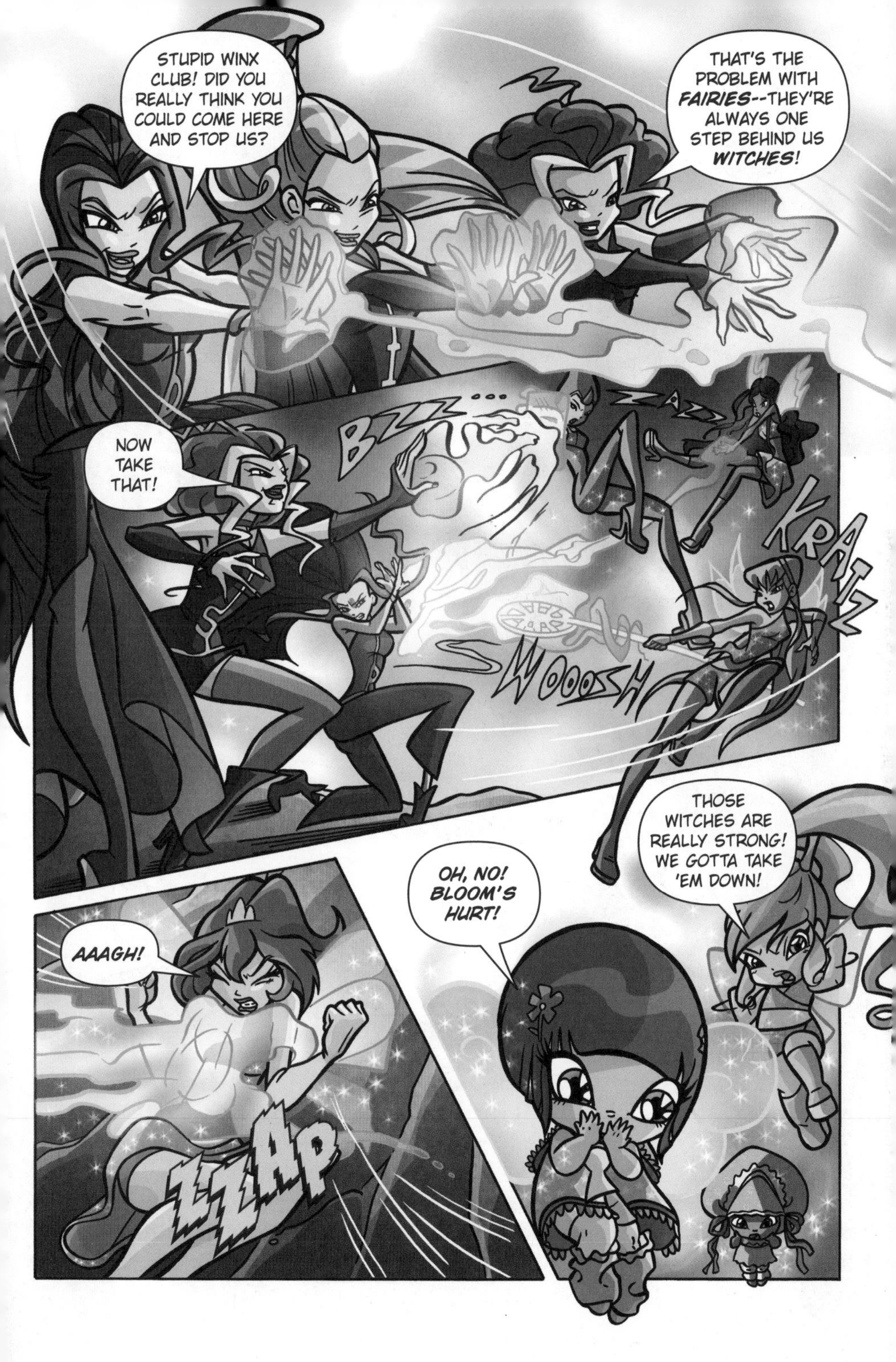

STUPID WINX CLUB! DID YOU REALLY THINK YOU COULD COME HERE AND STOP US?
THAT'S THE PROBLEM WITH FAIRIES--THEY'RE ALWAYS ONE STEP BEHIND US WITCHES!
NOW TAKE THAT!
BZZZ...
ZAP
KRAZZ
SWOOOSH
AAAGH!
ZZAP
OH, NO! BLOOM'S HURT!
THOSE WITCHES ARE REALLY STRONG! WE GOTTA TAKE 'EM DOWN!

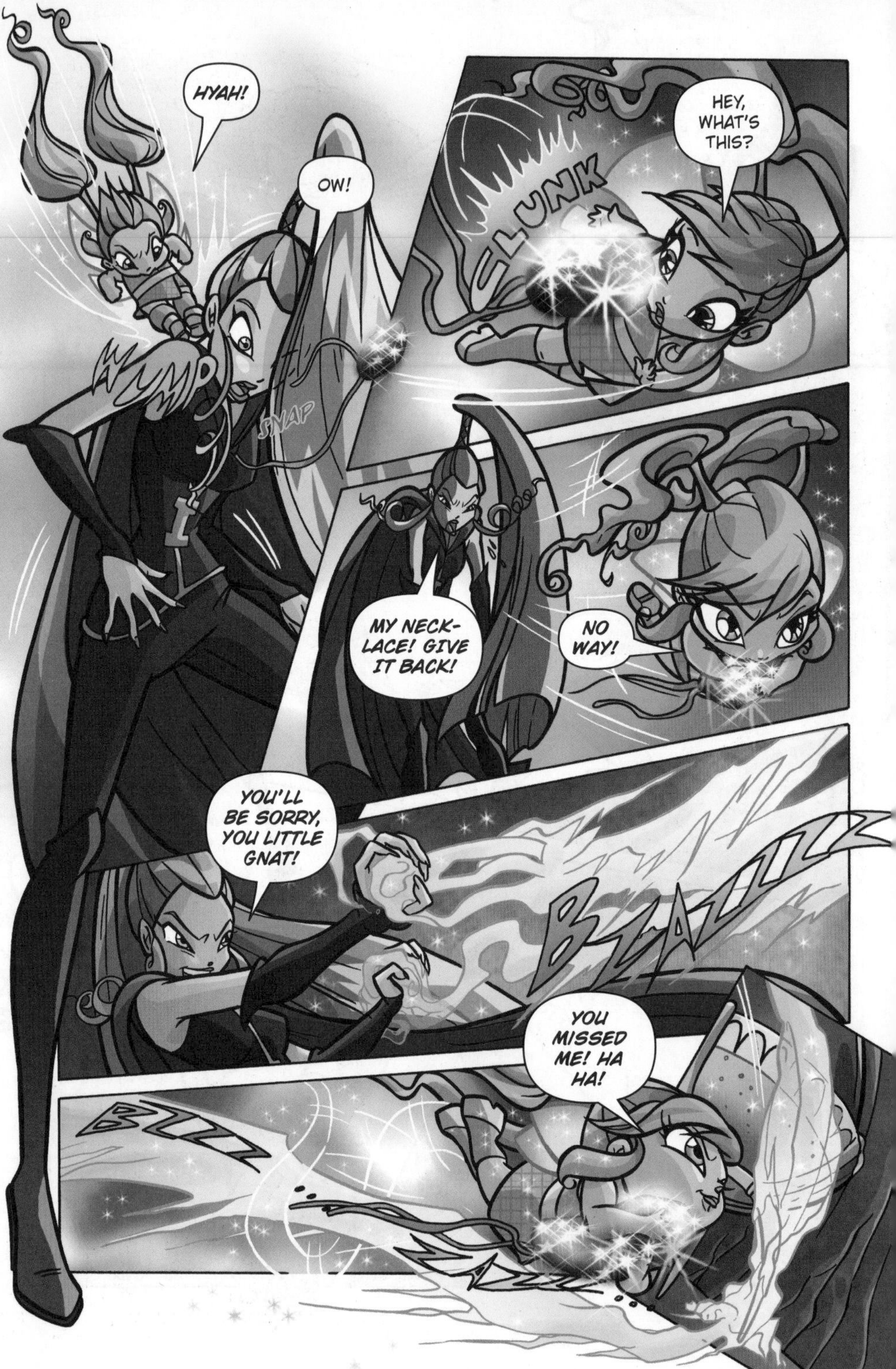
HYAH!
OW!
WHMP
SNAP
CLUNK
HEY, WHAT'S THIS?
MY NECK-LACE! GIVE IT BACK!
NO WAY!
YOU'LL BE SORRY, YOU LITTLE GNAT!
BLAZZZ
YOU MISSED ME! HA HA!
BZZZ

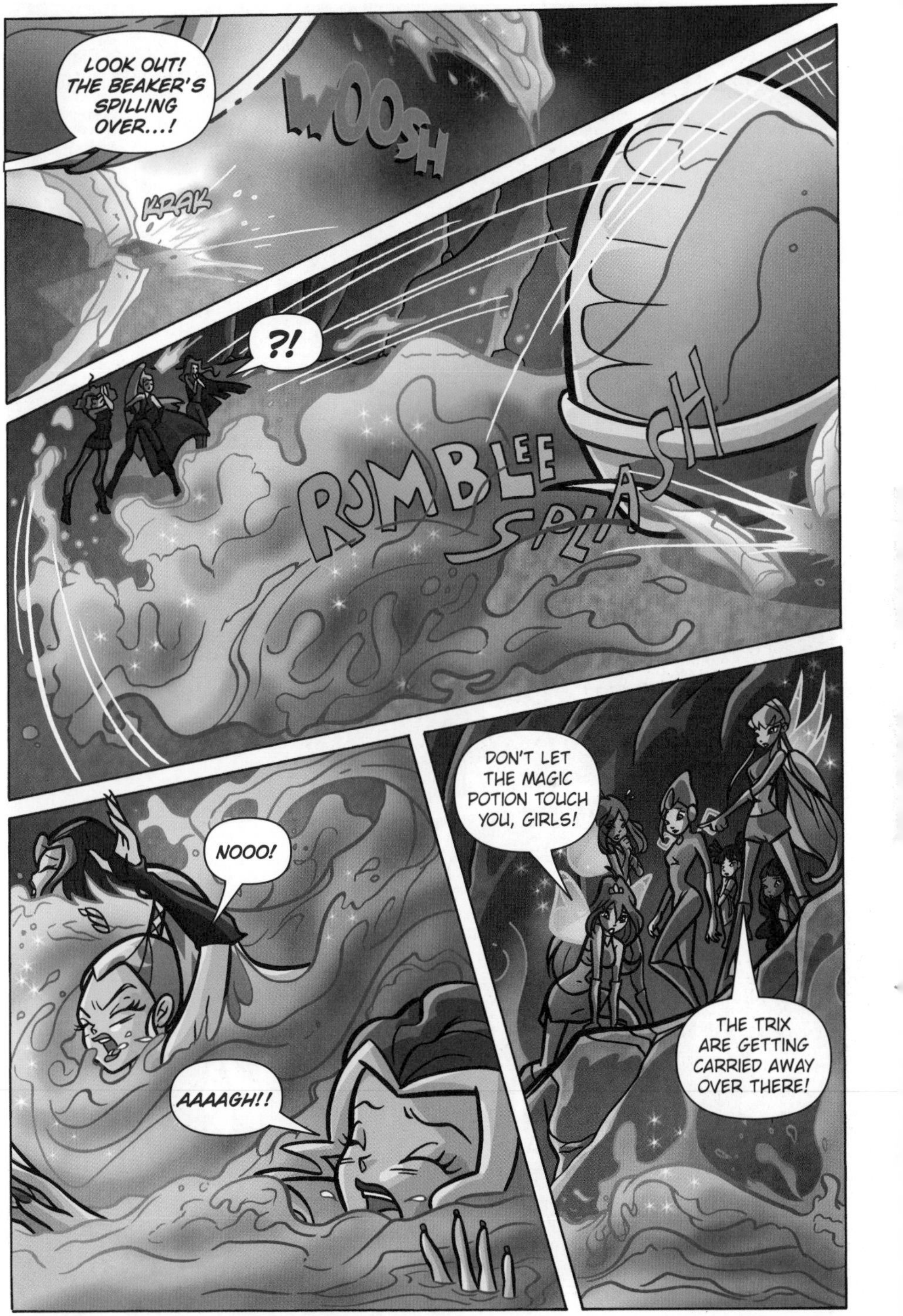
LOOK OUT! THE BEAKER'S SPILLING OVER...!
WOOSH
KRAK
?!
RUMBLEE
SPLLASH
NOOO!
AAAAGH!!
DON'T LET THE MAGIC POTION TOUCH YOU, GIRLS!
THE TRIX ARE GETTING CARRIED AWAY OVER THERE!

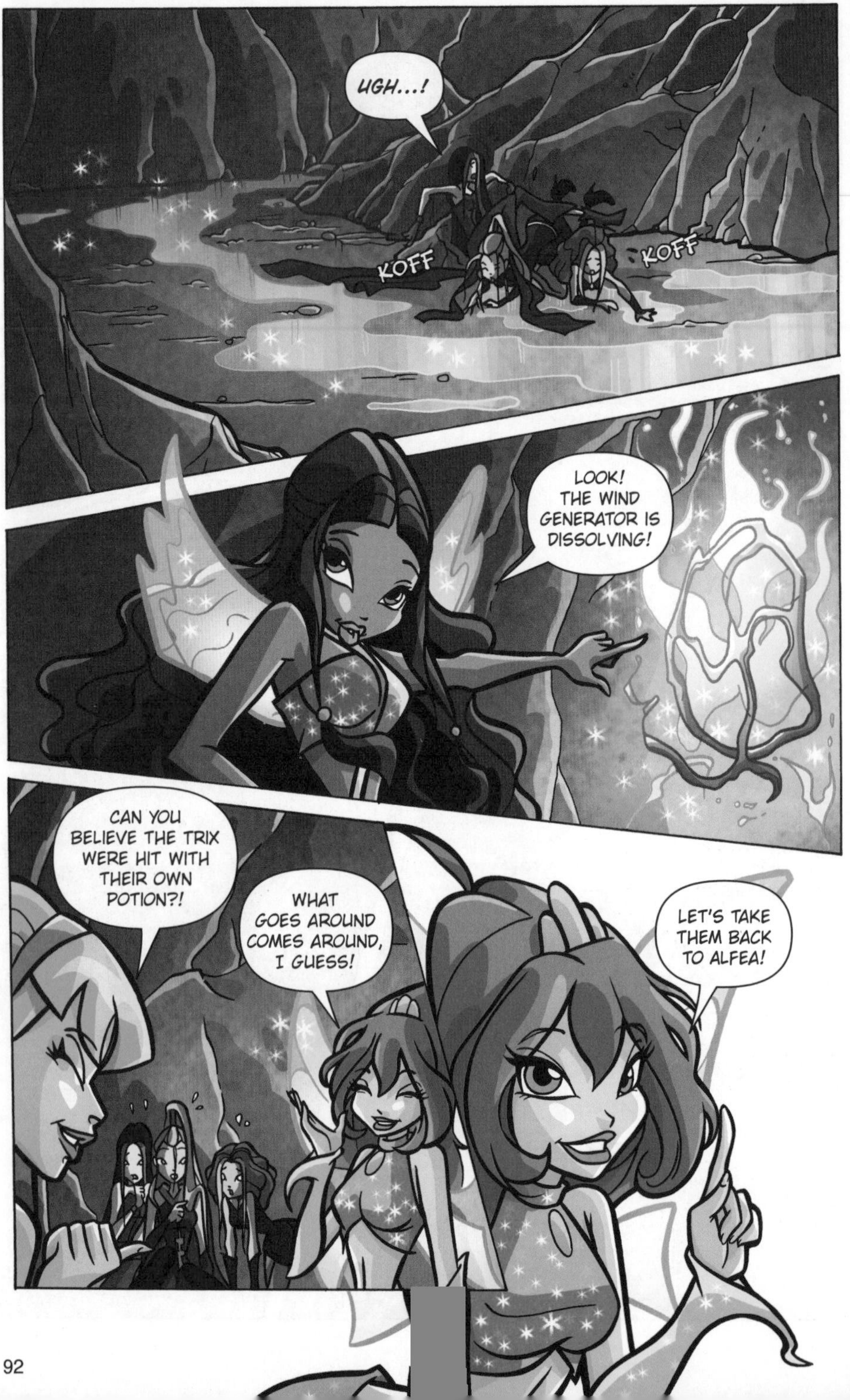
UGH...!
KOFF
KOFF
LOOK! THE WIND GENERATOR IS DISSOLVING!
CAN YOU BELIEVE THE TRIX WERE HIT WITH THEIR OWN POTION?!
WHAT GOES AROUND COMES AROUND, I GUESS!
LET'S TAKE THEM BACK TO ALFEA!

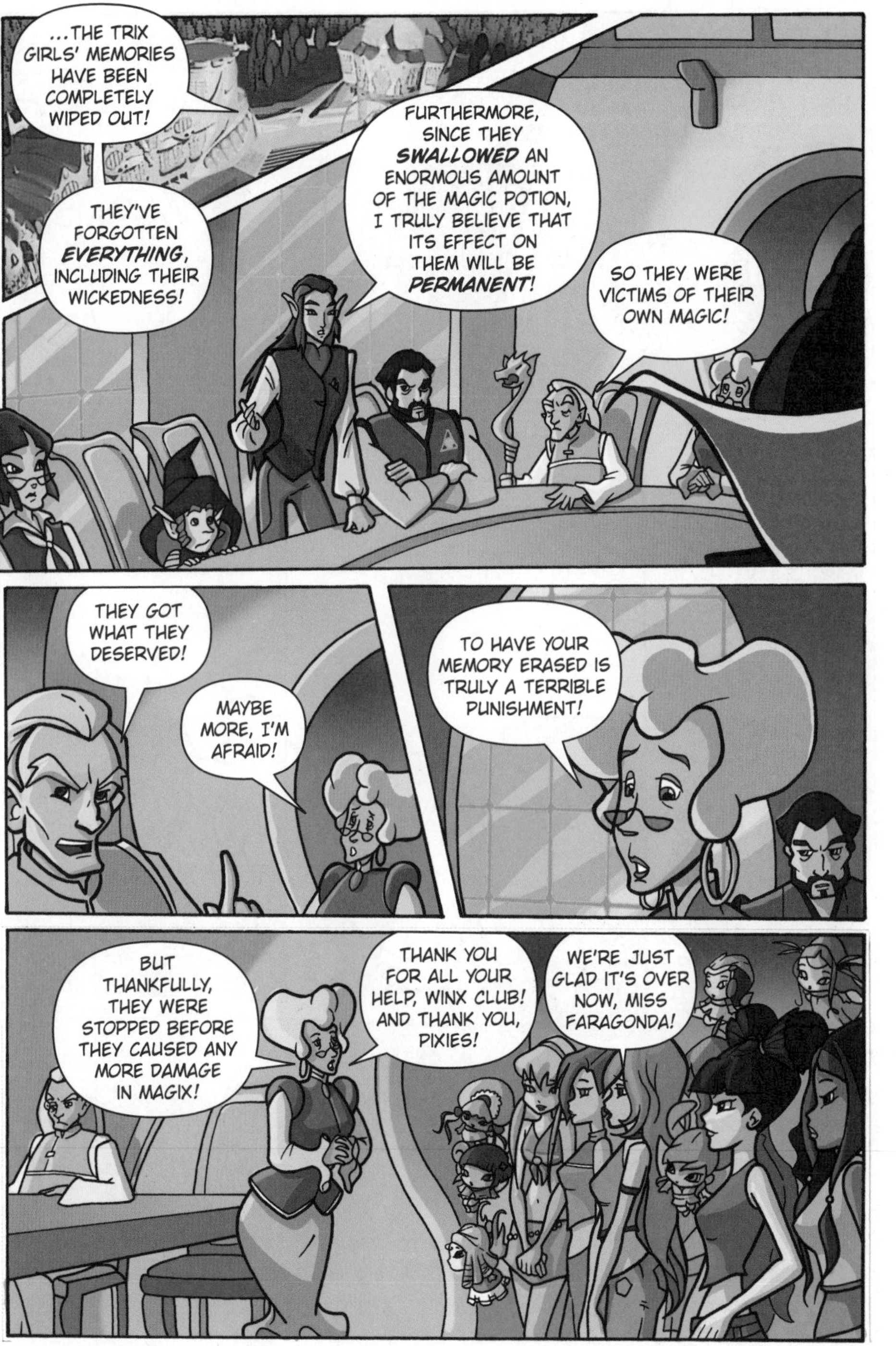
...THE TRIX GIRLS' MEMORIES HAVE BEEN COMPLETELY WIPED OUT!
THEY'VE FORGOTTEN EVERYTHING, INCLUDING THEIR WICKEDNESS!
FURTHERMORE, SINCE THEY SWALLOWED AN ENORMOUS AMOUNT OF THE MAGIC POTION, I TRULY BELIEVE THAT ITS EFFECT ON THEM WILL BE PERMANENT!
SO THEY WERE VICTIMS OF THEIR OWN MAGIC!
THEY GOT WHAT THEY DESERVED!
MAYBE MORE, I'M AFRAID!
TO HAVE YOUR MEMORY ERASED IS TRULY A TERRIBLE PUNISHMENT!
BUT THANKFULLY, THEY WERE STOPPED BEFORE THEY CAUSED ANY MORE DAMAGE IN MAGIX!
THANK YOU FOR ALL YOUR HELP, WINX CLUB! AND THANK YOU, PIXIES!
WE'RE JUST GLAD IT'S OVER NOW, MISS FARAGONDA!

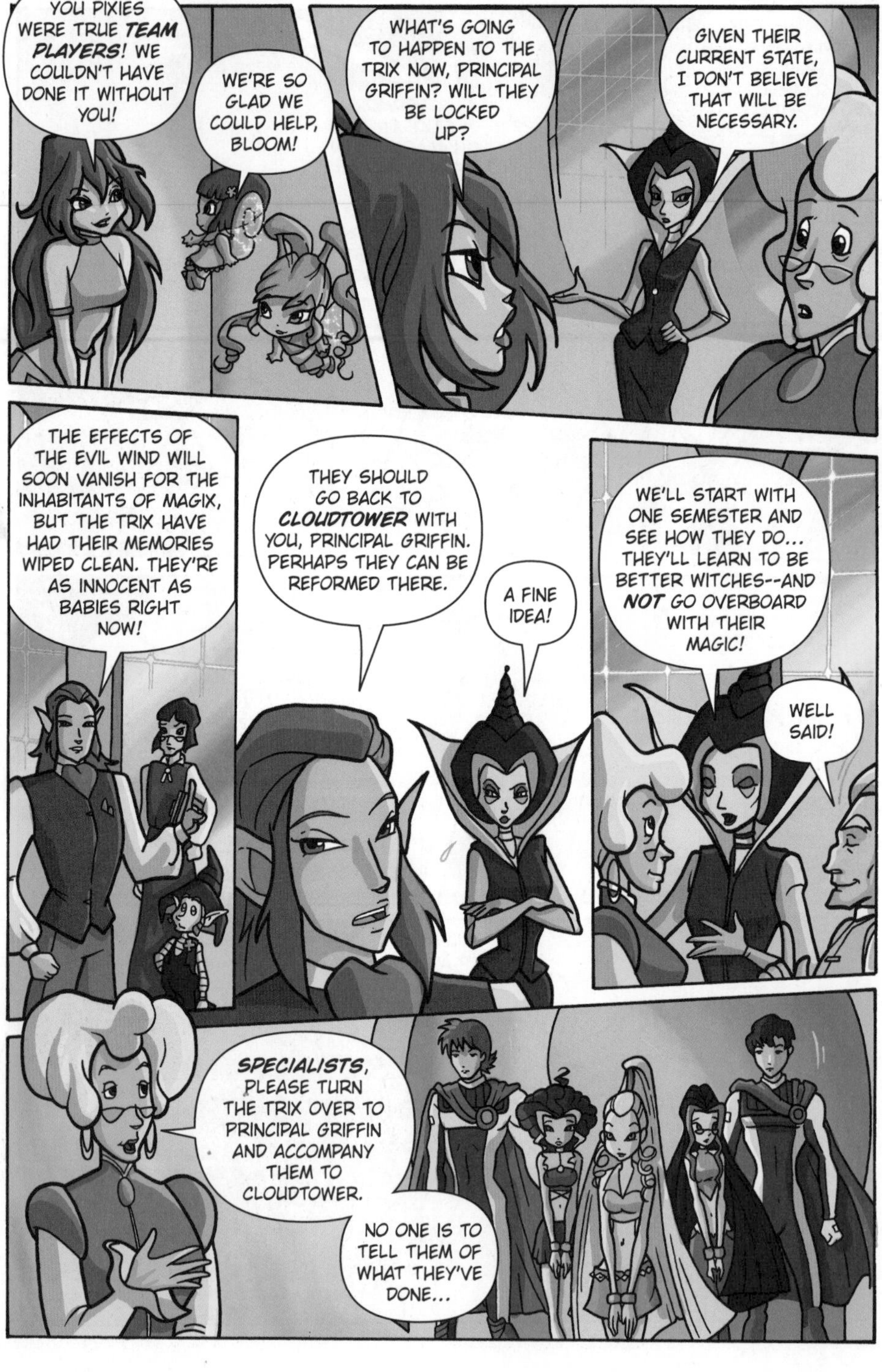
YOU PIXIES WERE TRUE **TEAM PLAYERS**! WE COULDN'T HAVE DONE IT WITHOUT YOU!
WE'RE SO GLAD WE COULD HELP, BLOOM!
WHAT'S GOING TO HAPPEN TO THE TRIX NOW, PRINCIPAL GRIFFIN? WILL THEY BE LOCKED UP?
GIVEN THEIR CURRENT STATE, I DON'T BELIEVE THAT WILL BE NECESSARY.
THE EFFECTS OF THE EVIL WIND WILL SOON VANISH FOR THE INHABITANTS OF MAGIX, BUT THE TRIX HAVE HAD THEIR MEMORIES WIPED CLEAN. THEY'RE AS INNOCENT AS BABIES RIGHT NOW!
THEY SHOULD GO BACK TO **CLOUDTOWER** WITH YOU, PRINCIPAL GRIFFIN. PERHAPS THEY CAN BE REFORMED THERE.
A FINE IDEA!
WE'LL START WITH ONE SEMESTER AND SEE HOW THEY DO... THEY'LL LEARN TO BE BETTER WITCHES--AND **NOT** GO OVERBOARD WITH THEIR MAGIC!
WELL SAID!
SPECIALISTS, PLEASE TURN THE TRIX OVER TO PRINCIPAL GRIFFIN AND ACCOMPANY THEM TO CLOUDTOWER.
NO ONE IS TO TELL THEM OF WHAT THEY'VE DONE...

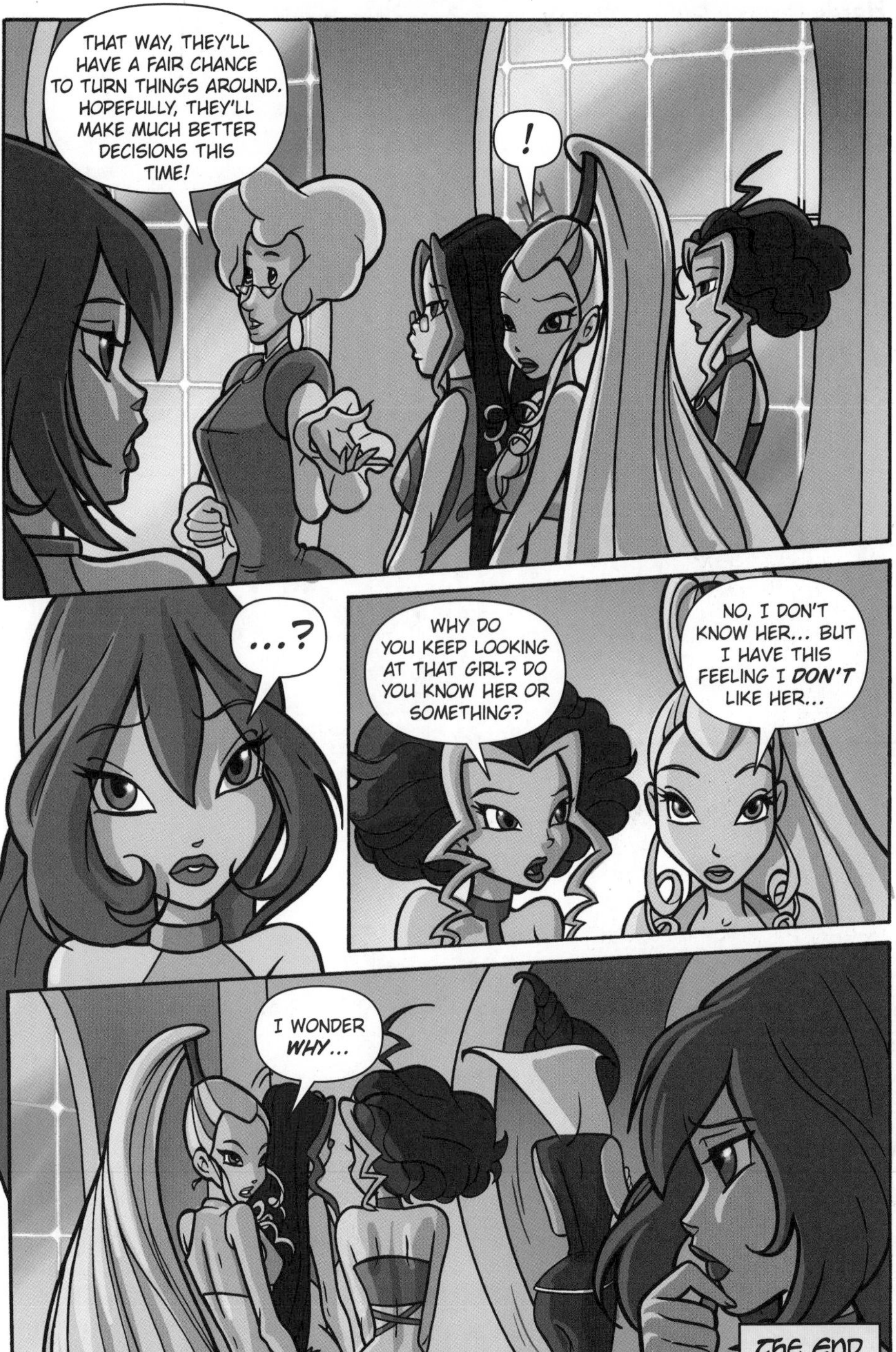
THAT WAY, THEY'LL HAVE A FAIR CHANCE TO TURN THINGS AROUND. HOPEFULLY, THEY'LL MAKE MUCH BETTER DECISIONS THIS TIME!
!
...?
WHY DO YOU KEEP LOOKING AT THAT GIRL? DO YOU KNOW HER OR SOMETHING?
NO, I DON'T KNOW HER... BUT I HAVE THIS FEELING I **DON'T** LIKE HER...
I WONDER **WHY**...
THE END

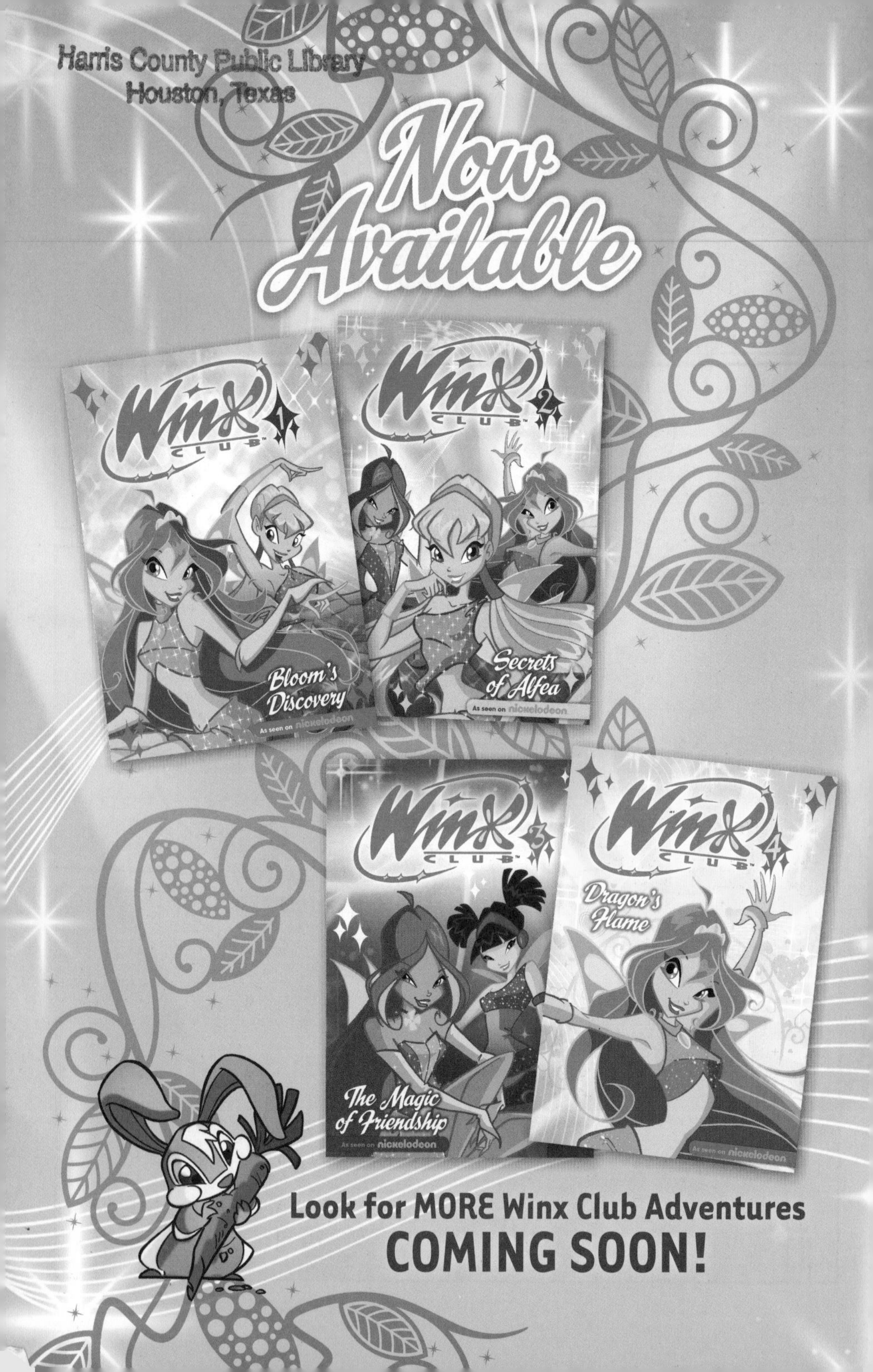
Now Available
Winx Club 1
Bloom's Discovery
As seen on nickelodeon
Winx Club 2
Secrets of Alfea
As seen on nickelodeon
Winx Club 3
The Magic of Friendship
As seen on nickelodeon
Winx Club 4
Dragon's Flame
As seen on nickelodeon
Look for MORE Winx Club Adventures
COMING SOON!